MW00424757

# THE SLEEPWALKERS

GORDON POPE THRILLERS, BOOK 1

B. B. GRIFFITH

Griffith Publishing
Denver

**Publication Information**

The Sleepwalkers: Gordon Pope Thrillers, #1

Copyright © 2020 by Griffith Publishing LLC

ISBN: 978-0-9963726-2-6

Written by B. B. Griffith

Cover design by James T. Egan of Bookfly Design

 Created with Vellum

*To Kit, who has cheered me on since day one.*

"Dreams are real while they last. Can we say more of life?"

-Havelock Ellis

# CHAPTER ONE

A t nine in the morning and not a moment earlier, Gordon Pope walked through the doors of the Baltimore City Circuit Courthouse and slowly shuffled through security. He nodded at Harold, the security guard, who watched benignly from behind a scuffed wall of bulletproof plastic as Gordon removed his watch and walked through the metal detector. He beeped, as always. The attendant wanded him, as always, and homed in on the tarnished brass belt buckle holding up his pair of ill-fitting khakis before waving him through. He'd taken his belt off every visit for months before realizing it saved him no time and just made for an awkward re-dressing. He'd lost weight since the divorce, and his pants were hanging on to his hips for dear life.

Harold pointed at the pass-through basin.

Gordon slid in his ID. "'Morning, Harold."

Harold grunted and checked his ID without seeming to see it. He noted the time and nodded him through.

One day, Gordon was going to get Harold to say something. After that, maybe he could get him to smile. That was a small microgoal of the type that Gordon often counseled his patients suffering from depression or signs of depression to set and strive toward in their daily lives. And recently he'd set it for himself.

No smile that day. Maybe next time.

Gordon weaved his way down the tracked marble floors and around harried government workers, following a path he knew by heart toward a bench by the vending machine on the second floor, where the criminal division was located. He sat heavily next to a large woman parked in a scooter, evidently asleep. He eyed the Moon Pies behind the glass for a solid minute before deciding against one. He pulled out his prep papers from a scuffed leather carryall, shuffled through them again, checked his watch. The woman beside him snored loudly once, startling him.

His session was starting in ten minutes. Where the hell was Brighton? He needed that three hundred bucks—knocked down from three fifty because Brighton was generally an asshole and knew Gordon was hard up.

Five minutes from his appearance time, Gordon heard a rapid clacking sound and stood as Brighton slid around the corner on his leather soles.

He held up his phone toward Gordon. "No service around here. I thought I told you. We're on the third floor today. Time to run." He smoothed his hair back then took off toward the stairway without looking back.

Gordon followed along at an awkward lope, holding up his pants with one hand in the pocket. "Third floor? We've never been to the third floor."

"You haven't. I have. Many times." Brighton fastened his double-breasted jacket and slowed to a power walk. He steadied his breathing as they climbed the stairs.

"What's on the third floor?"

"Don't worry about it. You just answer the questions exactly as the prep says. Nothing has changed."

Brighton didn't believe in going into detail with his expert witnesses about the cases in which they were to testify. He thought it muddied the waters. Expert witnesses were there to establish an objective point about which they knew an extensive amount and which had a bearing on the case. They didn't need to know what that bearing was. Quick, easy, clean. That was how Brighton & Associates had become the premier law firm for psychiatric defense. He paid three hundred a testimony. Three fifty if Gordon had stuck to his guns.

Brighton stopped outside of a door labeled Courtroom 7. He held out a hand to still Gordon, who was panting like a dog.

"We're at recess for another"—he looked at his gold watch—"three minutes. Sit in the back. Wait until you're called. You know the drill."

Gordon nodded, an unasked question on his lips, but Brighton patted him encouragingly on the shoulder and threw open the doors. Gordon followed and sat in the back as Brighton walked with a confidence just short of swagger to his place beside the defendant, who was a child. A boy, perhaps twelve years old. Gordon blinked.

"That son of a bitch," Gordon muttered. Brighton knew that Gordon had stopped practicing child psychiatry after the divorce. Gordon had explicitly told him he would not testify in cases involving children. That part of his life was behind him. Thomas Brighton apparently had not listened or, more likely, didn't care.

Gordon started sweating. Too late to back out now. He shuffled through his prep notes again. He skimmed the leading questions and reread his answers. Everything still rang true, from a professional standpoint, regardless of whether the defendant was an adult or a kid. But already his throat was dry. His mind jumped from memory to memory of how his life had been back then, with Karen, before this. His stomach rumbled with the vague nausea of loss. That was what kids did to him nowadays. He plucked his eyeglasses from his face and gave them a wipe down with the sleeve of his jacket. He could do this. He'd diagnosed a thousand kids before the divorce. The only thing that had changed since then was... well, everything.

"The defense calls Dr. Gordon James Pope."

Gordon stood and made his way to the stand, which was little more than a plastic chair behind a low wooden shelf. A glass of water gleamed there next to a microphone, turned off and pushed aside. Gordon counted only nine other people in the courtroom, and all but three sat on the side of the prosecution.

Gordon made himself look forward, and only after he'd been sworn in and turned to sit down did he chance an extended glance at the defendant. The boy was lanky, swimming in what was most likely a borrowed suit, hunched over and staring down at the table in front of him. He had dark-auburn hair that fell unkempt and moppish about his face. He didn't look up when Gordon was announced, didn't even move. He was flanked on either side by who Gordon assumed were his parents, a lean, red-haired man who was practically straining with the effort to appear composed and a fidgety blond woman with spooked eyes who looked about ready to bolt.

The boy seemed the calmest of any of them, on the surface, but Gordon knew better. That was a look of shock. Gordon doubted the boy would even be able to place himself on that day if asked a year or so down the line.

Thomas Brighton leisurely stood and smiled at Gordon as if he'd known him for years, then he approached the bench. He stopped and rested one hand lightly upon the worn wooden balustrade.

"Dr. Pope, would you please state your name and profession for the court."

Gordon cleared his throat and leaned forward as if the microphone were on. "Gordon James Pope, Doctor of Psychiatry from Johns Hopkins University, licensed and practicing psychiatrist with Jefferson and Pope, LP," Gordon said without skipping a beat.

"And how long have you been practicing psychiatry on behalf of Jefferson and Pope?"

"Seven years."

"Currently, you specialize in adult psychiatry, but when your firm first made a name for itself, what type of psychiatry were you practicing?"

That was off the script. Gordon clenched his teeth for the briefest moment before answering.

"Child psychiatry," Gordon said.

"So you have practiced both adult and child psychiatry extensively, for the record?"

"Yes."

Brighton nodded. "Dr. Pope, would you please describe, for the court, what parasomnia is?"

Back on script.

"Well, medically speaking, it's a category of sleep disorder arising from disruptions to the sleep stages," Gordon said, still wary. The script had been odd enough when he read it back at his office in preparation. It seemed even more so when taking into account the boy in front of him, who still hadn't looked up since Gordon's arrival.

"Layman's terms, please, Doctor." Brighton smiled warmly at the judge.

"It's when you do weird things when you're asleep." Gordon resisted the urge to bite the nail of his index finger.

"Things like what?"

"Well, anything from muttering all the way to walking, talking, eating... even driving."

"People drive while asleep?" Brighton asked with a perfect mixture of *are you kidding me?* and *of course they do*.

"Yes, it's been documented. Parasomniacs come in all shapes and sizes. There's a common belief that a sleep-walker has their eyes closed, bumping into walls, mumbling incoherent things, but that's not necessarily true. Many parasomniacs would look perfectly awake to you and me when in fact they are deeply asleep."

It was true, of course, all of it true. Gordon wouldn't sell himself out. He'd go into the poorhouse before he compro-mised the integrity of his profession. The medical facts stood true, no matter what age you were. But seeing the kid in front of him sent Gordon's mind suddenly racing toward the rest of the prep, extrapolating what it might mean. And it wasn't good.

"How is that possible?" Brighton peered into Gordon's eyes.

"It's simply a matter of missing chemicals in the sleeping brain. When you fall asleep, your brain eventually will become as active as it is when you're awake—this is called REM sleep—it's just that your sleeping brain has secreted a chemical to keep you paralyzed so you don't physically act on the random synapse firings in your head. Extreme parasomniacs don't get the release of this chemical at the right time, so they... aren't paralyzed in sleep."

Gordon grasped the glass of water on the stand and took a quick sip. He'd have liked to have downed the whole thing. He could feel his bald head start to glisten with sweat, but he knew wiping at it would look worse.

"*Extreme* parasomniacs? How extreme can we get here?" Brighton asked, unfazed.

"Quite extreme. There is a subset of sleep disorder called violent parasomnia, an estimated four to five percent of the parasomniac population. These individuals can sometimes throw things, like their bedside lamp, or punch walls. People have been known to attack their partners or hurt themselves. People have even killed others in their sleep."

Brighton let that last statement linger. Gordon looked from Brighton to the kid. *You've got to be kidding me.*

"And all of these examples are medically documented?" Brighton asked.

"Extensively. One particularly well-known case, the one we're taught early on in medical school, is the case of Richard Chee. The man in question drove for fourteen miles in his sleep and violently assaulted his in-laws. He actually killed his mother-in-law before turning himself in to the police with blood on his hands and no recollection of what had happened. It was pretty clear he'd been asleep the entire time."

The prosecutor, a woman dressed in a demure black knee-length skirt and jacket, scoffed loudly. "Objection, speculation."

"Sustained," said the judge.

Brighton bowed in allowance. "In the case of Richard Chee, was it the opinion of his medical staff that he'd been asleep the whole time?"

"Yes. It was their opinion," Gordon said.

"And Chee was acquitted?" Brighton added, looking briefly but meaningfully at the boy.

"Yes, he was."

"Objection," said the prosecutor. "Irrelevance."

"Mr. Brighton, let's keep Dr. Pope within the confines of his profession, please. And of this case," said the judge, eyeing them both over a heavy pair of plastic-framed glasses.

"Forgive me," Brighton said, as if he and Gordon hadn't rehearsed this exact back and forth. "One last question, Dr. Pope. When are sleep patterns most irregular in a person's life?"

"During times of stress: changes in environment or routine or changes to one's own person. Mental or physical trauma has been known to trigger parasomnias as well."

"And in your medical opinion, having treated both adults and children, would you say that adolescence is a time of stress?"

Off script again but undeniable. "Yes," Gordon said.

"A time in which one's environment and routine is particularly susceptible to change? Not to mention one's body, which is quite literally changing?"

"Yes."

"Thank you, Dr. Pope. That is all."

Gordon took another slug of water while the prosecuting attorney stood. She walked over to him and gazed directly into his eyes. Gordon wanted nothing more than to look away, but Brighton had counseled him never to look away. No matter what.

"Just a few questions, Dr. Pope," she said. "Have you ever personally treated a violent parasomniac?"

"No, not personally, but—"

"But you've read about them a great deal, yes, I'm sure.

Might that be because they are so rare that they're the stuff of collegiate case studies and not much more?"

"Like I said," Gordon stammered, "four to five percent—"

"An *estimated* four to five percent," she interjected.

"That's still a great number of people," Gordon said. "On the whole."

"And what about violent parasomnia in children, Dr. Pope? Do you have any statistics on that?"

Gordon didn't, of course. He hadn't planned on testifying on behalf of a child. He didn't plan on treating any child ever again.

"I don't," Gordon said.

Brighton furrowed his brow slightly, which on him, while in court, was as good as throwing in the towel.

"Neither do I, Dr. Pope. Do you know why? Because it is so rare that they don't keep them."

Brighton stood. "Objection!" he shouted. "Speculation, argumentative"—he ticked off each with his finger—"let's see here, assumption... I could go on."

"Sustained," said the judge, and Gordon thought he caught an eye roll.

The prosecutor backed away then turned. "No further questions."

Gordon nodded, gathered his things, and navigated his way down from the dais. As Gordon walked back down the aisle, he heard Thomas Brighton speaking. "I'd just like to make sure that the record shows that Ethan is twelve years old, just now entering adolescence..."

Gordon registered the boy's name, but he wasn't listening to Brighton any longer. He was a fairly good judge of age and wasn't surprised that his guess was spot on. What nearly stopped Gordon in the aisle was the brief flicker of a glance Ethan gave him as he passed the defendant's table. He'd seen thousands of kids back in the day, but none that looked like Ethan did just then. In fact, of all the kids Gordon had seen, only one reminded him even remotely of the way Ethan looked just then. Lost. Trapped. Cornered. But completely unaware of why.

The boy reminded Gordon of himself at that age.

# CHAPTER TWO

Gordon stood outside the closed doors of the courtroom for several minutes, pulling himself together, Ethan's face swimming in his mind. Even in that small glance, he had seen the marbled red of the boy's bloodshot eyes, puffy around the rims. Scratches ran down his face, small but noticeable, like a downward swipe from a cat's paw. Gordon had seen scratches like that before. They could've been from a lot of things. Or from one very particular thing.

He clomped down the stairs in a daze until he found himself back where he'd waited earlier. The electric whine and clunk of the vending machine brought him back to the humming hallway of the courthouse. The scooter lady grabbed the Moon Pie he'd been eyeing, sniffed at him with her nose held high, then whined off.

Why did he even care about the kid? He'd closed the door on that part of his life when Karen left him. Done. Over. He patted the breast pocket of his limp jacket. It crinkled with his measly paycheck, postdated because Brighton was an asshole like that, but still three hundred bucks. And three hundred bucks was three hundred bucks. That was his personal allowance, and he could do with it what he wanted. That was the rule he'd set himself. And usually, that meant booze. He checked his watch—eleven a.m. Too early. His mother would happily call it "brunch" and go hog wild—not at all out of the ordinary for Deborah Pope. He understood all too well the realities of children turning into their parents eventually, but he wasn't yet ready to turn into his mother in that respect.

So coffee it was, then. Good coffee, served by the judgmental baristas at Arnaud's down the block from his office. It was the closest he could come to a good scotch without the scotch. Gordon found himself looking forward to it. He pattered down the stairway, his mind on a perfectly foamed *cortado* and not where he was walking, when he nearly ran headlong into Dana Frisco. Dana sidestepped at the last moment and held out her hand to keep Gordon from taking them both down the stairs and into a wall. Gordon blubbered an apology until he recognized her, then he smiled.

"You always close your eyes when you go down stairs?" she asked.

"Sorry, Officer," he offered, bowing slightly. "Got a lot on my mind."

Dana straightened her gun belt over her sharp hips and moved both herself and Gordon out of the flow of traffic. "Yeah? Like what?"

"Well, money for one. Always money. Or lack thereof. Also booze. So sue me. And coffee." Gordon looked at the ceiling, counting on his fingers as he spoke. "Then there's my failing practice, there's my crazy mother, I'm sort of hungry, so there's that, too. And then the small matter of being an expert witness in a case that came out of the blue and settled right in the pit of my stomach."

Dana held out her hands in surrender. "Is this the sleep-walker?" she asked lightly. The com on her shoulder chattered, and she shut it off with a click.

"I don't know." Gordon looked briefly back up the stairs at the closed doors of the courtroom. "But he sure looked tired as hell."

Dana glanced back up the stairs and stepped in closer to Gordon. Gordon wasn't tall by any means, but Dana was shorter, built like a gymnast. He could smell the shampoo in her fine black hair.

"Brighton's case? The kid?" Dana asked, lowering her voice.

"That's the one," he said, finding himself whispering too. Dana nodded slowly, sadly.

"I processed that case," she said. "It happened on the edge of the city circuit, out in East Baltimore. The parents of the victim fought for jail time, but Brighton worked some magic, entered a temporary insanity plea because the kid had no priors, no history, nothing."

Gordon felt the heat that had flushed his throat while he was on the stand make a reappearance. He tried to swallow it away but struggled, and Dana noticed.

She looked sideways at him for a moment before moving on. "Not that it matters much. Odds are the kid ends up in Ditchfield anyway."

*Ditchfield.* The name brought back memories for Gordon, none of them good. "That's the juvie psychiatric hospital," he said. "For high-risk kids."

Dana nodded gravely. "You know about it, then."

"Back before... a while ago, I was the psychiatrist of record for a few kids mired in the Ditchfield system. They were..." Gordon sought the right words. He wanted to say, "ruined by the place." But while Dana was a friend, she was still a cop. He settled on "institutionalized."

"Institutionalized my ass," Dana said under her breath. "Cops are institutionalized. Lawyers, bankers, any nine-to-fiver working paycheck to paycheck—that's institutionalized. Those kids come out of Ditchfield like shells if they come out at all."

Gordon wasn't going to argue with that. "Brighton didn't prep me with the case specifics. He never does. I was going to keep talking like I knew what was going on with that kid, but if I don't ask you, I'll probably never know."

Dana looked at Gordon for a long moment. He and Dana had known each other for over a year. She did part-time work managing the holding cells in the basement, so she was often around the courthouse. The reason he'd met her the first time was that she'd struck up a conversation about how gross the water fountains were in the place, and from then on, they just kept running into each other. She knew about the divorce. He'd mentioned it in passing, trying to downplay it as though it was nothing more than a rainy vacation. She knew his practice was struggling, too. Come to think of it, she knew almost everything. Almost. She didn't know the whole of why he'd stopped treating kids, just part. But sometimes, the way she looked at him, he could have sworn she knew everything in his head.

"The kid almost murdered his friend at a sleepover," Dana said, keeping her voice low. "Strangled him in the middle of the night. Put him in a coma before the other kids could scream loud enough to wake up the poor guy's parents. He's at Hopkins Hospital right now. Still hasn't woken up."

Gordon nodded. He knew it must have been something

like that. He sensed it as soon as he saw the kid. But the truth still settled upon his shoulders like a slow stream of sand, heavier with each moment.

"Ethan, the defendant, he claims he did it in his sleep." Dana cocked an eyebrow. "Claims he has no memory of it." She paused. Her brow furrowed in concern, as if she could see Gordon slouching before her eyes under the weight. "Hey," she said. "Sorry if I..."

Suddenly, Gordon needed that drink, time of day be damned. Coffee wouldn't cut it.

"No, thank you for telling me. You're the only one around here who would. I'll see you around, Dana."

She only nodded and watched as Gordon made his way past her and down the stairs. Gordon didn't look back. He knew Dana had a thing for reading faces, and he didn't want to be read right then.

VERY FEW PEOPLE knew that Gordon's office was also his home. His lack of finances called for the double duty. When Karen left him, she basically took their entire child-psychiatry practice with her. Gordon had since come to understand that while she was half of Jefferson & Pope LP in name, she was a good deal more than that in substance. He'd lost half of his clients outright, and another twenty-five percent shuffled out the door in the years afterward.

No clients meant no referrals from clients, and so the stagnation built upon itself, his wheels spinning in the mud, until his career was basically swallowed up altogether. Almost as if it had never been. When he treated children in the aftermath, he stopped seeing their conditions as challenges with solutions to be unearthed and started seeing in their faces reminders of his loss. The divorce hobbled him, and nobody could sniff out uncertainty like kids, so he stopped treating them. Instead, he started treating their parents. His was a wonky, one-sided family practice. It had no heart, and so he doubted it would ever find legs.

The rare clients he saw these days were always window-shoppers who hadn't yet realized that the Karen Jefferson of *Baltimore's Top of the Town: Doctor Edition* and, more recently, of the *New England Journal of Medicine*, no longer physically practiced in Baltimore. They wandered into his Mount Vernon office building like tourists reading restaurant reviews years out of date—expecting to find a steakhouse but instead coming upon the dollar-a-scoop buffet that had taken over when the steakhouse moved to San Diego and married a powerhouse real-estate agent it had met through a pricey, high-caliber Internet-dating website.

Perhaps one in five of those tourists stayed for a session or two. That let him keep the lights on and the water running but either at his office or at his loft, not both. The loft reminded him too much of Karen, so the office it was. He still needed a place to live, though, so he'd turned the space into a half office, half apartment. The first-floor waiting room was where he worked, and the second floor he'd turned into a de facto studio apartment. He'd plugged in a two-burner stove and had an old college buddy jury-rig the guest bathroom to include a casket of a shower. It was a ramshackle affair, and very probably illegal from a zoning and fire-safety perspective, but it wasn't all bad. One block over and one block down from Gordon's home office stood a classic Baltimore pub. It was clean and dark and had all sorts of cold things on draft and more scotch and bourbon on the shelves than even he could name—the type of place the respectable pirates of old Baltimore would have gone, back a couple of hundred years before when the city was nothing but a smuggler's den. A lot of people, his mother included, would say not much had changed since then, but Gordon disagreed. The city held pockets of brilliance still, and Darrow's Barrel was one of them—especially with their crab-cake sandwich.

Gordon had four hours to kill before his appointment that afternoon, one of three he had scheduled for the entire week. He hadn't eaten out at a legitimate pub since his last expert testimony over a month before. He took his bites slowly, savoring. He'd earned them. He'd come into Darrow's thinking he'd earned an ice-cold mug of beer too. As it turned out, he'd actually earned three. And counting.

He watched the clock, an ancient thing shoved high up on a shelf, where the staff hoped patrons wouldn't see it and would keep drinking. But Gordon saw, and as his appointment approached, he grew increasingly grim. At the last possible minute, he stood up and paid his tab in cash and walked his way back to his office, his hands thrust into his pockets.

Once inside, he popped in a stick of gum, rolled his shoulders, and forced himself to smile as he straightened his office. He dusted off his client's chair and fluffed the pillows on an increasingly worn-looking loveseat. He dimmed the lights and cocked the shades, and by the time his front bell rang, he had halfway convinced himself he was excited to be working.

Gordon found himself tuning in partway through what was no doubt a cathartic story on the part of that afternoon's client, an overconfident, bull-necked executive named Mark Bowman. Mark's company paid for counseling for their Csuite executives, and Mark took everything he could from his company. In their second session together, Gordon had learned Mark was contemplating an affair with his kid's kindergarten teacher ever since they'd hit it off during a parent-teacher conference his wife couldn't attend because she worked nights at the hospital and slept during the days. He hadn't made a move yet, but he also hadn't shut up about it since.

Gordon was fully aware that Mark's plight, if you could call it that, would be the professional envy of many of his colleagues. Once or twice, he'd even thought about referring him to one of them, but then his bank account poked him in the chest again. Better to let the man vent while his company shelled out Gordon's hourly rate. With adult therapy, essentially what he had to do was let the clients run their mouths long enough to find their own solutions to their own problems.

He thought about how Karen would have rolled her eyes at him and told him he tended to wildly oversimplify things he didn't want to deal with, most likely as a coping mechanism. She would tell him to stop feeling vaguely threatened by the mere fact that a man had family enough to *have* marital problems, and she would tell him to do his job. And of course, she would've been right. But she was also in San Diego. Far from there. Far from him. And he was in Baltimore and a bit fuzzy from three beers over lunch. When Gordon blinked back to reality, Mark was in midsentence.

"She thinks it's unnatural to have only one. Says it warps the kid you've got."

Gordon made a noncommittal humming sound and gave a half nod. *What the hell is he talking about?*

"I mean, I'm an only child, and I think by any standard

you could call me successful. Frankly, it was a little insulting. Am I wrong?" Mark asked, leaning back in the client's chair with his knees spread wide.

"You're trying to have another child," Gordon said, setting himself back into the conversation.

"She wants three. I've bartered her down to two and a condo. She's not budging on the two, though. And she's got a ticking womb, you know. That's what I like about the teacher, Arielle. There's none of this..." Mark swiped his hand back and forth between his knees, looking for a word.

"Talk of children?" Gordon offered, trying to keep the remnants of that benign smile on his face. "That usually doesn't happen with mistresses, Mark. Not at first, at least. It's the offer they provide of freedom from the classic family model that is the initial allure."

Mark nodded as if he understood completely. "I wouldn't call her my mistress yet. We just text. A lot. But my wife's full of shit, right? About the single-child thing?"

"No, she's not full of shit. Studies have shown that children that grow up with a sibling are better adjusted socially." Gordon was done pandering to the man. So what if he walked away? Gordon was living like a broke college student already. He could stand to be a little bit more broke if it meant he never had to see Mark Bowman again. But Mark didn't counter him. In fact, he seemed not to even have heard him.

"Christ, the one kid is enough. Don't get me wrong, I love Jamie, but he's a train wreck. He's into all these magic card games, spends every waking second talking about them. Won't even consider a sport," Mark said, shaking his head to nobody in particular. "You got kids, doc?"

"No, I don't," Gordon replied evenly.

"Well, think twice. Jamie oughta be seeing a shrink. You

know anything about kids' brains?" Mark asked, looking out the window, grabbing blindly at the bowl of nuts on the table.

"Actually, Karen's and my first practice was exclusively child psychiatry," Gordon replied. "Years ago," he added.

"So you know what I'm talking about. You probably saw the real crazies. And now she wants another one?"

Back on the wife again. Gordon muffled his sigh into a yawn.

"Where is Karen? She's pretty famous, right?" Mark asked.

"She's quite talented, yes. And she's on sabbatical, pursuing a post-doctoral fellowship in San Diego for a time. But we both review each other's cases, so she is here in spirit." Gordon smiled blandly. How many times had he told that little white lie over the past five years? At some point, it wasn't going to hold water. Gordon wondered idly how long a fellowship could reasonably be said to continue. Most were for just the year, and Karen's was long done, so he was already pushing it.

Gordon felt particularly morose after Mark left, vaguely hungover and sluggish, his mind still stuffed with thoughts of the morning's testimony. Had he helped Ethan? Had he hurt Ethan's case? He'd answered everything by the book, aside from the few questions Brighton sprung on him, but those he felt he answered professionally. Dana Frisco's words echoed in his mind: "Strangled him in the middle of the night... said he did it in his sleep." And not just the words but the way she'd said them. Like she wanted to rib him with her elbow and add, "Can you believe that shit?"

Could he?

For the first time in six months, Gordon walked to the storage closet behind his buzzing computer. After Karen had left, he'd packed up everything even remotely related to their joint practice and shoved it into the closet, in the back, along with a bunch of junk he didn't know what to do with. He walked past his most recent castaways—a broken standing lamp, an old laptop he didn't know how to get rid of, and his ugly metal filing cabinets—and stopped, facing the far wall. Playsets and boxes of toys sat there: Matchbox cars and marbles, action figures by the bucketful, plastic dolls and plush dolls, and stuffed animals of every sort. They were covered in a light coating of dust, but otherwise, they stared at him as if not a day had passed.

Toys had been Gordon's tools back when he worked with Karen. Observing how kids played—or better yet, playing along with them—helped Gordon and Karen begin diagnosing their conditions the way a physician might examine a patient with a stethoscope or a blood-pressure cuff. That was the best part about working with kids. They didn't come out swinging like Mark Bowman, expecting you to validate their neuroses. In fact, a lot of the time, kids wouldn't even give you the time of day if you ask directly. But they will play. And if you're game, they'll let you join in. As to what was really bothering them? The root cause? That was up to the psychiatrist to figure out. Odds are the kid couldn't even tell you if they wanted to. Kids couldn't self-diagnose. They didn't read a bunch of articles on the Internet and proclaim a psychiatry expertise. They never walked in the door ready to tell you what was wrong with them, one hand out and waiting for the antidepressant script.

But coming back to the storage closet was bad. Gordon didn't have to be a shrink to know that. Closing this door in his mind had taken him a long time, and now he'd just opened it without thinking. That was called a regression.

Worse was the fact that he also had his phone in his hand and Karen on speed dial, and that he pressed Call before he could talk himself out of it.

He held the phone to his ear. Karen Jefferson picked up after four rings. He counted that as a victory. She hadn't yet shuffled him off to voicemail.

"Gordon, if this isn't some sort of emergency, I'm going to be very disappointed in you," she said. A judgment without sounding like a reprimand. Textbook therapist and not entirely unwarranted.

Right after the divorce, he'd called her a lot—too much. He cringed to think of it. He'd just broken a two-month streak—a personal best for Gordon and one he knew the struggles of which would be completely lost upon Karen.

"It is an emergency. Of sorts. Although not for me," Gordon said, his voice hollow and close in the closet. He was struck by an irrational fear that Karen would know he was staring at his toys, so he covered the receiver and scampered out into his office proper before flopping down on his patient chair.

Karen sighed. "Okay then, let's start at the beginning."

Gordon put his hand to his forehead and slumped deeper. "Is this really necessary? I'm not some pining teenager."

"If you want to talk, it is. You know the drill." Karen cleared her throat and paused. "Gordon, I'm not coming back to you or to Baltimore. You know that, right?" she asked as if reading off a script.

"Sort of," Gordon said, going off of his own script.

"Not *sort of*. Do you want to talk or not?" Karen asked, a note of annoyance in her voice, which was a rare thing and told Gordon more than anything that she took this stupid ritual seriously.

"Yes, I know. Okay? I know. You are not coming back." He paused for a moment. "But I'm keeping your name on the plate out front," he said quickly.

"I know, Gordon. I still get a few calls a month." Her voice was tired.

"You do? What do you tell them?"

"Exactly what we decided on the split, that we review each other's cases. Although I hadn't expected to be saying that still, almost *five years later*."

"Yeah, well, this time I actually do want to run something by you." He tried not to take her obvious pause of surprise personally. "Karen?" he asked after almost ten seconds.

"Yes. Well, yes, by all means. I'm happy to hear you've got work. What's the case?" she asked.

Gordon told her about his testimony and what Dana Frisco had told him about Ethan's crime. He even told her about how awful his afternoon session had been and how he'd had three beers just to get his mind right enough to even muster that smile for Mark Bowman and his bullshit. Then he took a deep breath and waited.

After a long moment of silence, Karen spoke. "You're telling me you're selling yourself as an expert witness for drinking money?"

Gordon coughed. It sounded bad when she said it out loud. "No. Well... yes. I suppose. In the strictest sense. But can we keep on topic here? Have you ever heard of violent parasomnia manifesting itself so young? Twelve years old?"

Karen made that soft ticking sound with her tongue that instantly took Gordon back to when their two desks shared one office and they would chart patients in the late afternoon, the lazy, heavy sunlight pouring through the big bay window between them, cutting through a ruby decanter of wine and settling upon them both as they worked to the tune of soft piano music in the background. He blinked, and the memory retreated.

"Off the top of my head? No. That type of extreme violence would most likely be the result of REM behavioral disorder, which has a median age of sixty-five, I believe. Children at that age exhibit your more garden-variety parasomnias, though."

"We treated hundreds of them," Gordon said, nodding, "but they were all of the slow-wave sleep variety. Sleep-talking, chronic bed-wetting, sleepwalking..."

"All very benign," Karen said. "I mean, I suppose it wouldn't be completely unheard of for an REM behavioral disorder to manifest at that age. Do you know anything about the child's emotional state? His health history? Violent parasomnia often runs in the family."

"No, I don't know anything about him," Gordon said softly. *Except how lost he looked. How defeated. How confused.* But looks could be deceiving. Gordon agreed with Karen. The science was against him.

"Do you feel some sort of residual guilt here? Is that why you're asking me this? You think you might have helped a killer kid go free?" Karen asked. "You testified that violent parasomnias exists. They do. Twelve is a tricky age. Studies show that children start dreaming as adults do as early as age nine. By twelve, he would be completely capable of exhibiting violent parasomnias. Likely? No. Capable? Yes."

Gordon rubbed his face. "I don't think he's going free. I think he's gonna end up in Ditchfield."

"Ah, I see," Karen said in that infuriating, two-steps-ahead-of-you way she had. "You think you let the child down somehow. Despite knowing nothing about him the second before you walked in the courtroom."

"That's not it," Gordon said weakly. Because he knew that was it—or at least part of it.

"You can't save every child that finds themselves stuck between a rock and a hard place. Not unless you have a time machine. Let me guess. You saw something in this kid that reminded you of someone. Maybe he reminded you of yourself. Maybe of the life you had when you used to treat kids like him. Like if he'd only come to you five years ago, maybe he wouldn't be sitting there on trial?"

Gordon felt depantsed. He couldn't say anything. She'd sniffed him out, and he knew his silence would only serve to confirm it.

"You're projecting, Gordon. And you're unsettled by the very nature of the case. When you get unsettled, you get neurotic. Obsessive." Despite her words, her tone was not impatient. If anything, she sounded a little sad. Still, she paused as if she knew she'd perhaps gone too far. They'd always used to throw diagnoses at each other across the office, half in jest, but Gordon knew that one had heart behind it.

"Well," he said. "This has been a fun chat, Karen. Thanks for talking."

"That was too much," Karen said. "I'm sorry."

"No, I think you're pretty much spot-on. Always were."

"Some part of you has loved every troubled kid you've ever come across. It's a noble thing. Insane, but noble. And part of the reason why I married you."

"Then divorced me," Gordon added. Karen took a deep breath, but he cut in before she could speak. "Divorced me when I couldn't love the one you cared about most." He was baiting her, he knew, lashing out a bit, doing what he could to turn the tables before all the food slid into his lap.

She didn't bite. "Get some sleep. Lay off the booze. Focus on your next patient," she said, not unkindly. "Good-bye, Gordon."

Gordon didn't respond.

"Good-bye, Gordon," she repeated more forcefully. She never used to let them end a phone conversation without a proper good-bye. He wasn't going to win that, either.

"Good-bye, Karen," he said.

That night Gordon had a dream he hadn't had in almost thirty years. He recognized what was happening instantly, and a wave of childlike terror washed over him. The nightmare always started the same way: he found himself standing at the edge of his parents' sprawling Bethesda estate. When he used to have the dream regularly, the place was his home, but he hadn't set foot there in decades. His parents moved after they divorced when he was in his early twenties. But in the dream, the estate was untouched from the days he would run its sprawling lawn as a child. He was facing back toward the house, a stout, four-story structure with two outspread wings, white-washed and shining in the distance. But he knew he wouldn't be looking at it for long. Very shortly, he would be pulled around, helpless to resist as he was dragged by some unseen force past the manicured edge of the lawn and into the rough outer growth before the forest. He would only be able to watch, paralyzed, as his toes dragged a line through the pine needles and brush into the darkness of the forest beyond. Where the cave was.

The nightmare had happened like that countless times in his youth. It was the single most recurring dream he could remember having, and it was always the same. So

Gordon faced his shining house, eyes closed, whimpering, waiting for the pull.

Except the pull never came.

He opened his eyes and looked down at himself and was surprised to find that he was not ten years old. He was a man, with a man's work clothing on and a man's soft paunch and a man's weathered hands. He touched his face and found stubble there. Yet the dream of his childhood remained. As his fear subsided, he turned himself around, prepared to confront the faceless kidnapper of his youth, but he saw nothing, only the forest waving at him like a heat mirage. He felt a strange compulsion to walk toward the woods he used to be pulled toward. And so he did. His feet hit the ground, but they made no sound. Silence stretched tightly between the trees. Had it always been like that? He didn't think so. Another difference.

He walked the route he knew well. He'd been there countless times in his dreams and also in real life. And so he found himself staring at the mouth of the cave head-on, the mouth that used to swallow him up until he cried out in terror, often awaking. If he was lucky. What was inside was worse. The Red. As a child, he could start to see it there at the mouth—tendrils of red mist snaking their way out of the black. But no red mist met him just then. And the weight of dread he used to feel was instead replaced by the weight of silence. A silence as heavy and unsettling as the terror he used to feel, but different. Manageable.

Gordon walked forward into the cave. Where once red mist had washed over everything like an incoming tide, now he saw only the inside of a cave. Half lit. Hot and damp. Empty. Gordon felt as though he was taking one last look at an apartment he'd moved out of before closing the door. An empty mark stained the rock underfoot where something should have been, a discoloration that meant something, but he no longer knew what. Gordon felt it very important that he remember what was there, that it was vital, even, and somehow connected to something. To... the boy. Ethan.

But as soon as Gordon recalled Ethan and the trial and testimony, the illusion of the dream started to break. He'd become too self-aware.

"No!" he screamed, but no sound came out. "Wait! What is it? What was it?" All his words died as soon as they left his mouth. He grabbed at the walls of the cave, but they came apart in his hands. The dream world crumbled around him. He ran. Not away—not this time—but deeper, deeper into the cave, as fast as he could, but his legs were putty and the cave disintegrating. He pleaded with himself to keep the projection alive for a moment longer until he could figure out what it meant, but his unconscious mind was uncaring.

Gordon shot awake and found himself standing again in his storage room. His heart raced. He felt alien to himself. He forced himself to take breaths. At first, he thought he'd fallen into another dream, but then he looked at the clock on the wall in his office. It ticked steadily. Four fifteen in the morning. So he'd sleepwalked. That was unsettling in and of itself, but it wasn't new to him. He used to do it all the time as a kid. After several minutes, he was able to pull himself together and pushed off the wall he'd been leaning upon. Karen was right—all this talk of the past was unhealthy for him. He was opening old wounds. He decided to go make himself some chamomile tea, absolutely not have a dram of scotch, and read his book in his office until he felt sleepy again. It was *Finnegan's Wake*, so it shouldn't take long.

He turned to close the closet door, and it caught on something—a Matchbox car, well used, more die-cast metal in color now than the cherry red it used to be. What was it doing out there? Had he picked up any of the old toys when he had been down there last? He couldn't quite remember, but he didn't think so. He'd grabbed it when he was asleep, then. He toed the car inside the closet and shut the door softly.

He was definitely not going to have a dram of scotch. But a sip never killed anyone.

# CHAPTER THREE

---

G ordon drank enough chamomile tea to drug a bear, but he still had a hard time sleeping after revisiting the cave in his dreams. He often counseled patients suffering from insomnia to give sleeping a shot for thirty minutes. If they weren't asleep in thirty minutes, they should leave the bedroom to do a simple task in low light—reading, doing the dishes, putting together a puzzle, things of that nature—until they felt sleepy again. Then they gave it another shot for another thirty minutes. Rinse and repeat. Each of these waking intervals he called a "sit session." Gordon went through four sit sessions before giving up on his own advice and simply lying awake in bed. He'd done all the dishes, read a full twenty pages of *Finnegan's Wake* —which was a minor miracle in and of itself—and didn't own any puzzles. He'd had the one slug of scotch, and the rest of the bottle beckoned to him, a solid, sturdy thing on the shelf in the shifting lights of the night, but he wasn't about to let himself fall down that rabbit hole just yet. So he lay in his bed, damp around the neck from the close heat, counting the number of times his feeble air-conditioning unit kicked on and shut off until he drifted for an hour or two around eight in the morning.

Then, of course, he was sleepy. But he had an appointment, not a professional appointment, but one that sometimes took at least as much out of him those days: lunch with his mother.

Deborah Pope came into the city of Baltimore twice a month, every other Thursday, for lunch with her son at Waterstones, an upscale bistro and grille in the swanky Harbor East neighborhood. Even that she considered risky, convinced as she was that the entirety of the city of Baltimore was one mean look away from erupting into anarchy at any moment. Gordon told her time and again that she didn't have to come if she didn't want to. She told him her love for her only son far outweighed her distaste for the city. But she never let him forget the sacrifice she was making, as if a twenty-five-dollar Cobb salad was the equivalent of a prison visit.

His mother was fond of Caesar, however. Her regular waiter at Waterstones greeted her as if she were royalty every time she came in and had so far resisted all her attempts to smuggle him out of Baltimore and into one of the many white-tablecloth dining establishments in Bethesda, where she still had a condo. When she was being especially pretentious, Gordon tried to slip him an extra ten bucks for putting up with her. Caesar always slipped it back while she was in the restroom. He said he found her hilarious, and besides, she tipped him as if she thought he was living hand-to-mouth in a war zone instead of across from the Walgreens ten blocks away.

"There he is. There's my son," she said, waving Gordon over to her regular table in the center of the garden patio. His mother enjoyed being outdoors but not out *of* doors.

She wore large-frame sunglasses with gold accents and had on a cigar-colored straw sunhat wrapped with a coral ribbon. She stood and smoothed her striped sundress before holding out her arms and pulling Gordon into a hug. She was a slight woman, not thin but with refined features that bordered on delicate. Her grip was rock solid though, and she planted a firm kiss on his cheek before pushing herself away and sitting. She settled her necklace and rings before grasping her martini glass, only to find it empty.

Caesar floated in. "Another, Mrs. Pope?"

"Oh, why the hell not. Thank you, Caesar."

Caesar nodded and looked at Gordon.

"Another? How long have you been here, Mother?" Gordon asked.

"Fifteen or so minutes. I get here early. I always assume some sort of breakdown will occur and I'll be reduced to one of those godawful taxi cabs. You might as well shoot me."

Gordon looked blankly at her. So they were having *that* kind of lunch today. He turned to Caesar. "I'll take a scotch on the rocks."

Caesar nodded and swept away. His mother gave him a disapproving eye.

"What, Mom?"

"Scotch? At noon?"

"You're on your second gin martini," Gordon said.

"I'm retired. It's different."

"I'm doing okay, Mom. Thanks for asking. I mean, I'm bleeding patients, and I called Karen last night for the first time in two months, and I'm not really sleeping well, but I'll live."

"Karen? You called her? Oh, Gordon."

"I had a legitimate medical question. She answered. She

was actually quite helpful." Gordon grabbed for his scotch as soon as Caesar set it down.

"The usual meal?" Caesar asked.

"Thank you, dear," his mother said. As he spun away, she picked up her own drink, elbow on the table. "Well, she's an outstanding doctor. Brilliant, you might say. As good as I was in my prime. Very talented."

"Mother, she ripped out my heart," Gordon said flatly.

"You didn't let me finish. I was going to say, 'Very talented, that bitch.'" She made no effort to lower her voice. A nearby table of young women turned to look at her, and she looked right back until they turned away.

Gordon stifled a smile. "Well, the fact is she brought in the business. And my current patients are catching on that she might not be coming back."

"*Might* not? She bought a two-and-a-half-million-dollar house in Laguna Beach. She had a kid with that new man of hers... What's his name? The big-shot agent?"

"Chad." Gordon rolled his eyes. As if she didn't know exactly who he was.

"Yes, *Chad*," she said with equal distaste. "The point is, there's no 'might.' She's never coming back."

"I know that. You think I don't know that?" He swirled his ice, the glass already sweating.

"Sometimes I wonder," his mother said over a sip.

"Her name has weight. That's why it's still on the plaque and the website and the phone listing. I can't do this without her."

"Nonsense. You're every bit as talented as she is."

Gordon looked up at his mother to find the sarcasm, but he found none.

"I mean it, Gordon," she said.

Gordon sighed. "Maybe once, but not anymore. She

kept doing what she loved, kept researching, kept publishing. That's why she's relevant, and I'm..." He held out his hands, encompassing himself.

His mother watched him through hooded eyes. She wasn't having it. "Oh, *that's* why you're stuck in that housing project with a smattering of clients you don't care about? *That's* why you're still single. Drinking scotch at noon?" She took a sip of gin. "Because you never got published?"

"Well, I was thinking the 'kept doing what she loved' part was more integral. But yes, that too. It goes a long way in our community to get published like she has."

"I am aware of that, Gordon. I was published many times in my day. And as for doing what you love, that's your fault. You made the decision to stop treating children. She didn't make it for you."

Caesar brought their food, and his mother smiled warmly at him in silence as it was presented. As soon as he left, she turned back to Gordon with a sniff. He crossed his arms and eyed the salad, no longer hungry.

"What I'm saying is it's in your head," she said.

"It's definitely not my head that's the problem," Gordon said.

His mother held up her hand, stopping him.

Caesar stepped up. "Is something wrong with the salad, Mrs. Pope?"

"Oh, I wasn't waving for you, sweetheart. My son was getting vulgar. I'll have one more martini since you're here."

Caesar nodded and breezed away.

His mother ate in silence, ignoring Gordon's stare. She looked up after a bite. "What, you never heard of a three-martini lunch? We used to do it all the time back when I practiced. Then the country got into yoga. The damage was irreparable."

Gordon laughed and took up his fork. "I don't blame you. You did couples therapy for three decades. I'm going on three years, and I feel like it's already driving me to the bottle." He savored the crunch of the chopped peppers and the tang of the mustard vinaigrette. He wouldn't go begging his mother for cash, but he sure as hell would take the Waterstones' Cobb, every time.

"No, dear. See, I actually liked couples therapy— despite being married to your father all those years. Or perhaps because of it. Living in a disaster of a relationship helped me see the signs in others. That was the secret to my success."

Gordon recalled the scattered toys in his closet, the Matchbox car that had seemed to roll itself free. It put Gordon in mind of reliving his own childhood.

"Mom, you remember that night when you found me wandering on the north end of the Bethesda property in that... that cave?" Gordon tried to keep his voice light, picking at his salad as he spoke.

His mother stopped midsip and watched him carefully. "Of course I remember. What brought that up? Is this because I mentioned your father? Did he do something to you? Because if he did and you're coming out with it now, I'll dig that bastard up and kill him again, myself."

"No, Mom. Christ. How many times... He was an asshole, not a criminal," Gordon said. "Forget it."

But his mother wouldn't forget it. "Then why are you bringing up my single most terrifying moment as a parent at an otherwise pleasant lunch?"

"I was an expert witness yesterday in a case where a sleepwalking boy allegedly strangled another child, nearly killed him," Gordon said, lowering his voice. "It really messed with me. It's like it opened up a window in my brain to all this stuff I thought I'd put away."

"Strangled another child? My God. All we ever worried about with you was if you'd sleepwalk into something and kill yourself. And that was plenty to worry about, believe me." When Caesar came around again, she handed him her credit card without looking at it. "For the bill, dear. And would you mind getting me a chilled glass for what's left of my drink? I'd love you forever." Caesar produced one from behind his back, and she hooted. The gin was swapped, and Caesar moved on.

"I do remember you fretting over me. And you rarely fret. So I know I must have been a pretty serious sleepwalker," Gordon said.

His mother snorted. "*Pretty* serious? A sprained ankle is pretty serious, Gordon. We had to lock you in your bedroom at night for years."

"But that night was different. At the cave. That night was worse, right?"

His mother took a deep breath and then a dainty sip of gin. "Yes. Usually, you bumped around your room for a bit. Maybe walked into ours to bump around there. Once, we found you in the garden, bumping around the tomatoes— startling but not frightening. Then, that night. Bam, out of nowhere, you walk nearly a quarter of a mile to that washed-out culvert and end up in this little cave." She shivered at the memory.

"And then what?" Gordon asked. He'd heard it before, many times, but he felt that hearing it again was important.

"You know. You were growling, holding on to a big rock there and swaying a little. I was so horrified and relieved at the same time that I didn't do anything at first. Just watched you. Until you stopped."

"I stopped?"

"Yes, you stopped, and then you sat down, then lay down. Fast asleep. The paramedics took you to the hospital because they thought something was wrong. Turns out you were just deeply asleep. You woke up twelve hours later, smiling. We took you home. Then I went and had several stiff drinks with your father and ended up in some sort of horrible row with him that I can't recall the details of. I think we each accused each other of putting too much pressure on you." She waved the rest of the story off with one hand.

"What happened after that?" Gordon asked.

"Well, we ended up tying your little leg to your superhero bed. Remember that?" His mother smiled out of the corner of her mouth.

Gordon nodded. *That alone would be grounds for therapy.* But that wasn't what he'd meant. "No, I mean, what happened after that night with the sleepwalking? Any more episodes that you can remember?"

"No. Nothing. Eventually, we forgot to strap you in, and then when nothing happened, we even stopped locking the door."

"Just like that. Sleepwalking from the day I could walk, then... bam. Nothing. Over." Gordon was speaking to himself as much as to his mother.

"You outgrew that stage. Thank God. Although you moved from that to picking your nose. You remember that? You still haven't quite outgrown that one completely."

"I don't see how you outgrow something like that in one night," Gordon said. He wasn't about to tell his mother that he'd revisited that cave, that the dream he'd had throughout all those sleepwalking years had come back. The dream was different from before, but the cave was still there. Things weren't quite as buttoned up as his mother thought.

"You're thinking too much about the past, Gordon. Whatever you were working through in that brain of yours as a little boy, you did it. It broke like a fever." His mother signed the bill and tucked her credit card into her clutch. "Now, I have another lunch to get to, with my bridge club, all the way over in Travilah. I need to run. Those witches wait for nobody." She stood and kissed her son on the forehead. "See you in two weeks, sweetheart." Gordon nodded, his mind elsewhere.

As his mother left the table, he turned to her. "Mom, how old was I then? Ten? Eleven?"

She thought for a moment. "You were twelve years old," she said, nodding definitively. "I remember because it was the week before your thirteenth birthday, and I was dreading the questions from the neighbors." She waved again and turned away.

Gordon had thought to finish his food, but he was slowly losing his appetite again. The fact that Gordon's own parasomnia had come to a head at the same age as Ethan might be nothing more than a strange coincidence. Or not.

He could hear Karen's voice in his head. *"You're projecting, Gordon. Leave it alone. Focus your energy elsewhere."* But to Gordon, Ethan was looking less and less like a projection and more like a reflection—a reflection of the boy Gordon had been when he wound up in that cave.

# CHAPTER FOUR

W hen Gordon returned home, he made himself two promises. The first was that he would not call Karen again, not even to discuss her thoughts on how his own parasomnia symptoms could have stopped seemingly overnight. That was a legitimate medical question, but he already knew what she'd say—that the lessening of parasom-niac symptoms was well documented at that age although nobody knew why. *"But you already knew that, didn't you, Gordon? So why are you calling me again?"*

Because he missed Karen? Not exactly.

Because he missed working with Karen? Missed the doctor he had been when he was with her? That was more like it.

Bottom line, the call would seem exactly as desperate as it was.

The second promise was that he would not go through the boxes of past case files he had stored right next to his toys in an effort to find anything that resembled Ethan's violent parasomnia, no matter how badly he wanted to. That would be textbook regression. He'd double-taped those boxes shut for a reason. How quickly he'd managed to forget the toll that seeing each kid had taken on him, like a sliver of stone chipped from a statue with each visit. Over the years, he'd been worn down and blunted. That he was good at treating kids almost made it worse. He considered it a special kind of curse to be drawn to a profession that forced him daily to confront his greatest failure.

He turned from the closet door and trekked upstairs to his apartment, but each step seemed to slow him. He might have turned himself around and gone back down and into the closet on the way toward breaking his second promise were it not for his phone ringing in his pocket. He fished it out to silence it and saw who it was: Dana Frisco. He was surprised he had her info in his phone. Had they exchanged numbers? Perhaps, now that he thought about it, many months ago. Something about her offering to keep an eye out for more courthouse work for him. He felt a lurch in his stomach, the kind he got whenever he knew a phone call wasn't going to be good news. He picked up.

"Dana?" he asked. "Are you all right?"

Dana spoke softly. "Hi, Gordon," she began and then paused. "Yeah, I'm fine. I wanted to see if I could... run something by you." She almost sounded embarrassed.

It occurred to him that she might be asking him out. Could that possibly be it? *She gave you her phone number*, he told himself. Stranger things had happened. Of course, he'd taken her number and then sat on it for four months like a hibernating bear. Still, he found himself smiling. Dana would like Darrow's Barrel. He'd buy her the crab-cake sandwich. She'd be impressed. *"Best-kept secret in Baltimore,"* he'd say, leaning in and winking. Maybe not winking. Nobody winks in real life. But the scene was all there. He could picture it: cold beer, the smell of oil on old wood underneath the subtle scent of her shampoo, the sizzle of the fry line in the back—

"Listen, this isn't standard," she said. "Far from it, and they might have my badge if they knew I was calling you like this."

Gordon smirked. He hadn't known he had such a bad-boy reputation down at the precinct.

"We're about to hit that twenty-four-hour window, and I gotta pull out all the stops," she said.

Gordon paused. "What?" he asked.

"It's another kid. A little girl, twelve years old. She's been missing for almost fifteen hours now," Dana said, her voice tight.

"What?" Gordon asked again, partly to cover himself and partly to let his mind catch back up with the reality of the situation. "What can *I* do?"

"I saw the way the Ethan Barret case hit you, and I know you used to work with kids a lot, and I thought maybe you could—"

"Dana, I'm a psychiatrist, not a private eye. I'd rather just disappoint you now," Gordon said.

"I know, I know, but hear me out." Dana took a deep breath. "The girl disappeared from her bed. Okay? A neighbor kid, a young boy, reported seeing a girl in a white nightie walk past his window sometime in the early morning hours."

Gordon went cold. "Sleepwalking?"

"That's the running theory."

"Nobody tried to stop her?"

"The kid thought she was a ghost. He hid under his covers then fell asleep. You know how kids are," Dana said, trying to calm herself. She sounded as though some small part of her wanted to wring that kid's neck. "I know you don't do this stuff anymore. I know. And the last thing I want to do is overstep here, but I don't think I have to tell you the statistics on kids that go missing for over twenty-four hours."

Gordon knew.

"There's something else, too," Dana said. "The missing girl is Ethan Barret's best friend."

The nervous sweat on Gordon's brow sprouted anew.

"Apparently they are, or were, very close," Dana continued. "Sort of like a first boyfriend, girlfriend thing. It was too weird of a coincidence not to call you. See if you could just take a look at the scene here."

Gordon's unfocused gaze fell upon the closet door.

"Tell me where you are," he said.

DANA FRISCO TUCKED her phone away and pointedly ignored the lingering stare of her partner, Marty. She focused instead out the windshield, on the buzzing orange streetlight above their squad car. The big bugs of the Baltimore summer slammed into it with the sound of wet hail.

Marty Cicero had been working with her for seven months, which was four months longer than her last partner. He wasn't the type of guy to be the first to look away, even when she was pointedly ignoring him. At a glance, you would lump him in the Jersey Shore brigade. He was dark and built, his chest half again as wide as Dana's. He wore a gold chain, shaved his legs, and had a tribal armband tattoo. Dana had wanted to write him off as nothing more than an East Coast gym rat at first. The problem was he was too damn perceptive, his gaze too keen. And he was too much of a straight cop. He shuffled his mass to face her more fully.

"Did you seriously just call in a psychiatrist?"

Dana nodded slowly.

Marty sat back in his seat, and the fake leather creaked. "Does Lieutenant Duke know about this?"

He already knew the answer was no. Dana knew he wanted her to say it out loud.

"No, Marty. But if Duke ran everything the way he wanted, we'd all be dead of paper cuts long before we found Erica Denbrook."

Dana knew she wasn't quite herself when it came to missing kids. She got a certain look, glassy and dangerous. Marty had been on missing-children calls with Dana before. He was watching her as if she was drunk on moonshine and might snap at any moment. She knew he'd heard the talk around the station about her reputation. She'd had four partners in the past five years. Three of them had gone on to make detective, which in the BPD meant they were on their way. Not her. Never her. In the men's locker room at the station, they called her the bull. That wasn't a flattering thing. The idea was that if you rode with her long enough, if you put in your eight seconds, you'd get promoted. As for why she still sat in a squad car? Dana knew Marty was trying to figure that out. If he asked her directly, which he hadn't yet, she would say it had an awful lot to do with Warren Duke.

"We either find this girl in the next six hours, or odds are she's gone," Dana said. She struggled to keep her voice even and cold, but she could see in Marty's eyes that he knew better. Dana had a daughter of her own, seven years old, named Chloe. She pictured Chloe in every one of these situations. Every call like this she got. She couldn't help it.

Dana watched a fat cicada slam again and again into the streetlight until it hit a broken panel and started to fry in the heat.

"Gordon Pope knows how kids think. He can help us," Dana said.

"More cops is what we need. More cops will find this kid, not some psychiatrist," Marty said.

"More cops? We've already got six of them running down the neighborhood from top to bottom. There are three in that spillway alone. They'll just start running into each other."

Dana sat back and waited, turning the car's weak air vents onto her face. Their cruiser sat down the street from a blockaded intersection outside a halfway-constructed tenement neighborhood. A low-lying brick façade to her right read Tivoli Estates, or was supposed to. The *Ti* was missing from Tivoli, and the *E* was missing from Estates. Someone had had great plans for Tivoli Estates. Then the recession hit. The money pulled out and left the handful of families that had moved into the duplexes and single-story ranch houses to fend for themselves. Since then, it had been the *Voli States*. The neighborhood, if you could call it that, was built on an incline leading up to the old Tivoli theatre at the top, so it was easy for Dana to see that, at best, one-third of the buildings were occupied. The rest were abandoned or unfinished.

To her left, three flashlight beams swung like nooses in the wind as they made their way into the neighborhood up a graffiti-pocked spillway clogged with trash and construction debris. To her far right, a flashing cruiser slowed what sparse traffic there was to a stop until two policemen waved each car clear. The cicadas sounded like chainsaws, and Dana could see the mosquitoes already swarming over the heat of the cruiser's engine block. Piles of bricks and rotten wood and pools of standing water lined the sides of the two-lane street leading into the neighborhood, where God willing, a little girl was still just lost somewhere. But more likely than not, in that neighborhood and in that city, if they found anything, it would be a body.

GORDON TOOK the back route Dana had told him about, pulling off Highway 40 a little before the Tivoli Estates exit and meandering down some ugly-looking side streets. The sky was near full dark now, and he could see the blue and red lights flashing in the night haze well before he came upon them, which was the idea. Dana had made no bones about smuggling him in. He realized he was most likely a dead ringer for the profile of somebody that might have taken the girl: a single white male in his midforties. Rumpled and unshaven, smelling vaguely of booze. Driving a shitty car through the scene. Knowing his luck, he'd get arrested while trying to get into the neighborhood to help the girl. But Dana knew what she was doing. She and her partner were waiting back of the blockade, parked along a residential street. She waved him behind her and took the lead, her lights flashing in silence. She spoke a few words at the cordon, and both cars passed by. The policeman stared him down as he crept through, but Gordon looked straight ahead.

Four blocks into the neighborhood, they stopped. Dana threw her car into park, and Gordon did the same. The sound of their car doors slamming echoed against the dark houses. A curtain rustled in a window then stilled. Gordon couldn't help thinking they were walking the neighborhood Ethan lived in as well—the basement of one of these houses was almost a murder scene. The halted development here lent the place a broken air, not so much quiet as empty. He saw signs everywhere of what it might have been—a vibrant neighborhood where kids splashed around the spillway, biked along the sidewalks that zigzagged up the hill, or hiked to the Tivoli to catch a rainy afternoon movie—but all of its potential was clipped, not unlike the future of Ethan himself.

Dana walked right up to him and wasted no time. "The focus is on a spillway that rings the south side of the neighborhood. There's a small sluice of runoff there that they're combing. It's not very deep, but if she hurt herself or fell into it somehow, it's enough to drown in."

Dana's flat, unflinching tone chilled Gordon. She didn't sound like herself. He wanted a better look at her, at her face, but the streetlights above were burned out, so all he saw was the muted shine of her black hair and the silver of her badge reflecting in the ambient light of the cruiser. Her partner was no warmer. He was a squat, powerful-looking man, his arms crossed over a shelf of a chest. Gordon had met him before at the courthouse—Marty Cicero. The man didn't have to say a word for Gordon to know he wasn't exactly happy with Gordon being there. He wondered if the officer might warm to him if he knew Gordon shared the sentiment.

"The roadblocks and sweeps haven't caught anything," she said. "The few neighbors there are said they saw nothing, heard nothing. No cars, no sounds of struggle. It's the type of neighborhood where a sound like that would carry."

"So you think she's still here somewhere?" Gordon asked.

Dana nodded. "The neighbor kid saw her walking south from her house, there, towards the spillway." She pointed at a flat ranch house down the street that was lit up like a stadium, swarming with people, several of them police. "I thought you may have some insight as to how long these things last, you know, or maybe how kids act when they're sleepwalking."

"If she was sleepwalking," he said.

"We don't have a lot to work with here. I think it's as good a theory as any at this point."

"Children shamble when they sleepwalk. They're like cows. It would be unusual for her... What's her name?" he asked, realizing he still didn't know.

"Erica Denbrook," she said softly.

"And she's twelve?" he asked, clearing his throat. That age kept coming back to haunt him.

She nodded.

"It would be unusual for Erica, at her age, to sleepwalk with purpose, with direction. And kids who sleepwalk don't just disappear. If anything, they make themselves conspicuous, like drunkards. If she's been gone for over ten hours, I guarantee you she's woken up by now. Probably some time ago. But she's still not back. That's what should be worrying you," he said.

Cicero snuffled and shifted his stance. Dana scanned the street up and down as if it might offer something new, but Gordon was willing to bet she'd been up and down the street for hours already, to no avail. Her gaze moved in tiny jerks, like a nervous bird, and she swallowed several times as though her fear would come bubbling up out of her if she let it. Gordon felt that anything that might stem that panic, even pretending he could be useful, was better than letting her fear take hold of her, so he spoke again.

"That's the window? The one where the neighbor kid saw her?"

Dana nodded eagerly. "You want to take a look?"

"What about her bedroom?"

"We dusted the bedroom. No forced entry. No foreign prints."

"Can I see the bedroom?"

Dana was quiet. Apprehensively, she eyed the house, still buzzing with activity and the low hum of conversations heard over the still night.

"If I can do anything for you, it's gonna start in there."

Dana nodded. "I'll... I'll make it work. Follow me. Don't say anything."

Gordon heard a soft popping sound when Cicero stepped in behind him. He turned briefly to see the officer tapping his teeth together, eyes set grimly forward.

A policeman in plainclothes was speaking with a distraught man and woman just inside the front door. Erica's parents were young, in their thirties. Dana said their names were Marcus and McKayla. Neither looked to have showered, eaten, or slept in twenty-four hours.

A fat policeman standing on the front lawn stepped up and then paused when he saw Dana. He looked at Gordon, then at Cicero, then back at Gordon.

"He's with me," Dana said, more of a command than an explanation.

The officer shrugged and stepped aside. The plainclothes officer just inside the door wasn't as accommodating. He was a tall man with clean-cut salt-and-pepper hair. He wore dark jeans and a light-pink dress shirt under a gold-buttoned navy jacket. His badge flashed from his hip.

"No press," the man said. "No outside visitors of any sort."

"He's with me, Lieutenant," Dana said again, less forcefully this time.

"Of course he is, Frisco. But he's not with me. And

unless you cleared it back at the station, he's not getting in. I'm not having another Rockhurst on my watch."

Dana paused. "I cleared it with the station. And Rockhurst was a simple misunderstanding that—"

The lieutenant held up his hand, stopping Dana cold. He turned to Gordon. "You, what's your name?"

"Gordon Pope."

"Marty, hold him here while I run this guy down." He turned away from them without another word and stepped out of the porchlight. Dana clenched her jaw and watched him go.

"Well, looks like you got about three minutes, Gordon," she said.

Cicero turned broadside to her. "What? Lieutenant Duke said to stay put, Dana."

She looked at him. "You're not Lieutenant Duke's partner. So either you tackle us both, which I have no doubt you could do, by the way, or you be *my* partner."

Cicero's breathing quickened. He flicked his eyes back and forth between Dana and Gordon.

"Don't worry, Marty. You'll have plenty of time to become best buds with Warren Duke when they promote you." She turned to Gordon. "It's down the hall, the room on the right. Three minutes."

Gordon looked at Cicero and took a step toward the hallway, and when Cicero did nothing more than stare bullets at him, he set off. He was in Erica's room in seconds, smiling and feeling as though he'd done something important until he realized he had no idea what he was looking for.

Gordon panned the room. He saw a twin bed in the corner with a brightly striped bedspread, rumpled and pushed to the floor. Posters of bands he didn't recognize. An open pink retainer case on a thin blue side table next to the bed, empty. That was evidence for the sleepwalking theory —Gordon had worn retainers as a kid, and while he wasn't the most social boy, even he wouldn't have been caught dead wearing them outside while under his own power. A whirring laptop, slim and silver, sat on a small corner desk, casting a faint blue pall. The screen constantly refreshed some sort of live chat feed. He moved in for a closer look when Dana's voice suddenly carried down the hall, and he knew he had to go. Gordon had just turned the corner when Warren Duke came back.

The lieutenant stepped inside the foyer and paused, staring at Gordon as if his presence was personally insulting. Then he turned to Dana and said, "He isn't cleared, Dana," his voice terse and low, a school principal's voice. One vein flickered purple at the edge of his tanned temple.

"Must be some mistake, Lieutenant," Dana said. Gordon wanted to shrink back down the hall, but Dana stood her ground. If anything, she stood taller. "I'll take him out, check it out with dispatch myself."

"You do that," Duke said, his voice flat as slate, eyes unblinking.

"This way, Dr. Pope," she said, as if she'd never met him before in her life. Gordon slid sideways around Duke, trying to smile. They left the house along with Cicero and paused in the street outside, beyond the light of the porch.

"Dana, that is exactly the type of shit that I'm talking about," Cicero whispered. "That's the reason you—"

A look from Dana stilled him. Out there, in the darkness, Gordon thought he saw a chink in the armor she'd shown inside. It was in her eyes. They were hurt, but her face was a grim mask. He wondered how many small barbs and jabs that mask had taken over the years from men like Warren Duke.

"Warren Duke, huh?" Gordon said, breaking the silence. "You know, I read a paper once that hypothesized a link between single-syllable last names and social entitlement. It was in the *Saskatchewan Journal of Anthropology*. Hand to God."

Cicero turned to Gordon with narrowed eyes, but Dana laughed. It was a deep laugh, not a high-pitched, nervous laugh. And it snapped the tension between them like a brittle stick. "What about 'Pope'?" she asked. "That's one syllable."

Gordon scratched at his collar for a second. "Eh, it was a garbage paper anyway."

"Did you get anything? From the bedroom?" Dana asked.

"Well, I think you're right about the sleepwalking," Gordon said, "but that's about all I could get. I'm sorry." And try as he might, he couldn't keep the bitter disappointment from his own voice. Nobody had asked for his professional help in something that mattered for a long time. That it was Dana made it all the more biting, especially since she seemed to be taking the weight of this case on her own shoulders.

"It's my fault," Dana said. "I'm not sure what I thought you'd find. And you had no time anyway." She watched Duke still interviewing Erica's parents through the dining room window.

"You could have tried to clear him first," Cicero said, as if telling her the night was black.

"Oh, please. This is the Warren Duke show. I doubt he'd approve of Gordon even if I'd submitted it the second the call came through. I just wanted to act quickly, do what I could to find her in the first twenty-four hours."

Gordon followed her gaze. He watched McKayla Denbrook take a sip of coffee, and her hand shook, but Gordon doubted that was from the caffeine. He looked back at Dana, recalling that she had a child, a girl. He guessed she was placing herself inside, by that window, with that coffee. The remnants of a board game were spread out on the dining room table just past where Duke stood. It looked paused midgame, probably from the evening before, when the family had still been whole. He squinted, stepping forward. The game looked like Chutes and Ladders. He walked forward again, on the porch now. Gordon and his mother had done their fair share of board gaming back in the day. He recognized the old-school yellow checkerboard, the classic design. It was indeed a very well-worn game of Chutes and Ladders, fading around the edges. Buttons stood in for some of the missing pieces. He took another step and nearly walked right into Warren Duke's chest.

"I'm sorry, maybe you didn't understand me," Duke said, holding up a hand that flashed with a gold signet ring. "Interfering with a police investigation is a—"

"That's Chutes and Ladders," Gordon said, ignoring him and speaking to Erica's parents just inside.

Whatever prepared response Duke had died on his lips. McKayla turned toward him, cup in hand. Gordon could see she was so tired and overrun that she was willing to assume any stranger in her house might be a detective or official of some sort.

"Yes," she said. "We've had game night every Wednesday since Erica was five."

"And she likes Chutes and Ladders?"

"She used to like them all, anything we put out there to

play," said Marcus. His hair was unsettled, as if he'd been running his hands through it repeatedly. "But nowadays, this is the only one that can get her to the table. If it was up to her, I think she'd be on her phone or in her room on her computer."

"But you still played last night?" Gordon asked, resisting the urge to roll his fingers as if he could speed the man up. Warren Duke already had his hand on Gordon's shoulder and was squeezing sharply.

Marcus nodded. "It's all that's left of family time. She can play online whenever she wants other days, and she does. But Wednesday night is always our night." He spoke as if he was lecturing her. Then his eyes softened again.

His wife began to cry and pressed herself to his chest.

Duke led Gordon away, outside again, past the lights. He was breathing hard through his nose, and once out of earshot of the house, he shoved Gordon forward, off the lawn and into the street next to Dana and Cicero, who didn't look pleased with him either.

"Frisco, I'm writing this up," Duke said. "And if you don't keep this guy under control, I'll make sure everyone knows about it."

With one last shove, he turned away, and that time he closed the front door behind him.

Dana shook her head, her hands on her hips. "As if I didn't fuck this up enough already." Cicero made a move toward him that Gordon knew would end up with him being escorted to his car with a sore shoulder.

"Wait." Gordon held up his hands. He looked around the lawn in a slow spin, his eyes darting everywhere. He settled his gaze on the sidewalk, the one that went past the neighbor's window. "I think I have an idea."

## CHAPTER FIVE

Dana watched Gordon walk down the sidewalk and past the neighbor's window, left to right, the direction the boy had seen Erica walk. The streetlights buzzed above him, the dust of a score of moths sifting down to be blown away in the weak breeze of the night. His eyes were wide as his head did a slow pan. Marty watched him with open skepticism, his hands half-clawed, as if they itched to collar Gordon and toss him from the scene. Dana shot a glance back at Erica's house. Warren Duke was the type of guy to have a strict three-strikes-and-you're-out policy. If he caught her dragging her feet again, she was most likely out of a job.

"I'm guessing Erica went to bed around ten? When do kids go to bed these days?" Gordon asked, still scanning the street.

"Her parents said she went to her room around ten. Most likely fell asleep shortly thereafter. The parents went to bed at ten thirty and said the light in her room was off."

"Your timeline puts the neighbor kid's sighting at what... eleven thirty?" Gordon asked.

Dana straightened. "Yes. Approximately eleven thirty. The neighbor said he looked at his bedside clock. But I don't remember telling you that."

"You didn't. But it makes sense. It takes anywhere from fifty to seventy minutes to go from awake to late-stage and REM sleep, where the strongest dreams occur. Let's call it an even sixty." Gordon pulled up his khaki slacks at the pockets and crouched as he peered down the sidewalk where Erica had last been seen. He leaned slightly against the brick of the low retaining wall to his right, sighting along it with one eye squinted.

"So that puts us at eleven thirty," Marty said flatly. "And Erica dreaming in her bed. Which isn't what happened."

Gordon popped up and turned toward them, his expression intense, as if he'd been staring at the numbers for hours and they were finally starting to come together. "Exactly," he said, pointing at Marty. "It isn't what happened, because she never got to dream."

"With all due respect," Marty said, his tone making it clear he had little to none, "unless you have something concrete to give us that can help, I need to get you out of here before it costs me and my partner our jobs." He looked sidelong at Dana.

Gordon nodded. "There are five stages of sleep," he said. "Stages one and two are light. Hypnagogic. Fleeting images from the day, no real cohesion"—he ticked off the stages on his fingers—"but stages three and four are what's called slow wave. This is where most sleepwalking occurs. Extreme parasomniacs rarely get to stage five, which is REM, deep sleep. They get up before then. Instead of being able to work out whatever their brain needs to work out in their sleep, they act on it. One of the most common reports coming from these cases is that the individual went to sleep dreaming of something on their to-do list and then acted that thing out while unconscious."

"No shit," Dana said, her mind already catching up with Gordon. "The unfinished board game. Chutes and Ladders."

Gordon nodded, a small smile at the corner of his mouth. "And what does this look like to you?" Gordon asked, pointing at the concrete at their feet and the small retaining walls on either side.

"A sidewalk?" Marty offered, holding his hands out.

"See, to me, this looks like a chute."

Gordon stood and massaged his lower back. Above him, the streetlight fizzled brightly for a moment before blinking off, joining most of its kind in the neighborhood as a dark sentry. Gordon looked up at it then swatted at a dive-bombing bug. Dana almost smiled. Even when Gordon got his moment, he couldn't quite get his moment.

"Are you serious?" Marty asked. "You think she's, what, acting out the game?"

"Yes. That is exactly what I think. At least she was when she walked past this window almost twenty-four hours ago."

Hearing the time passed put Dana back in the trenches. The heavy air seemed weighted with the loss of the girl. When you have a little girl of your own and another child goes missing, some part of you goes with that child. Some part of you is that child's mother, clinging to her tea cup as if it held leaves she could divine.

"Well, let's play the game, then," Dana said.

Gordon nodded then spun around again, facing forward. He started walking at an even pace, his head on a swivel. "We're looking for anything that might resemble a chute or a ladder to a child. Think out of the box. The dreaming mind makes wild leaps of connectivity and association, particularly the sleeping mind of a child, but they'll often share a common theme or kernel of similarity—"

"How about that actual ladder?" Marty asked, pointing to the right. Behind the retaining wall and through a break in the overgrown hedge running parallel to the sidewalk was a small access ladder, no more than five feet high.

"Where does that go?" Gordon asked.

"The next block. The neighborhood was supposed to be built at a soft tier, with the Tivoli up top and a greenbelt and runoff plain at the bottom," Dana said. She'd spent nearly an hour staring at the city-planning specs for Tivoli Estates and could picture the layout in her mind. The more she thought about it, the more it seemed set up as a series of steps with runoff chutes and access ladders. She gripped the first rung and climbed up. The men followed.

"What's the Tivoli?" Gordon asked, straining his eyes in the dim streetlights. The next block consisted of a handful of dimly lit houses and the stark skeletons of half again as many abandoned ones, but at the very top was a single structure with a turreted outline.

"The old Tivoli theatre. It has historic status with the city and county. It was supposed to be the centerpiece of the neighborhood, but the restoration money never came through, so it's just as dilapidated as it ever was. We already looked there. Ran the whole place down first thing. There was no sign of her."

The three of them turned to look at the scene below. Spread across the neighborhood were fifteen or so bobbing flashlights—more lights than cops. Good to see that some neighbors cared, at least.

"They were that close? Ethan and Erica?" Gordon asked.

"Marcus Denbrook said they were always together. And when they weren't, they chatted online. Up until the assault. They refused to let her to contact him after that. Apparently, Erica didn't take it well. They got into a fight about it last night, over the board game," Dana said.

"Why didn't you tell me this?" Gordon asked.

"Does it matter? If anything, it gives more credence to the runaway theory, not the sleepwalking theory."

Gordon shook his head. "Trauma and stress before slow-wave sleep is a trigger mechanism for parasomnia."

"What the hell is a trigger mechanism?" Marty asked, tucking the back of his shirt in flush with the rest of his uniform. Gordon turned to him and started to answer but paused. From somewhere above, they heard the faint sound of the neighborhood search party calling Erica's name.

"C'mon," Dana said. "Stay on target. Chutes and Ladders." Dana crouched lower, to the level of what she guessed would be Chloe's line of sight. She pictured Chloe here, walking on a sidewalk that was not a sidewalk. She'd be in her sleep shirt, an XXL freebie her dad had caught out of an air cannon at an Orioles game years before, back before he left them both to go build his beloved bar in Florida. It was still Chloe's favorite shirt. She wouldn't have shoes on, of course, or even socks. *God, the poor girl is barefoot.* The realization quickened her heart—tiny feet walking obliviously through the wreckage of this place.

To their left, the sidewalk continued in a more-or-less straight layout, but to the right it curved upward in a wide arch. "That way," Dana said. "Chute." Dana handed Gordon a spare flashlight and clicked her own on as they walked. "Marty, check the addresses against the all-clear list." Marty nodded and clicked on a Maglite the size of a ladle.

"So you're telling me a person can climb a friggin' ladder in their sleep?" Marty asked, panning toward the sudden barking of a dog behind darkened blinds in the house to his left. He checked the address against a sheet of paper he fished out of his pocket, then moved on.

"Yep," Gordon said.

"And if she cut her feet all up, she wouldn't wake up?" Dana asked.

"Not necessarily. There have been cases where para-somniacs set off in the snow in their sleep and walked to the point of frostbite without waking up. Amputating frostbite."

"That's freaky as hell," Marty said, flashing from his list to the houses and alleys they passed.

"That's the mind at night," Gordon replied. "Anybody see anything? The game jumps around. If she took this road, she won't have stayed on it for long."

"It just drops off over here." Marty ran his flashlight over the open space to his right. "Dana, you got anything?"

Dana was eyeing a drain pipe set into the left side of the road about twenty feet down, a metal hole in the slope of earth, perhaps three feet across. It gaped at her like a darkened basement from the top of the stairs.

"That'll do," Gordon said, following her eye. He walked quickly up to it and ducked underneath the corrugated metal lip. "It goes somewhere, that's for sure, and it's not clogged," he said, his voice echoing. He scurried inside on his elbows. Dana turned around, fully expecting to have to drag Marty behind her, but found him adjusting his belt and unbuttoning the top button on his uniform.

"Time's ticking," he said. "But if there's a flash flood and

I'm spit out into the harbor somewhere, I'm gonna be very disappointed in both of you."

Dana smirked, turned around, and ducked in ahead of him.

The three of them crawled on hands and knees through the storm drain in silence. The air was hot and still, but the metal was cold to the touch. A thin layer of scattered debris coated the center bottom, and leaves crunched underneath them. Dana put her hand on something wet and spongy and cringed.

"You all right?" Marty asked.

"Just fabulous," she said.

Sweat was dripping down her face by the time Gordon popped up and out just ahead of her. Moments later, Dana was able to stand. She climbed out of the pipe and found Gordon pondering an offset grate in the dirt.

He took off his steaming glasses and wiped his face of sweat, smearing a fine line of dust into the creases on his forehead. Then he picked up the grate. "Doesn't weigh much. Clearly not bolted in."

"Something a young girl could have lifted?" Dana moved aside as Marty popped out behind her.

He dusted his lapels. "I never liked this game." Marty blew his nose clear. "Not even as a kid. I was more of a Battleship guy." He panned the ground beneath them and paused over a brief trail of crushed leaves.

"It was Risk for me," Gordon said absently. "Hours and hours of Risk. I think she came this way. I think we're on the right track."

"This is the third block," Dana said. "One before the Tivoli. None of these houses were finished."

"This fella barely made it past the skeleton stage," Gordon said. His flashlight traveled from bottom to top of what was supposed to be a split duplex, two stories, with a nice offset porch and a small balcony for each unit. As it stood, it was an off-kilter rectangle of browning particle board, half-covered in tattered plastic that waved at them in the night wind.

Dana walked around the base of the structure, but it was boarded up tight. She stopped in front of a forgotten trellis, two stories tall. *A ladder?* She shook it lightly. It groaned. Dust and yellow paint flaked down through the beam of her light. She looked back at Gordon.

"Looks climbable," Gordon said begrudgingly.

His simple tone—the way he made it entirely plausible that a twelve-year-old girl could have treated this neighborhood like her own personal board game when every other person walking these streets right now probably thought she was already trussed up in the back seat of some shitty van with electrical tape around her tiny ankles—made her question whether she wasn't losing her own mind. It was insane to hope like that. She felt a disparaging comment on her lips but knew that if she let it out, the search would be over and Erica would be gone, so she turned it into a loud, almost angry call of the girl's name. The two men were startled into silence then listened for any reply. There was none. Only the search groups below, who swung their flashlights toward them. One group nearby started moving their way.

"There's an open window well up there," Gordon said, one hand on his hip as he lit up a break in the wall, perhaps ten feet up. It gaped at them, dusty and dark. Dana knew what she had to do. She unbuttoned her collar, slid her flashlight into her belt, and flicked on the smaller light on her shoulder. She took a firm grip of the trellis and started climbing. Marty looked as though he wanted to argue, but Dana shook her head. Before he could say anything, she'd expertly maneuvered up the old trellis, switching her grip and threading inside the bars when she needed to. The trellis shook, and the metal squeaked, but it held. Then she was up and in, her flashlight flickering in the darkness like a jack-o-lantern flame. Below, Gordon told her to be careful in an awkward, motherly whisper that might have made her smile under other circumstances, but he was right about being cautious. The walls were framed with swollen wood that sagged drunkenly inward, and here and there, the floorboards sported the telltale bruise coloring of rot. One wrong step and she would be right back where she started, only with a broken leg.

Then Dana saw something that almost made her cheer out loud. Little footprints, barefoot, about the size of her hand, but clear enough. She followed them with her flashlight, wincing when she saw they'd passed right over a rotten spot on the floor and continued on. They marked the old wood with little dimples of mud and headed toward the back of the second floor.

"Erica? Sweetheart?" Dana asked, trying to keep her voice conversational, trying to keep a reflux of panic from rising in her throat and ultimately failing because what she saw next made her go cold.

Another chute, and this one was real. A trash chute cut into the wall, a long tube of ridged plastic the workers used to toss junk from the upper stories to the ground below. It was basically just a drop.

"Erica?" she called again, louder this time. She picked her way across the room. No answer.

"What's going on up there?" Gordon asked, his voice distant in the rushing of blood to her head.

Erica's path was unmistakable. The tracks led to the chute and nowhere but the chute.

"She went down a garbage chute! Go around back!" She took a step forward, and the floor crunched heavily beneath her. She froze. The ground steadied. She was perhaps ten feet from the chute. She heard Gordon running around the outside of the building. She heard, more distantly, Marty's voice in concert with other, deeper voices —cop voices.

"I see it!" Gordon said. "There's a dumpster here! Erica! Erica, are you there?"

Dana listened, frozen in place, wide-eyed as Gordon hammered at the top of the dumpster and swore. "The stupid thing's locked!" More metallic slamming. Then still- ness. "Dana! I hear her! I hear something! She's crying!" More hammering. Or was that her own heart? "Stupid-ass thing, there's a huge metal bar across it. Dana, I think she's hurt."

Dana's mind was already made up. It had been made up as soon as she saw those footprints end. She could hear the crying too, a soft mewling, like a kitten fallen between the slots of a grate.

"Erica, honey, I want you to get away from the opening of the chute if you can, okay? I'm coming in," she said. She secured her utility belt and tied back her hair. The top lip of the chute was already pulling away from the building. Old nails hung from the ribbed plastic like teeth. She flexed her fingers. She didn't weigh much, but she knew the chute wouldn't hold her, not for long. But neither would the trellis if she tried to climb back down that, and the longer she stood there gaping, the less the floor seemed to want to hold her either. She thought light thoughts—feathers, bubbles, dandelion seeds—took a deep breath, and soft-stepped the ten feet to the chute. She heard a big *crack* behind her but didn't stop. The chute was like those slides she hated at the water parks as a kid—the big, steep ones the boys all loved, so she made herself ride them too—the key was just doing the damn thing. She picked up her feet and went in shoes first.

The chute smelled like rotten banana peels and hot street tar. It was rough and tattered, broken from both use and neglect, so she was able to skid to only a half-fall by the time she hit the opening into the dumpster. Still, she slammed her shoulder on the metal lip, which sent a lightning bolt of pain up her neck, and the floor came up to meet her with the force of a slamming door. She sat hard on her tailbone, and all the air left her in a *whuff*. Her chin bounced into her shoulder light and sent the lamp careening into a pile of trash, where it rested, shining directly back into her eyes for a moment before it popped out. The dumpster went black as ink. She'd bitten her tongue too. She spat blood, cursing to herself.

Gordon was slapping on the dumpster from the outside, making the air ring inside. "Dana! Are you all right? Talk to me!" His voice was muffled, but she could hear the panic.

"I'm all right," Dana said. "Stop that banging, I've already got one hell of a headache." She fished her penlight from her breast pocket, clicked it on, and froze. There, illuminated between sharp-angled shadows, huddled against a pile of bricks, and surrounded by the sparkle of shattered glass, lay Erica. Dana scrambled over to her and hovered her hands over the girl for only a brief moment before brushing at her sweat-streaked brow. Her eyes were closed, and she wasn't crying anymore. Her hair was pinned here and there with butterfly clips, but her trip had shaken much of it loose so that it haloed around her head. *Please, please, please...* Dana wasn't even sure who she was pleading with—Erica, sure, but also whatever god had thrown this poor girl down here, broken among the trash. She checked for bleeding but found none. She felt for a pulse, but if it was there, it was weak, and her hands were shaking too much to sense it. She went back to brushing the girl's hair, gently feeling for cuts and wiping her brow. *Please, please, please.*

And then an answer. A flutter. That soft mewling sound.

And then a ripping sound. A puncturing *thunk* followed by more ripping, and a whoosh of cooler night air and yellow moonlight. A grating pop, and then the whole chute was torn away from the opening. Gordon's head shoved through. Marty's voice just behind him, directing. The tinny whine of an approaching ambulance.

"Is she alive?" Gordon asked.

Dana could only gather the little girl slowly to her chest and hold her and smile grimly through her tears because the two of them were crying in the dumpster—both she and Erica—and Dana knew damn well from personal experience that if someone was crying, it meant she was very much alive.

# CHAPTER SIX

That night, Gordon took a forty-minute shower, poured himself three fingers of scotch from his dwindling stock, and sat down to watch the news. When he saw Warren Duke take all the credit for finding Erica Denbrook in a snippet from a press conference, he poured himself a fourth finger.

Duke relayed to the press that Erica was dehydrated and had suffered a badly dislocated shoulder but was expected to make a full recovery within the week. He looked exhausted, as if he'd carried her to the hospital himself. Dana was the one who'd risked her job, Dana had climbed into that hellhouse and thrown herself down a trash chute, Dana had literally waded through jagged garbage to find the girl, Dana's was the touch that had brought her back.

*And not to be a dick, but some small mention of an intrepid psychiatrist might be nice, Warren.* A certain Maryland native, perhaps? Office conveniently located in Baltimore's historic Mount Vernon neighborhood. Currently taking clients. Offering extremely competitive rates.

Gordon snorted into his scotch. He'd known Lieutenant Duke for all of one day, and he already knew the man would do no such thing. The way Duke framed things when he'd joined the brigade at the dumpster, Dana was lucky she wasn't fired on sight. And Gordon was lucky not to be in jail. Charming fellow. But not surprising. Gordon knew his type. He'd seen them all over Johns Hopkins when he was getting his doctorate there. They were the boat-shoe-clad, pastel-short-wearing, popped-collared undergraduates, the newest generation of East Coast privilege just hitting the upper-management circle. Gordon was willing to bet Duke hadn't so much *made* lieutenant as been *born into* lieutenant. And was on his way up. Gordon knew his type because he'd run in many of the very same circles not too long before Duke came along—bright, privileged, good pedigree—only Gordon had never felt much of a connection with his contemporaries, even back then. Did the generations that came before Gordon find him as foreign as Gordon found Duke?

*Probably, but that doesn't make Duke any less of a jackass.*

Gordon's glass was empty. He looked at the handle of fire-sale scotch to the left of his television—also empty. He'd hit his dollar limit for the week, as well, and since moonlighting with Brighton wasn't on the horizon anymore, he was going to have to go dry for the next several days.

Or he could call his mother.

He was a phone call away from an allowance, a phone call away from slipping back twenty years and getting a folded check from his mother every month, her holding it out to him with that shine in her eye that said, *"Take it, Gordon. Really. You can't possibly be expected to fend for yourself in a world gone this crazy."*

Gordon shook his head. That was as much as admitting the past twenty years had never happened, and they'd sure as shit happened. Sobriety was nothing compared to a two-decade brain wipe. He could go without his plastic bottle of scotch for a week. He was almost one hundred percent sure of that. Ninety-five percent sure. Okay, at least ninety percent sure.

Gordon wasn't sure when it happened, but one second he was watching the news, sinking into his old chair with the soft weight of a hot shower and a scotch kicker lulling him to sleep, and the next he was back in his cave. He felt a half-second stab of panic, just as in the old days, and a tendril of red mist snaked along the floor, but he slapped it with his loafer to dissipate it, and just like that, he placed himself. His shoes did it. Loafers were adult shoes. He was an adult. The cave couldn't hurt him anymore.

But it *had* once—or very nearly had. He remembered. The mist was an echo of an imprint, but it had held something once. He turned toward the entrance of the cave. It was open, just as it had been when he'd revisited a few nights before. But the cave hadn't always been open. At one point, it had been closed, and he'd been trapped inside of it. With that realization, the dream wavered. He shouted in frustration, but the color of the place was already fading. The damp smell too. Those were the first things to go when someone woke up. He spun around, drinking in the scene with the eyes of his subconscious, trying to see what it was that his brain thought he should see there, and that's when he noticed the rock.

A big, round stone sat just to one side of the entrance—a big, round stone *he* had pushed aside, once. Gordon knew it. But that had taken him years. Years and years to push that stone aside. And before he could do it, he'd been trapped.

He'd ripped at it with his fingernails. He ran to it, his feet already sloughing away and back to the waking world. He reached the stone, standing on the stumps of his knees. There, in the large rock, were several gouges, like a pen dragged through wet paper. And bits of fingernail too.

Gordon opened his eyes. He didn't shoot awake. No startled yelp, no bolt of understanding from the sky. He was in his chair again, in front of his droning television, and his hand was out, reaching for something. As the fog of sleep left him, his fingers grasped at something unseen, forgetting they were holding his empty scotch glass. It dropped to the floor and shattered. He stared at it, reminded of the fragmented light in the dumpster, the thousands of pieces of shattered glass that surrounded Dana and Erica in the darkness of their own cave.

After a moment, he realized he wasn't reaching for something he'd seen in the dream but rather reaching for his dream journal, which he'd stopped keeping many years before. His mother had foisted the journal upon him when he was a child in order to deal with his sleepwalking. It was classic Deborah Pope parenting: suggesting a therapeutic dream journal might help calm her son's roiling subconscious and then not so subtly suggesting he was only hurting himself if he didn't produce it every morning for her professional eye. He was nearly a teenager by the end of it, for God's sake. For every dream that ended up in the cave, he'd had two that ended up with morning wood. He wasn't about to write that down for his mother to read.

But he had written almost every dream down. His journaling got so routine that he'd reach for his nightstand first thing in the morning, grasping for his little black Moleskine notebook while still half asleep, determined to capture what he could before it fled him. He'd gone through probably fifty notebooks. Notebooks that his mother had kept and then given him when he said he was going to start a child-psychiatry practice with his now ex-wife. Notebooks that he'd boxed and taped and stashed in a dusty, forgotten corner when he closed the practice.

Notebooks that were in the closet downstairs. Behind the toys. Behind the case files.

The realization made him slowly sit up, then stand. He almost put his left foot down on a jagged edge of glass, his broken tumbler momentarily forgotten. He managed to avoid it with a skipping stumble and then walked right past his dustpan and broom and took the stairs down two at a time. The bare bulb in the closet clicked on and then popped out with a bright flash and a hiss that made Gordon yelp like a child then curse like a sailor. *Where are the damn light bulbs? Do I even have any more light bulbs?* Karen had kept everything in labeled drawers. Gordon tended to leave the lightbulbs on the floor wherever he last changed them. *Forget it.* He knew where the flashlight was.

The boxes holding his old dream journals were in the very back and looked to have been tossed out of a moving van into the rain and then kicked into the closet. Which made sense because they'd been in there so long that Gordon couldn't remember unpacking them for the first move to set up the joint practice, much less the second move that broke apart said practice in all but name. He stripped the tape easily and sat down on another, sturdier box with his flashlight in hand to start rifling.

He found stacks and stacks of black notebooks, smelling like ancient newspaper and looking far more scandalous than they actually were. The first one Gordon picked up detailed a long stretch of nights in his eleventh year, when he'd ended up wetting the bed twice in the span of three months. Same dream—nothing Freudian or Jungian about it. He'd just dreamed he was peeing in a huge toilet. He remembered his father near hysterics, talking about how he wouldn't abide a bed-wetting son, and his mother rolling her eyes in silence when she could have stepped in on his behalf. She knew as well as any psychiatrist that the last thing you do to a bed-wetter is shame him. But she'd held her tongue. *A skill she seems recently to have pointedly forgotten.* He tossed the book away—picked up the whole stack, in fact, and set it aside. That wasn't what he was looking for.

Not until he searched the second box did he find something promising: a series of journals near the bottom, dated to when he was twelve years old, around the Fourth of July. He remembered the wet heat of the cave then, the real cave on the north of the property, and how when he'd come back to himself after sleepwalking, he was shivering and sweating at the same time because of how stifling July was. He flipped through each page, scanning it for any reference to the cave, wiping his damp forehead and leaving fingerprints on the paper. Then he found one entry dated June thirtieth.

*I dreamed I went to a red cave. I felt that I had to meet someone there. But when I got there, I was terrified. I wasn't ready. I tried to run, but the cave was blocked. I scraped at the walls of the cave until I woke up. My nails had cut my face. It stings in the shower.*

He flipped forward, certain he'd find more entries, at least a mention about the night he woke up in the cave itself. But the next entry was dated July twentieth and detailed some nonsense about finding himself at a math exam he'd never studied for. He flipped back to the cave dream. Forward to the math dream. That was a huge gap. He nearly threw the journal in frustration. The cave dream was the single most traumatizing dream of his childhood. He'd spoken of it countless times with his mother at their lunches.

*As an adult*, he added to himself. As an adult Gordon.

As a child, he'd apparently written about it once then never again. Could he be remembering things wrong? Had he not dreamt of it as much as he thought he had?

Or had those dreams frightened him so much that he didn't want to remember them?

The journals from there on out had the feel of censored letters from a war front—general platitudes, basic ideas, many things blacked out or left unsaid.

With nothing more to say for himself and the cave dream, he found himself reading again and again the passage he had written. *Red cave?* The cave he'd visited minutes before had a mere dusting of red, no more. *Had to meet someone?* Gordon remembered whatever was in that cave as being something to run from, not to meet. *But I wasn't ready.* Ready for what?

Gordon had a nagging feeling that everything was connected, from Ethan's trial to his own sleepwalking and even to Erica's near-death experience in the dumpster. But the common thread was eluding him. He was missing something. He felt it was there, in his dreams, but he couldn't stay within them long enough to figure it out. The half-formed picture was frustrating enough to drive a man to drink, and the last drink in the house was dried into the carpet upstairs.

He had a sudden, almost desperate urge to call Karen. Either that or to go out to Darrow's Barrel and see how much Riggs the bartender could extend him on credit. Gordon had his spreadsheets, and his spreadsheets said there was no more cash for booze, but a bar tab was different. Gordon looked at his cell phone. He had reasonable cause to call Karen. He could run down his thoughts on the dreams and sound almost as though he wasn't calling just to hear her voice. Or he could just go get a beer.

As it turned out, Riggs said Gordon was good for several beers. Four pints was the final number. Gordon vaguely remembered the kind offer of a fifth, which he politely declined, reasoning that leaving some water in the well was how one continued to get credit, and one never knew when that pint might come in handy. When he went back home, he had no urge to call anyone, which was a victory. His only urge was to hit his pillow.

Gordon woke up in the damp heat of his bedroom the next morning. Baltimore sometimes did a trick where it rained, but the rain made things hotter. He stumbled up, turned on the air-conditioning window-unit he'd neglected, stripped off his damp T-shirt, and fell back into bed again. He fumbled for his cell phone on the nightstand and checked his call history.

No calls to Karen. He did a little fist pump.

He clomped out of his bedroom and toward the sink, eyeing the shattered glass still on the floor with reproach, as if someone else had done it. In fact, all of the day before felt to Gordon as if it had been lived by another man, from running up and down the Tivoli Estates neighborhood to find Erica all the way to washing away the sour taste of his journals with whatever beer Riggs was willing to front him. His time hunched over a flashlight in the storage closet seemed like a strange mania to him in the light of a new day.

Karen would tell him his dreams might say a bit about where his mind dwelled but nothing more. He could hear her in his head, her patient voice saying, *"Dreams are just dreams, Gordon. Don't go all Freudian on me."* And she was right. He wouldn't. The time had come to turn the corner. He needed to confirm his handful of appointments for the remainder of the month and hammer out a concrete plan for getting new clients. Did psychiatrists have social-media accounts nowadays? Could he maybe do some sort of blog? He wasn't much of a writer, but he could at least get his name out there more, figure out how to use a tablet, or something.

Gordon sat at his computer, his browser open, ready to research how to market a small, struggling psychiatry practice. He had a hot cup of fresh French-press coffee steaming next to a dripping glass of ice water. Ambient electronica was playing on his handheld speaker. A steady rain was falling outside, tapping his windows. For once, he was happy he didn't have an appointment all day. He felt so good, in fact, that he pulled out his Brain Journal, a mishmash of medical ideas that he thought stood a chance of growing into publishable journal articles. He felt inspiration fluttering about the eaves of his brain. Something not quite defined was coming, the beginnings of an idea that could bring him professional recognition as Gordon Pope. Not Karen Jefferson and Gordon Pope. Gordon Pope. He tapped the tattered journal in time with the music, sipped his coffee, and watched the rain.

And then his doorbell buzzed. He blinked rapidly. It couldn't be a package. He hadn't ordered a book in months. He wasn't expecting any visitors—hadn't had one of those in months, either. *Probably just a solicitor or someone mistaken about the address.* He decided not to answer and leaned back in his chair and lifted his coffee mug to his lips.

The doorbell buzzed again, longer that time. Too long for a solicitor, too long for a mistaken address. He stood, tucked his robe over himself, and moved to his intercom.

"Yes?" he asked, not quite managing to keep the annoyance from his voice.

"Dr. Pope?" came the reply, a man's voice, small in the background wash of rain.

"Yes?" Gordon replied hesitantly.

"My name is Andrew Barret. You... I believe you testified at my son's hearing? Ethan?"

All of the cozy warmth of the morning slowly seeped from the room. Gordon found himself leaning against the com as if it was the only thing keeping him up.

He pressed the receiver with a trembling hand. "Can I help you?"

"May I speak with you?"

"I'm really not... I have a pretty hectic schedule at the moment—"

"Please. We're sort of at the end of our rope, here."

His voice held an air of desperation, as well as a touch of shame, as if he was hesitant to speak up, even into the com. That made Gordon feel a little ashamed too, of his fumbling and his excuses. Years before, he would have had the man upstairs already, one hand out to take his coat, the other holding out a mug of coffee. Where had that Gordon gone?

He hesitated another moment then pressed the com again. "All right. I'll buzz you in. Take a seat in the study on the main floor. I'll be down in a moment."

Before he could talk himself out of it, he pressed the button that snapped the lock open. He heard the door open and lingered a moment more before dashing back to change, narrowly avoiding the shattered glass a second time. As he threw his robe onto his unmade bed and rifled around his closet for the most professional-looking outfit he had that was also still moderately clean, he recalled Andrew Barret's face. He'd been the strained-looking man sitting at the defense table next to his son, his back straight, gripping his hands in his lap as if he thought he might lose them otherwise. His wife, Jane, was the skittish blond woman on the opposite side of Ethan, looking as though she'd walked into a bad dream, not a courtroom. And in a lot of ways, she had.

They'd probably want coffee or tea, caffeine of some sort. Gordon doubted they'd been sleeping all that well. Gordon wouldn't be sleeping well either if his son was known to assault people in their sleep. In fact, he might never sleep again. He tucked his shirt in, slipped his bare feet into some loafers, checked that his fly was zipped, popped the kettle on, and refilled the press. Then he took a deep breath, grabbed a pair of cups in one hand and the coffee in the other, and took the stairs slowly.

At the bottom, he turned to his guest, only to find not Andrew and Jane, but Andrew and Ethan. Gordon almost made it three shattered cups in twenty-four hours, but he caught himself at the last second and awkwardly set the service down before the whole thing slipped from his hands. Ethan looked thin as a waif, even thinner than he had in the courtroom. His auburn hair was long and a bit stringy and pushed back behind his ears. He had a long chin but a small nose and pensive green eyes. His skin was pale and wet from the rain. His arms were tucked around himself, and he was eyeing the photo of Karen and Gordon that still hung prominently in the foyer, the one where Karen sat on a low-backed leather chair and Gordon rested his arm gently on her shoulder, both of them cheesing for the camera. He turned to Gordon at the sound of the clanking mugs. He looked as though he did not want to be there. In fact, he looked like he did not want to be anywhere but his bed. His father stepped forward between them, hand outstretched.

"Dr. Pope, I'm Andrew Barret," he said a little too eagerly. "Thank you for seeing us."

Gordon shook his clammy hand. "Yes... What is this about?"

"Ethan is out on temporary release," Barret said, his voice low, as if the boy might be spared what had no doubt been emphasized with a gavel in the courtroom.

"What was his sentence?" Gordon asked although he already knew. Ethan watched them both, and he could see it on the boy's face.

"He's to be sent to Ditchfield Medical Facility," Barret said, his voice thin and reedy. He cleared his throat as if the name had stuck there. In the silence that followed, the rain sanded the windows in a flaring gust.

Gordon closed his eyes. He'd expected it, but to hear it spoken as truth hit him surprisingly hard.

"But we have thirty days to appeal," Barret added, craning his neck toward Gordon, his brow furrowed. "Thomas Brighton—you remember Thomas, our attorney?"

"Yeah, I know Thomas."

"Thomas told us that it would be damn near impossible to win an appeal unless Ethan's... condition... was clinically proven and some sort of treatment plan could be outlined."

Gordon said nothing. He turned to look at Ethan, who watched him flatly. So Gordon's testimony alone hadn't been enough to sway the court. He wasn't surprised. Violent parasomnia was tough for people to understand. It was hard enough for clinical psychiatrists to understand, much less a judge or a jury.

"Thomas said that, huh?" Gordon said. "And let me guess, Thomas also gave you my contact information." Thomas didn't like to lose. If he thought there was a chance he could improve his win percentage or up his profile, he'd take it.

"Sort of," Barret said. "He told us the name of your practice and told us to look you up." He clasped his hands together nervously and spun his wedding ring on his finger.

"Did Thomas also tell you I... that Karen and I don't see kids anymore?" Gordon asked. "That it's a policy of mine? Has been for years now?"

"He said you might take some convincing. That's why I've waited until now to come see you. We've approached several practicing child psychiatrists already." Barret looked at his son, who slowly shifted his gaze in return before pulling his phone from the baggy front pocket of his raincoat and tapping idly on it. "They were either booked or out of town or... The fact is, none were willing to take up Ethan's cause. I think that some of them..." He struggled to find the words to finish, so Ethan did it for him.

"They were afraid of me," Ethan said, still focused on his phone, still tapping. His voice was high, and his childish tone made his words all the more surreal.

Gordon had no response. He was still coming to terms with the fact that the boy and his father were standing in his office to begin with.

"Thomas said that with a diagnosis and plan of care, he might stand a chance of appeal," Barret said. "But the deadline to file is in three weeks."

"Look, Mr. Barret, I don't know what Thomas thinks I can do for you, but even if I wanted to, I can't just rubberstamp a diagnosis and plan of care here. I gave that testimony because I was a compensated expert witness. I had no idea that it would be Ethan's case. I've been meaning to have some words with Thomas about that. He knows my policy on treating children."

"Do you believe he was sleepwalking?" Barret asked point-blank.

Ethan looked up from his phone, his face a blue glow.

Gordon remembered the look of the boy in the courtroom, hunched and frightened, but not just because of what he'd been accused of, not just because he'd nearly killed his friend. But because he didn't understand how he'd ended up there. Gordon knew that because he'd felt the same thing once.

"Yes," Gordon said. He felt what he felt. But that didn't change anything about treating the kid.

Ethan eyed Gordon a moment longer then nodded slightly before looking down at his phone again.

"I knew it," Barret said. "That's what the cop said, but I could see it on the stand. You believe us."

"What cop?" Gordon asked.

"Brighton's office is right next to the courthouse, and there's this police officer that we've bumped into a few times there. She said she helped find Erica Denbrook. Actually, she said without you, the girl wouldn't have been found."

"Dana said that?" Gordon asked.

He nodded. "Which is strange because they never said anything like that on the news."

"Tell me about it."

Gordon doubted that Dana "happened" to run into Andrew Barret. She was in and out of the courthouse in an official capacity often enough, yes, but Gordon was beginning to think that very little Dana Frisco did was by chance.

"Erica and Ethan are friends," Barret said.

"*Were* friends," Ethan said suddenly, his head snapping up from his phone.

"Right," Barret said sadly. "Were friends. But the point is Dana and I struck up a conversation over it, and she suggested I look you up as well. She said you could help. That was twice your name was mentioned. So here we are."

The Chutes and Ladders gamble was one thing, a lucky break he'd pulled out of a snapshot of Erica's life. Diagnosing and crafting a plan of care for a convicted criminal was another. Because that's what Ethan was. Whether or not he was asleep at the time didn't change the fact that he'd come very close to killing another child. Those were the facts. The question was why... and whether he was culpable at the time.

And Dana Frisco thought Gordon could figure it out.

Gordon suddenly felt a little bit warm, and he doubted it was from all the coffee.

"Can you help us?" Barret asked.

"I can't promise anything," Gordon found himself saying, as if his mouth had skipped permission from his brain. "But the least I can do is chat with him."

Barret sagged a little. "Thank God. And thank you. When can you start? Like I said, we have a time frame here—"

"How about right now?"

# CHAPTER SEVEN

For the first time in nearly five years, a child sat in the patient chair opposite Gordon Pope. When he'd worked with kids, he had a kid's chair, an identical version of his own leather chair at one-third the size. The kids had loved it, but in his self-cleanse after the divorce, he'd sold it online for a quarter of what he'd paid for it. He was regretting that decision, seeing Ethan's feet dangle from the floor as he sat back and watched Gordon quietly.

Ethan's phone was tucked beside him, and in the silence, he stole occasional glances at the screen. His green eyes were hollowed, the color of dry grass, and lidded with exhaustion. He had the weary, wary air of a child who had been passed from examination room to examination room.

His father tried to join them at first, but Gordon insisted that he meet with Ethan alone. Gordon had forgotten how personally parents often took the one-on-one sessions between psychiatrist and patient. The fact was very few breakthroughs occur with parents in the room. Gordon wanted to know the boy himself, not the son that came out when his dad was around. Barret acquiesced quickly. He seemed to know not to push his luck.

Gordon doubted he would get any sort of immediate opening up, and he wasn't surprised. He was reminded of a well-used quote from Dr. Mort Gladwell, the psychiatry chair at Hopkins in Gordon's day, and an unabashed eccentric. He'd said that the difference between child therapy and adult therapy can be broken down to one statement: With adults, you had to help them find the words, but with children, you had to help them make the words. That was where Gordon came in.

Sitting across from Ethan, he had hoped to find familiarity, a clicking-into-place, a welcome-back feeling. Instead, he was reminded of why his practice with Karen had fallen apart. His heart twinged like an old war wound, which was what he was afraid of. The question for Gordon wasn't so much if he could treat the boy—it was whether he could set aside the broken feeling it gave him long enough to try.

*Ground zero,* Gordon told himself. *We are at ground zero here.* The basis of every connection made between therapist and patient was built upon trust, and Gordon knew that didn't exist with Ethan. Yet. Still, Gordon had seen worse first visits. He'd had children yell until they were taken out of the room. He'd had children stare at the walls. Scream at him. Run circles around his chair. Throw things at the windows. Honk, grunt, and spit. Anything to avoid the silence that Ethan seemed to have cloaked himself in already. He sat awkwardly on the wide lounger, like a novel teetering between bookends.

"You want to sit on the rug?" Gordon asked, pointing to the round sheepskin rug on the floor beneath them. Ethan said nothing, but nothing wasn't a no.

"C'mon, that chair is way too big. I got it because I was

told I needed to be sensitive to the fat people I saw. Turns out I don't even have any fat clients." Gordon slid to the floor himself first. He managed to disguise a grimace as his knees popped. He settled himself with his knees up and his back against the chair.

Ethan slid to the floor much more naturally, the way only kids can do, like a settling Slinky. He reached up for his phone without looking and set it down next to him and started tapping at it, although without any real aim.

*I suppose we should start at the beginning.* "Hi, Ethan. My name is Gordon."

Ethan nodded, turned from his phone, and picked at the thick carpet for a moment.

"Your dad is right outside, but for now it's just you and me. Do you remember me? From the trial?"

Ethan looked up at Gordon briefly and nodded. "You tried to help me," he said.

Gordon nodded. *Technically, I got paid to say that it was theoretically possible that you could be a violent parasomniac at twelve years old.* But he would take what he could get. "I did what I could."

"It didn't work. Now I've gotta go to jail," Ethan said. His voice held no malice, but his words seemed carefully chosen, as if he was gauging Gordon's response.

"You're not going to jail. Ditchfield is a hospital," Gordon said. Then he paused and decided he wouldn't lie to the boy. "But it's not really any better."

Ethan nodded, seeming to appreciate the blunt answer. "Mom called it a nuthouse for kids." He made eye contact with Gordon in intervals, switching between him, the rug, and the phone with the ease of a driver checking his mirrors. Gordon felt he didn't have the boy's full attention, but he wondered if anything actually did.

"Have you had any more dreams? Any more sleep-walking since the incident at the sleepover?"

"I don't have dreams," Ethan said.

"Everybody has dreams every night. It's just a matter of if you remember them or not."

"Not me. Not anymore. And no, I haven't tried to kill anyone else yet, if that's what you're asking," Ethan snapped his words with a flash of aggression that seemed out of place, as if his brain had flared for a moment. Gordon noted it while appearing to ignore it.

"Forget killing. I'm talking about anything. Any thoughts when you wake up in the middle of the night? Any twitches before you fall asleep? Do you find yourself sitting up or maybe at the door to your bedroom before you know what's going on?"

Ethan stopped scrolling on his phone, and he stopped picking at the rug, and he stopped looking at Gordon. His head inched down, and he stared at his shoes.

"I'm tied to my bed," he whispered.

"Does your dad tie you to the bed?" Gordon asked, keeping his voice neutral. He almost looked past the door to his office, where Andrew Barret sat. It occurred to him that he knew nothing about the man and had assumed good faith on his part. How quickly he had forgotten that the majority of neuroses that manifested themselves in children were directly attributable to their parents in some way. But Ethan cut his thoughts short with a quick shake of his head.

"I tie myself," he said. "With a rope. I took it from the garage without Dad seeing."

"Why do you tie yourself to your own bed?"

"In case."

"In case what?"

Ethan was silent again.

"Do you think you would try to hurt your parents, Ethan?"

Ethan shrugged. "No. But I didn't think I'd hurt Jimmy Tanner either." He left it at that for a moment, but Gordon knew when not to speak. "And sometimes I wake up... twisted. Like I've been fighting in my sleep."

Gordon made another mental note. He'd found that kids didn't like it when he took physical notes, scratching away on a pad while they spoke. To adults, the scratching meant they were getting their money's worth. To kids, it was like he was writing secrets that they couldn't read. It unnerved them. Ethan picked his phone up with both hands and kept refreshing the screen.

"What are you doing on that thing?" Gordon asked.

"Nothing," Ethan said.

"Are you talking to somebody?"

Ethan took a big breath and blew it out. "Not anymore." He tossed the phone gently onto the rug. "What's the point anyway, of all this? It doesn't matter. I've told everyone a billion times everything I thought. Everything I felt. Everything I dreamed. Everything I don't dream. Nobody believes that I don't remember. Erica used to believe me"—he nodded at the phone—"but she won't talk to me anymore either. So now it's nobody."

"I do," Gordon said simply.

Ethan paused, clearly weighing whether he believed Gordon or not. Then he shrugged. "Doesn't matter anyway. Jimmy is in the hospital. He might die. Everyone knows that I did it. Even I know I did it." Despite his attempt at nonchalance, his voice cracked at the end like a blown reed. "It doesn't matter that I don't know why."

"It does matter. It means everything, Ethan. That you were asleep means everything."

"Yeah? What if Jimmy was your kid? You wouldn't be saying that. How would you feel then?"

Another Gladwell-ism came to Gordon's mind: Nobody on earth can smell out a dodged question better than a kid.

"I don't know what I'd do," Gordon said.

"Yeah, you do. You probably have a kid my age." He leaned forward, and the hollow green of his eyes wetted to a sparkle. "Think if I killed him. Like this." He held out his bony fingers and squeezed the air, concentrating to the point where a vein popped up on his temple.

"I can't say how I'd feel," Gordon said, trying to rein in the situation, "because I don't have kids."

Ethan stopped speaking and looked at Gordon as though he'd just dropped a plate of food. "That's weird. Why not?"

Gordon rested his arms on his knees and then his chin on his forearms. A thought occurred to him. He could take a gamble. Everything about the past five years told him not to, but everything about the past five years seemed to be slowly sifting away that afternoon. Gordon took in a small, barely perceptible breath and peered intently at Ethan.

"I'll tell you a secret if you tell me a secret," Gordon said, his voice low.

Ethan's finger paused above his phone. Secrets were powerful things for children. They often burdened adults, but in Gordon's experience, kids held secrets in almost mystical esteem. Ethan looked as though he was weighing Gordon's words carefully. Gordon was banking on it.

"Okay," Ethan said.

Gordon nodded. "I don't have kids because I can't have kids."

"You mean you don't have a girl," Ethan said, half asking, half stating the obvious.

Gordon snorted. "Well, yes. There's that too. But even when I did have a girl... I couldn't. I can't."

Ethan cocked an eye at Gordon but nodded slowly. He seemed to get it. At least, Gordon thought that whatever Ethan assumed was probably close enough. Gordon was firmly in his forties now, and every day he still had to wrap his head around what it meant to be sterile, around the reason he existed on the earth, if not to continue his little sliver of the human race. He'd been yoked by a solid, steady weight of existential depression since he'd been diagnosed years ago. It grew heavier when Karen had left him because of it, heaviest when he'd had to close up shop because every child reminded him of one that would never spring forth from him.

There, sitting with Ethan, he'd expected the yoke to be heaviest of all, to pin him to the floor next to the boy, but it didn't happen. After he spoke his secret aloud, he sat a little straighter, and was reminded of another reason he'd loved working with kids: they took those things in stride. It was what it was. Children were dealt new cards every day. They shuffled everything into the deck regardless, and to them every card weighed the same. *These things only crush middle-aged men.*

"You're only the third person in the world besides me that knows that," Gordon said, amazing himself with the statement. Other than him, only his mother and Karen knew. That was it.

Ethan sat still, letting the secret settle.

"My turn," Ethan whispered.

Gordon watched him patiently.

"I'm trying to chat with Erica on the phone. She won't talk with me anymore. Not after what happened."

Gordon covered his disappointment. That was hardly

quid pro quo. He already knew Erica and Ethan had been tied at the hip once, but it was hardly surprising that she'd keep her distance now, given what she knew he'd done to his other friend. Still, it was a disclosure, and as Karen used to say, every disclosure was a victory. Gordon opened his mouth to speak, but Ethan kept talking.

"We used to sleepwalk together," Ethan said.

Gordon froze and settled again. Ethan seemed not to notice.

"Together?" Gordon asked.

"We'd end up in the same place together, wake up there next to each other. At the Tivoli. It's this old abandoned movie theater at the top of the neighborhood."

"I know of it," Gordon said softly, as if speaking loudly would scare the boy from his train of thought. "You both would wake up there? Not walk there together, but wake up there?"

Ethan nodded but already was moving on. "But that's not my secret. Mom and Dad know about that although they think it only happened once. Here's my secret." Ethan leaned over, close to the ground, his hands buried in the rug. "Whenever we ended up there, we both dreamed the same dream."

Gordon kept a still face. It wasn't unheard of for close friends to dream along similar lines, but for some reason he didn't think that was what Ethan was referring to. When he said same dream, he meant the *same dream*.

"What was the dream?" Gordon asked. Ethan seemed prepared for it.

"Every time we ended up there, it was because we were being chased by Red."

"Red?"

"It's our name for him, except it's not a *him*, really. Not even a thing I can describe, just... Red."

"Like a red mist?" Gordon asked, suddenly sweating, suddenly brought back to his own cave, to the tendrils of red mist that remained there, the last vestiges of a thing he'd clawed his fingernails out to run from.

Ethan nodded. "It's a mist that's not a mist. It makes me feel... like I should kill Jimmy." The last words were barely a whisper, and after Ethan said them, he sat back and watched Gordon wrestle with his own thoughts.

"I know Red," Gordon said. "Do you believe me when I say I know Red?"

"How?"

"I don't know, but I know him. Or I knew him, once."

Ethan nodded. He believed. "But he's gone now. Which is good, right? I wasn't lying when I said I don't dream. I don't see Red anymore. I don't dream at all."

Gordon thought about how the boy who claimed he no longer dreamed still had to tie himself to the bed.

"Everybody dreams, Ethan," Gordon said.

"But if I can't see Red anymore, he must be gone, right? That's good, right?"

Gordon shook his head sadly, deciding not to coddle the boy. "I don't think it is good. And I don't think Red is gone just because you don't see him."

Gordon tucked his knees up and hid his chin behind them. "Where'd he go?"

"I don't know. But you and me are gonna figure it out."

# CHAPTER EIGHT

After Ethan and Andrew Barret left his office, and with Ethan's words still ringing in his head, Gordon's willpower finally cracked. He found himself sitting on the floor in his closet with his box of dream journals in front of him, rifling through book after book with the phone cradled in his neck, pressed to his ear and ringing.

"Gordon—" Karen said after picking up.

He heard the barest hint of reprimand on the tip of her tongue, so he cut her off. "I know you're not coming back to me or to Baltimore," Gordon said quickly, getting Karen's ground rules out of the way. "I have a question about dreams. A professional question."

Karen was quiet on the other end. Gordon heard the high wail of a young child somewhere in the background, along with the bark of a dog. And was that a lawn mower? The domestic bliss of it all soured his stomach.

"Okay then," Karen said. "What is it?"

"You're gonna think I'm crazy, but hear me out."

"I already think you're crazy, Gordon. What is it? Chad and I are taking Maggie to the park here in a minute."

Gordon knew he must really be trying Karen's patience. She purposely avoided bringing up Chad or their little girl whenever they spoke. She wasn't a gloater. Gordon had always appreciated that.

"I'll make it quick. I'm seeing a patient who claims he and his neighbor friend have the same dream."

"Well, that's not unusual, especially if they inhabit the same general environment," Karen said.

"No, the *same dream*, Karen. He told me that on several different occasions, they sleepwalked out of their houses at the same time and ended up in the same place with recollections of the same dream."

"Well, that's ridiculous. I think you need to switch track here and start to diagnose why your patient might be constructing this fantasy."

Gordon flipped through his journal again. He'd marked the cave dream with a sticky note. The entries to the front and back were smudged with thumbprints, but he was no closer to understanding what was happening in his twelve-year-old brain than he'd been when he first stumbled into the closet.

"Normally, I'd agree with you," Gordon said, bracing himself for his next words, "but what if I told you that I sort of had the same type of dream back when I was a kid?"

Karen didn't respond. Maggie's crying turned to laughing for a second. Gordon imagined Chad working to entertain the little girl, waving things or picking her up, tossing her above his head. He shut the image out. No good would come from going down that route.

"You're treating that Ethan boy, aren't you?" Karen asked. "The sleepwalker."

"He lost his case. They're sending him to Ditchfield

unless they can get an appeal together, and that hinges on a clinical diagnosis and plan of care."

"Remember what I said about projecting? And remember why you left child therapy in the first place? Because you—"

"Get too invested, I know. But—"

"The boy isn't your kid, Gordon. None of them are your kids. They can't substitute. But you still try, and then when you can't help them, you think you've failed them. Hell, even when you can help them, you never think you can help them enough. You lose objectivity. You get obsessive."

Gordon looked at himself in the wall mirror opposite the closet. He was sitting on the floor amid the drifting dust of his past, surrounded by twenty little black books. Karen had a point. But she didn't understand. The similarities between Ethan's dreams and Gordon's own at Ethan's age were too strong to ignore.

"He had nowhere else to turn. I said I'd talk with him, see what he had to say, that's all."

"Well, maybe you ought to just keep it at that. Did it ever occur to you that maybe the child *should* go to Ditch-field? He did nearly kill his friend."

"I'm not so sure he did. At least, not in the way the court thinks he did," Gordon said. "And that's why I need to know, have you ever heard of anything like the exact same dream occurring in the minds of two separate people?"

Karen sighed heavily into the phone. Chad said something in the background, and Gordon could hear the heavy silence of Karen's hand covering the receiver. Then she came back.

"If I believed in the Jungian analysis of dreams—which I highly suggest you take with as much, if not more, of a grain of salt than the Freudian side of things because both of them will get you laughed out of a clinical setting—but if I *did* hold with Jungian analysis, I'd say that what you're describing is an example of an archetype of some sort, one of a set of several general themes or occurrences that have been found to inhabit the dreams of the majority of people of this earth. Things like being chased. Sinking. Flying. Certain colors. Jung would say that they trace back to an ancient response."

"How about an encroaching figure made of red mist?"

Karen snorted in laughter. "No. See, that is way too specific. That is why what Ethan claims happened cannot have happened. And if you think it happened to you too, maybe you ought to think about how easy it is to rewrite memories to tailor specific outcomes. Like wanting to find a connection to this boy, for instance."

Gordon shook his head but held his tongue. He wasn't tailoring anything, the proof was there, in those journals... until it wasn't anymore. Until the sleepwalking episode itself, of which he'd written nothing. And then thereafter, nothing.

"I'm sorry, Gordon, I really have to go," Karen said.

"Yeah, okay. Thanks for talking," Gordon mumbled.

"Take care of yourself, okay? I mean that," she said before hanging up.

Gordon sat for a long time on the floor, at first staring at nothing in particular, then flipping through journals again, finding nothing new in the entries but reading them through all the same.

Empty spaces in his memory. Nights when dreams flitted away from his grasp before he could journal them. And the same thing was happening to Ethan as well. *"I don't dream,"* he'd said. And now, Gordon had had two separate but distinct dream episodes wherein he'd revisited a place he'd thought his brain shuttered thirty years before.

Gordon wanted to run one more thing by Karen, but he decided to hold back after he got the distinct impression that she already thought he was going through a minor melt-down. Something was lurking in the recesses of Ethan's brain—something tied to the cave of Gordon's own dreams. A corner piece to the puzzle he'd found himself in a race against time to solve. So he'd wanted to ask Karen about her thoughts on the validity of induced REM sleep. If Ethan's brain kept forgetting, maybe Gordon could force it to remember.

The problem was, induced REM required more than just a willing patient. It required the use of specialized machinery, the likes of which existed only in a sleep lab.

But again, Gordon found himself availed of a window when he should be hitting a locked door. Johns Hopkins had a world-class sleep lab. Also, for better or for worse, Gordon knew someone who could get him access. If he was willing to be indebted, that was.

# CHAPTER NINE

Gordon took up Caesar's offer of a cocktail before he'd even arranged his napkin on his lap.

"Full tumbler of ice, generous pour of scotch please. Nothing fancy. A blend is just fine."

Gordon couldn't be sure, but he thought he saw a knowing look in Caesar's eye as the waiter nodded and backed his way out. Gordon made a mental note to ask the man ten or so years down the line if he might be hired away as his mother's caretaker. Would he be ready for that? Could anyone be ready for that? Sure, Caesar looked like he had the patience of a saint, but it was one thing to serve the woman cocktails twice a month and quite another to be at her side daily. She had a way of making people feel as though they owed her without actually doing anything. And Gordon was there to actually ask her for a favor.

Caesar produced Gordon's scotch with a minor flourish, and Gordon let it sit and sweat for a bit in the noon heat of the patio. Even in the shade, the temperature had to be nearly ninety degrees, with enough humidity to swell a wooden door shut. He thought about his approach but was pre-empted by his mother's hooting hello to Caesar at the front door. *Too late.* He'd never been good with prepared words, anyway. He took a decent swig of his scotch and stood, waiting.

"My son! My son!" said his mother, and she hugged him and kissed him on both cheeks. "And a week before our normal lunch date? Have you been missing your mother?"

She waved off whatever response Gordon might have mustered. Her silver-and-turquoise bracelets clanked gently. She settled her linen pantsuit at the sharp creases as she sat and allowed Caesar to jump her chair in a bit. She set her earrings and gently adjusted her watch before clasping her hands before her and smiling kindly at him. *Happy as a clam.* She always seemed to know when Gordon was coming to her for help.

"How are things, Gordon?" she asked, pinching the stem of her chilled martini between two fingers and letting it hover over her mouth before sipping.

"To tell you the truth, Mom, I've been feeling a little odd lately."

Her brow furrowed, and she set her martini down. "Are you ill? When was the last time you had a physical?"

"A *physical*? I'd say probably the eighth grade, to clear me for baseball," Gordon said, rolling his eyes. "But it's nothing like that."

"This is why I told you to get that baseline lipid panel at thirty. Now, we'll be able to see if there's been any sort of—"

"Mom. Stop. It's this sleepwalking stuff. It started with the testimony, and it's got me looking at how weird my whole episode was and what I wrote about it and didn't write about it," Gordon said.

His mother snapped her fingers delightedly. "I *told* you that you'd look back at those dream journals. Didn't I? I said, 'Gordon, do not throw those out. You will regret it if you do—'" Caesar had appeared at the snap, and both of them watched him for a moment. "Oh, dear. No. I wasn't snapping for you. Good lord. I'd have to slap myself. I'm not that far gone. Escort me out the second I do, Caesar," she said, deadly serious as Caesar smiled and bowed himself out. She turned back to Gordon, but he cut her off before she could crow any longer.

"The boy in the assault case. Ethan Barret. He came to my office. His father asked if I'd evaluate him. It's his only shot at an appeal."

His mother paused then blew past all of the implications of her son spearheading therapy for a convicted criminal and instead asked, with a wry smile, "You're treating children again?"

"No. I mean maybe. Just this one. He reminds me too much of myself, and there's something weird going on here."

"That's wonderful, Gordon," she said and hooted once more before controlling herself. "It's about time you took another crack at child therapy. It's where your heart lies."

Gordon swirled his scotch and stared into the dripping amber. "Tell Karen that. She thinks I'm projecting. Says I get too invested, that I turn these kids into my own kids. The kids I can't have."

"That frigid bitch," she said offhandedly, "telling you you're projecting. What right does she have?"

"She's very probably correct, Mother."

"Of course she's correct. She's always correct. She's a brilliant psychiatrist. That doesn't make it a bad thing, though. People forget that *projecting* is just another word for *empathy*. Which is a concept Karen wouldn't understand if I beat her over the head with it." His mother waved a dismissive hand over the conversation as if that closed things. Gordon found himself smiling.

"The court gave Ethan thirty days," Gordon said. "And I've hit a bit of a brick wall." Gordon drained his scotch. "What I'm gonna tell you here might be hard to believe. Okay? But just hear me out."

His mother sat back, martini in hand.

"Ethan described to me dreams he was having around the time of the assault, dreams that sounded a lot like the kind of thing I wrote about in my journal with the cave before everything went blank. Ethan doesn't recall his dreams any longer, either. And just this past weekend, I helped Dana find a young girl who also sleepwalked. She was Ethan's friend, Erica, who Ethan said was having the same dreams too. When we found her, Dana asked if she remembered what she was dreaming about. Nothing. Each of us had the same type of dream, and then it disappeared. I managed to stop sleepwalking, but these kids are still doing it—and more dangerously. I think if I can monitor Ethan's dreaming, I can maybe figure out why. It could go a long way towards treating him. And maybe stop something horrible from happening to Erica too."

Gordon sat back and looked longingly at his empty glass for a moment before glancing at his mother. He readied himself for some sort of dismissal, not unlike the waving of hands that had put a nail in her previous point. His mother jutted out her lower lip in consideration.

"You're telling me," she began, her voice conspiratorial, "that you've been padding around with a girl named Dana?"

Gordon blinked. "That's what you got out of all that?"

"Who is this Dana? Is she single?"

"Mother!"

"Fine, don't tell me. Look, I'm just thrilled you're doing something outside of your apartment for once. And with a woman!"

Gordon looked plaintively for Caesar.

"I mean, even if it is chasing down some child's boogie monster. Have you told her all that you just told me? If she hasn't run off yet, she's probably worth looking at seriously. Even if she has run off. It's not like you're swimming in it."

"Wait, what exactly are we talking about here, Mother?" Gordon asked, his voice a sharp whisper.

"The girl of course. Dana."

"Officer Frisco," he said. "And no, I haven't told her any of this yet. I'm not stupid. I know how it sounds." But even as he said it, he felt fairly confident that while most people might run from him, Dana was not one of them. "She actually sort of got me involved in all this."

"I'm saying that if this woman believes there's something more here than meets the eye, and she's a cop with a decent head on her shoulders, maybe you're not completely insane," his mother said as if pointing out the color of the sky.

Gordon saw his opening, so he clipped his retort, "There's only one way I can think of to make sure I'm not insane. But I need your help."

Her eyes widened in mock surprise. She signaled to Caesar that she'd like a refresh on her martini and both of them would be having the usual meal. Gordon knew she was taking the time to enjoy her moment.

"What can I do for you, dear?" she asked after settling again.

"You're still an Elliot Society member at Hopkins, right?"

"Of course. It's what got you into the medical school."

Gordon looked at her sidelong.

"Oh, please. Of course you had the resume, too. But nobody gets into these places anymore without a little grease. Don't be naive. I kept it up because Maude from bridge club seemed to think an Elliot recommendation might get her oaf of a son into the undergraduate program."

"How altruistic of you."

"It is, isn't it? Maude also happens to be a council-woman on the greater Bethesda zoning committee, which damn well better come in handy when I decide to put in a water feature out front that might be a hair against code. Just a hair."

"Ah, there it is," Gordon said. "Always a plan in mind. Well, you do whatever it takes. I don't care. What I care about is access to the Elliot Sleep Lab."

"For your boogie man?"

"Call it whatever you want. Can you get me lab time? I have to run tests on Ethan. I have some theories I need to confirm."

"And this poor child's parents are on board?"

"They're desperate, so yes. Does this mean you think you can get me lab time?" Gordon pressed.

She waved her hand again. "Of course I can get you lab time. Even if I wasn't an Elliot fellow. Keith Burback still runs that place, and he's always had a thing for me. We were in the same class, you know. He was too fat for my liking. Still is. But he's a good man."

Gordon sighed with relief. Maybe, just maybe, he'd be able to take a swing at this screwball of a situation after all.

Then his mother held up a finger. "On one condition, of course."

"Mom, please—"

"Oh, come off yourself. It's for your own good. You need to pursue this Dana Frisco. That's it. That's all I ask."

"Pursue her? She's not a lady-in-waiting."

"You know what I mean. I know you like this girl. Don't even try to dance around it. A mother always knows." She finished her martini with a delicate sip and set it aside to make room for the lunch, which arrived on cue.

Gordon couldn't say anything. He sat there with his mouth open, trying to form words. How did she know? Had he mentioned Dana before? It would be just like her to file away a casual mentioning for just such an occasion in which to corner him.

She took a bite of salad, even happier now than when he asked her outright for her help.

Gordon cleared his throat. "Fine. Yeah. I think she's... pretty great."

"Pretty great? What are you, twelve?"

*It seems like it these days.* He was dreaming the dreams of his twelve-year-old self, so why not bring back the twelve-year-old awkwardness as well? Or maybe it had never really left—he'd just managed to get married and divorced in the interim.

"She's got her own life, Mom. She has a daughter, and she's up to her ears in garbage just trying to do her job."

"I have no doubt. She's a police officer in Baltimore. There are worse places to do your job, but they require enlistment."

"Spoken like a true tourist. You have no idea what this city is really like. You haven't ever lived here. There's more to it than Waterstones Grille."

"I'm sure there is. I don't care to see it."

"My point is Dana is very busy, and she doesn't think of me that way."

"And my point is that she called you when she needed help. And you delivered. You helped find the young girl. That means something."

"That was luck. I had a hunch, and it paid off. That's part of the reason I'm hesitant here. Now, she thinks I can magic my way to an acquittal for Ethan. This is why you never set the bar high on your first day on the job."

"It wasn't luck, Gordon. You've never needed luck. You think when Karen left, she sucked all the talent from the room, but you're wrong." She set her fork down and dabbed carefully at her mouth, avoiding the lipstick. "Anyway, those are my terms. Do something. Anything. To let this girl know how you feel."

Gordon knew that if he protested vigorously enough, if he complained or bartered or bitched or sulked, his mother would pull the strings and get him in the lab anyway. Conversations were a kind of dance for her, but at the end of the day, she would help him however she could. In the end, he could either keep those lunches amicable or give her rounds and rounds of ammunition to go with her martinis, so he nodded. He would approach Dana. Because if he set aside all the banter and the snobbery, his mother was right. He was falling for Dana Frisco. He could be a twelve-year-old about it, or he could man up.

# CHAPTER TEN

The Elliot Center for Sleep Disorders was located in the northeast corner of the Johns Hopkins School of Medicine campus. It was near the Welch Medical Library, where Gordon Pope had spent nearly a full quarter of his life, more or less, from pre-med classes all the way through his doctorate. He walked the campus grounds at last light, surprised by how hard the nostalgia hit him. The last time he'd walked around Hopkins was for his ten-year reunion, over ten years before, and then he'd had Karen at his side and a boatload of chardonnay in his stomach. This evening, he was alone.

He'd told Andrew Barret that he would meet him and Ethan at the lab, but he wanted to make the walk himself. He was a sucker for nostalgia. That was part of the reason he kept calling Karen. He passed the library to his right and imagined himself there as he used to be, a loopy pre-med student, then a haggard med student, then a terrified resident, moving about the stacks, slamming cup after cup of coffee. He remembered sleeping there, waking there, crying there, and meeting Karen there. They'd even had sex there once, in the deserted journals section back by the microfiche machines at three in the morning, a nervous, clutching, sweaty, wonderful thing that lasted a quarter as long as Gordon had hoped it would. He could see himself through the glowing windows as he'd been then, a ghost moving from level to level. He doubted they even had microfiche any longer.

From the outside, the Elliot Center looked exactly the same as it had for decades—a square, Bauhaus structure two stories high, made entirely of brick on concrete. Not exactly the type of place that inspired a good night's rest, but then again, if you ended up there, you weren't sleeping right anyway. Rumor was the university was building a massive, multimillion-dollar pediatric sleep center that was supposed to be a bit softer, but as always, that was just a few years out. So the Elliot Center was it.

He met the student worker behind the desk and was ushered into the Elliot Lab without question. The Barret family was already waiting in the mauve appointment room. Ethan sat uncomfortably in a small chair in the corner, tapping away on his phone, a small overnight bag at his side. Andrew Barret stood and welcomed Gordon with a vigorous handshake, as if still afraid he might bolt. Gordon was surprised to see Jane Barret, Ethan's mother, also in attendance. She looked up at him with wide eyes resting on half-moon bags the color of storm clouds, her blond hair slightly disheveled. She gripped the arms of her chair as if it were moving and didn't get up to meet him.

After greeting them and waving awkwardly at Mrs. Barret, Gordon excused himself to ready the lab. He went through the double doors into a large, rectangular room with four beds that looked as though someone had tried very hard to make them appear as anything but rank-and-file hospital beds and had almost succeeded. He took in the room. It wasn't bad. It was painted a calming blue, and each bed had a different patterned bedspread. Framed pictures of calming desert and ocean scenes were spaced evenly along the walls. Still, it was very hard to make a hospital *not* look like a hospital. Gordon walked around the room, taking down several sterile-looking medical charts and unplugging every superfluous blinking machine he could. He took the pamphlets off the small table by the entrance and dimmed the lights. The corner bed would be best—it would feel the least like a dorm-room bed. Gordon fluffed the pillow and eased the hospital tightness of the sheets. He stood and crossed his arms. The place was still a medical lab, no bones about that, but it was far better than most, and it would do.

Gordon brought Ethan to the lab and showed him his bed. The boy stared at it numbly. He looked as though he hadn't slept in weeks, as though the room was yet another in a sequence of small rooms with strange people that would ultimately do nothing to help him. He sat down heavily on the duvet and kicked off his shoes. He was already in his pajamas.

"You sleepy?" Gordon asked.

"Yeah," Ethan said.

"When was the last time you got a full night of sleep?"

Ethan shrugged. If Gordon were to guess, he'd say the boy couldn't recall, it had been so long. That was written plainly on his face. He was terrified to give in to his exhaustion.

"Let me run all this strange machinery by you, all right? None of it will hurt you. But it is sort of weird to sleep with it all on."

Ethan looked blankly at the rig beside his bed through hooded eyelids, his phone hanging limply from both hands.

Gordon had a striking impression then that the boy wasn't even fully with him there in the lab, that he was already half asleep, that his entire life now was battling against that liminal line of unconsciousness that presses and presses, more insistent the more it is denied. Still, Gordon went through the gear for the benefit of Ethan's parents watching behind a small, disguised panel of glass if for no one else.

"This is an EEG. This little guy will record your brain waves as you sleep," Gordon said, tapping a small tan box at the end of a clipped bundle of wires. "It has this funny hat that I need to put on you, okay? So just pop under the covers and lie like you normally would."

Ethan swung his feet up and kicked his way into bed, knocking the duvet off and scrambling the sheets. "Okay," he said quietly.

"Sorry about this, buddy," Gordon said, peeling off the backing of a ring of sticky tape at the base of what looked like a child's hairnet with little suction cups stuck in the webbing. "It's not all that comfortable, I know—unless you like sleeping with nets on your head. I have to get these electrode ends to touch your scalp, so I'm gonna root around here for a sec, okay?"

Ethan nodded his assent, and his eyes flicked from his phone up to the glass panel in the wall as Gordon settled the skullcap on his head.

*Not so hidden after all.* Gordon ran a baseline test on the output monitor several times, adjusting certain electrodes here and there until he got the readout he wanted. He was surprised at how intuitively everything was coming back to him. He'd done a fair amount of study in that lab, with older equipment. He was a little sad to see how little had changed in the field of sleep study. They'd had EEGs back when he was contemplating doing his doctoral thesis on sleep deprivation. What he was attaching to Ethan was sleeker and fancier, but it was the same thing.

When Gordon finished, he stepped back and checked the fit. Ethan looked as if he was trying to sleep while getting a perm, but it would give Gordon what he needed. The boy himself seemed remarkably nonplussed, almost drugged. He kept forgetting he held his phone, letting it fall and snatching it up at the last second.

"Last thing," Gordon said, holding up a little blue clip. "This monitors your heart. I'm just gonna clip it to your finger, okay?"

Ethan nodded, watching the two-way mirror as Gordon attached the clip to his forefinger.

Gordon followed Ethan's gaze back and forth. "Are you okay, buddy?" he asked, his voice a whisper.

"Are they gonna stay out there?" Ethan asked, his voice small.

"They can come in if you want. Sit by you while you try to sleep. No big deal. Whatever helps you get comfortable."

Ethan turned to Gordon and really looked at him for the first time that night. "No," he whispered, and his voice brought goose bumps to Gordon's neck. "They can't come in. Nobody can come in. Not even you." He rubbed with one foot at the ankle of his other, where Gordon had noticed a small rope burn as the boy was getting into bed.

"Ethan, you're safe here. Understand? This is a safe place. Nothing can get to you, and... and you can't get to anybody else, okay?"

"Promise me," Ethan said. "Promise me that they won't come in."

"I promise."

"You too. You can't come in either. Just look at the machines from back there. Behind the wall."

"I can't promise that. I may have to adjust things. Check stuff. Make sure you're all right."

"I'm not all right," Ethan said. "I'm just warning you."

"It's okay, Ethan. I've done this stuff before—"

"Be careful," Ethan whispered, and the genuine fear in his face brought back the goose bumps twofold. Gordon fought down a shiver. He needed to make Ethan feel as though the entire experiment was normal, which was a joke in and of itself. Nothing about it was normal. Normal seemed to have left the building of Gordon Pope's life as soon as he walked into that courtroom.

"Sleep tight," he said lamely. As if anyone could sleep tight while strapped to an electrode array and a heart monitor. But Ethan was already leaning back on his pillow. He tried to take the phone from Ethan's hands to set it on the nightstand next to the bed, but as soon as he grabbed it, Ethan held on.

"I need it to sleep," he mumbled. So Gordon let it be.

He flicked off the overhead lights at the door. The monitors were in sleep mode. A small floor light of soft blue allowed the attending doctors to see the sleeping patients if need be, but it was low, more of a night-light than anything. The room was as dark as it could get. He closed the door behind him and moved to the monitoring station behind the glass, where he sat down next to Mr. and Mrs. Barret.

"Ethan wants everyone out of the room," Gordon said, glancing at them out of the corner of his eye while watching the EEG output on the monitor in front of him. All receptors were active. The readout showed a line swinging in patterned peaks and valleys, slightly slower than a normally functioning brain wave, but that was to be expected given how exhausted Ethan looked.

"He thinks he's going to hurt us," Mr. Barret said,

shaking his head. "It's ridiculous, but he won't let us near him at night. He locks his doors." He looked at his son in the bed, glowing faintly blue with the light of the phone in his hand.

"I noticed lesions around his ankles," Gordon said carefully, and as soon as he did, Mrs. Barret started to tear up.

"I swear to God I would never hurt him. You have to believe me. Not me, not Andrew. Nobody," she said, her voice quivering.

"I do. Otherwise, I would have called CPS the second I saw them. I've seen abuse, and I've seen abusers. You aren't them. But that leaves one alternative. He's giving them to himself, which means he's not only tying himself up, but he's also struggling enough against those restraints to burn himself."

She lifted a shaky hand to cover her mouth.

Mr. Barret looked at his son in utter confusion. "What is going on with you, my man?" he whispered.

"That's what I'm trying to figure out. He told me he doesn't dream. Everyone dreams, but not everyone remembers dreams. He was having no problem recalling his dreams up until the night he attacked his friend. Then his recall left him, for some reason. I'm going to try and get it back by inducing REM sleep."

They watched as Ethan fumbled to put his earbuds in, attached to his phone with a long white cord.

"He falls asleep to music?" Gordon asked.

"Sometimes. Sometimes to podcasts or video-game broadcasts. There are these people that broadcast themselves playing video games. All the time. He says he needs them to sleep. They're like his white noise."

Gordon watched Ethan in silence then turned to Mr. Barret. "When does he normally get up for the day?"

"He's up before we are, which is usually around seven."

That was completely medically unhealthy for a preteen. Preteens could comfortably sleep until noon without batting an eye. The only reason Ethan would be up at seven was if he wasn't really sleeping. Or sleeping in such short bursts that his body was neither here nor there subconsciously. That, ironically, was good news for the study because, even as Gordon watched, the boy was falling asleep. His brain waves settled into a regular rhythm of alpha waves. He was already tuning everything out. And if he hadn't slept for as long as Gordon thought he hadn't slept, he was going to sleep hard.

"Are you sure you want to be here for this, Mrs. Barret?" Gordon asked. He could hear the woman's rapid rabbit breaths, and they were making him nervous.

"Why?" she asked. "Is it going to be bad? Is he going to hurt himself?"

"I don't know what he's going to do. But my theory is that whatever it is, it's happening in or around the REM stage of sleep. REM sleep is like a bank. Every time you deny yourself REM sleep, your body remembers, charges interest. Then, when you finally do sleep, it hits you hard."

She watched him, horrified. Her husband squeezed her hand.

"Which is to say that whatever he's been doing to himself is going to come out here. Tonight. And you might not want to see it."

Mrs. Barret blinked away tears but shook her head resolutely. "It's in God's hands. Not ours. Not even yours, Dr. Pope."

Gordon watched the monitor. That was an odd thing to say, and it seemed to make Mr. Barret uncomfortable as they watched Ethan fight to stay awake in his bed. His head dipped again and again into his shoulder until it settled there. The phone dropped from his grip and slipped to the blanket. His mouth opened slightly, and his heartbeat regulated, then slowed. His brain-wave activity shifted to a steadier and more rhythmic pattern.

"He's in stage-one sleep right now," Gordon said, standing to get a better look at the boy over the monitors. "In stage one, we sort of rehash the day, but it's like a Dali painting. Disconnected images from our experiences, colors, snippets of thought—all of it floating around in our brain like a swirling pot of soup."

Ethan twitched his lip but offered nothing more revealing than that. Gordon sat back down, and the three of them waited in the low light of the monitoring station. At first, the Barrets couldn't take their eyes off their son, but as the night wore on, they settled into their seats and waited for Gordon to tell them of any changes in his condition. Mr. Barret sat with his legs apart, elbows resting on his knees. Mrs. Barret looked as if she was either sleeping or praying—Gordon couldn't tell which.

"He's downshifting now," Gordon said quietly, his eyes on the monitor where, here and there, a more severe peak and valley distinguished itself on the readout, "going into stage-two sleep."

Gordon stood again and watched Ethan. The boy had closed his mouth, and a small tapping sound began to come from the com system.

"What's that?" Mrs. Barret asked, her voice soft but high.

"His teeth," Gordon said. "He's tapping his teeth." Ethan was also moving his lips in the barest approximation of words. Gordon checked his watch and monitored the wavelengths. "Slower, slower. I'd say stage three now.

He's progressing faster than normal, but that's to be expected."

"Is he dreaming?" Mr. Barret asked. "Can you tell what he's dreaming?"

"I think he's trying to dream," Gordon said. "But these waves are interrupted, see? Here." Gordon pointed to a staccato tightening in the rolling wavelengths. "He's fighting himself somehow."

Ethan settled again, his body slack. His phone slipped off his bed and clattered onto the floor, taking his earbuds with it. He didn't notice.

"We've broken two phones that way," Mr. Barret said.

Gordon nodded blankly, paying attention to the monitor, where the wave activity was now solidly delta. "This is deep sleep. Delta waves. He's either late stage three or early stage four. This is where sleepwalking typically occurs."

"Not in REM?" Mr. Barret asked.

"No. I have a theory that for some reason Ethan's body isn't allowing itself to get to the fifth stage of sleep. I don't think he's had REM sleep for some time."

Gordon's eyes flicked from the monitor to the boy, glowing in the low light. He watched as Ethan's legs moved, slowly at first, as if testing to see if they were still bound. His head rested calmly on the pillow, which made the independent movement of his limbs all the more alien. Andrew and Jane were silent. They watched Ethan as if they were strapped down and stunned.

"REM sleep is what heals us," Gordon said. "It's where we're free to spin the story of our lives on our own terms. There are theories, well-respected theories, which pin REM sleep to the development of consciousness itself."

In his bed, Ethan suddenly calmed.

"Without REM, we devolve. It's what separates us from

beasts," Gordon said, speaking as if to himself, his hand pressed on the glass, his face inches from it, fogging it.

"Are you calling my son a beast?" Mr. Barret asked, standing to look through the window next to Gordon. His wife curled up in her seat, staring forward at nothing, gripping her hands together.

Gordon's reply was cut short when Ethan sat up smoothly in his bed, his eyes still closed. Both men froze, waiting for the anger, the rage Ethan feared, but it didn't come. He sat up, face forward, like a marionette. Gordon looked at the monitor.

"REM waves are erratic and rapid in their patterns. They look almost exactly like the neural patterns of a conscious brain," Gordon said, tapping the monitor. "These are not them. He's still in stage-four sleep. His dreams are not his own. He should be in the first wave of REM by now, but he isn't."

As if he'd heard Gordon, Ethan slowly turned his head toward them until it settled at the point where it faced directly at the one-way glass. Both men stood back involuntarily.

"He can't hear us, can he?" his father asked.

"No. This booth is soundproof, and he's deeply asleep," Gordon said, but his mouth had gone chalky.

Ethan's eyes were closed, his arms limp at his sides, his hands palm up and open, but Gordon would have sworn that somehow the boy knew what was happening, knew where they were. He relaxed by degrees until his head was fully rolled to one side, his mouth open. His teeth started tapping once more. Behind Gordon, Mrs. Barret started to mumble a Hail Mary. Mr. Barret bowed his head, but not in prayer.

"My wife," he said, taking no pains to lower his voice,

"she thinks our son is possessed." The way he spoke showed how little he thought of her belief. But Gordon caught the fear in his voice, just a note of it, a tremulous crack in his stolid veneer, which had appeared when Ethan sat up. Mr. Barret looked toward Gordon out of the corner of his eye, but for reassurance or for refutation, Gordon couldn't say.

"Your son is sick, Mr. Barret. He is not possessed," Gordon said with far more vehemence than he felt. He had been raised Catholic, but his parents treated religion more as a social necessity and community obligation than a demonstration of faith. As for himself, he'd let God fall by the wayside around the time he learned his balls didn't work and he personally would be the end of a million years of striving and thriving ancestors. He couldn't square himself with a God that wasteful.

"Then what was all that about?" Mrs. Barret asked, suddenly behind him.

"I don't know, but he's fallen back into stage-one and - two activity. Hypnagogic imagery again, snippets of the day."

"So we start over?" Mr. Barret asked.

"Theoretically, yes," Gordon said. "A healthy sleeper will cycle through to REM about five times a night. Ethan tried once, and it didn't work. He's going to try again."

And so they waited.

Gordon noted as Ethan began his second cycle through the sleep stages. His teeth tapping turned to a grind at stage three. Five minutes later, he started to slide his feet, putting his knees up and down under the sheet. Gordon turned the microphone up, but not even a murmur came from the boy —no sound at all in the room other than the grinding of his teeth and the susurrous slide of his feet on the fabric.

"Stage four again," Gordon said. He marked the time—

thirty-two minutes from stage one to stage four, faster than the last cycle. Ethan's body was rushing things, trying hard to reach REM, but again it was falling short. If anything, the sweeping patterns of his delta waves were even more consistent, less indicative of the rapid waking pattern that characterized REM sleep. The three of them watched through the glass side by side as Ethan sat up and threw his sheet off himself in one sweeping toss. His eyes remained closed as his hands probed the bed to either side of his body, his fingers snaking and then pausing in rictus forms. He tipped his head back and seemed guided by his nose like a hound, weaving and pausing, weaving and pausing. His hands gripped two fists full of the bed and started pulling in opposite directions. The bottom sheet stretched and stretched and then slowly ripped. Through the microphone, it sounded oddly like a plow through dirt. Then Ethan pressed a strip of sheet to his sweating brow, then to his mouth, licking it.

His mother turned away, crossing herself. Mr. Barret appeared to be blinking back tears. "People do all sorts of strange things when they're asleep," Gordon said, by way of reassurance. "Especially when their REM bank is dry. This isn't some demon. It's your son, and he's exhausted. He's acting out his hallucinations because his brain isn't producing the acetylene that paralyzes us in REM sleep. What should be going on in his head is going on in his body. That's all."

But even as he said it, he wondered if that really was all. Something about the movements Ethan made unsettled him beyond the obvious. They were far too practiced. He should be in the midst of a fragmented dream narrative, but instead he looked more like an animal who had woken up in a strange cage and was subtly feeling out his surroundings.

And then Ethan fell back to his pillow once again, jaw slack. "He didn't reach REM this time either. He's cycling through a third time," Gordon said.

Already, Ethan's brain waves had gone delta.

"Much faster now. He's already stage three again." Gordon flicked his eyes from the monitor back to where the boy lay. The tapping and grinding that had characterized the first hour and a half of sleep were gone. In its place was a steady, measured white noise, rising and falling.

"What is that?" Mr. Barret asked, cocking his ear to the speaker.

"Breathing," Gordon said. "He's breathing loudly." *And strangely.* The breaths were nearly unbroken, the rising and falling following one another instantly. It sounded more like panting.

Ethan sat up again, slower that time, more measured. Gordon would have thought

*more aware* if he believed that the boy was aware. But he didn't. He didn't think the child he'd sat with on the floor of his office was anywhere to be found right now. But *something* was aware. He felt that distinctly. Not a demon. Not a spirit. Nothing like that. He couldn't put it into words, not yet. He felt he'd need to sit in silence over about five fingers of scotch to figure it out. But for the time, all he could think to call this thing was *primal.* That word kept coming back to him, again and again. Stuck behind the one-way glass, he felt distinctly as though he was at the zoo.

Ethan began to feel at the wires attaching him to the machines. He started first with the vital-sign finger clip. He traced the cord gently to where it was attached to his forefinger, eyes closed. When he found it, he ripped it off. The vitals monitor flatlined, and a small, insistent beeping began, oddly quieted, as if not to wake the patients even in the case of a medical emergency. Gordon cursed. Ethan was starting to claw at his face. The EEG machine was already beeping an unsettled warning.

"He's gonna rip the EEG equipment off," Gordon said, pushing his chair back and going for the door. "Stay here, I'm going in."

Mr. Barret stood but acquiesced. His wife set a hand briefly on Gordon as if to bless him, but she seemed to think the better of it and turned toward the glass instead.

Gordon opened the door to the lab, and Ethan froze instantly. He was sitting upright on his bed, his eyes closed. One hand was wrapped around his sheets, the other already slipped underneath the mesh webbing of his hairnet. His teeth were clenched, but he was completely silent. Gordon could just barely make out the tinny sound of whatever Ethan had been listening to through his headphones, like the tapping of a bug scratching its way across the floor. Gordon started towards Ethan but stopped as the boy nosed the air and took a deep breath and let it out in stepped exhale. Gordon pointedly tried not to think of how Ethan had almost killed another person in just that type of state. It took the combined efforts of every professional bone in his body to start walking toward him again, but walk he did.

"Ethan, can you hear me?" he asked calmly, feet from the bed.

Ethan's face went slack. Then Ethan turned to Gordon and opened his eyes. Gordon nearly fell backward over the bed behind him. The boy's eyes were wide, too wide for his drooping face. His eyes were screaming, but his face was asleep. Gordon thought back to a case Gladwell loved to bring up in Psych 101, which was his wheelhouse back in the day, about a man in Canada who had driven fourteen miles along the interstate while asleep and managed to do it well. It was completely within the realm of medical science that Ethan could still be asleep right then. Still, Gordon had never before come face to face with anyone who slept with their eyes open. It seemed like something out of folklore. He wondered how many hysterical Hail Marys Ethan's mother was reciting back behind the glass. Admittedly, the situation was looking less and less like typical parasomnia—even less like extreme parasomnia. But Gordon was a medical man. He wouldn't brook nonsense like possession, especially when the boy's future was on the line.

And then Ethan spoke, and Gordon wondered if the hysterical Mrs. Barret might have the right of things after all.

"It is too late," Ethan croaked. They sounded like the words of a person who had just woken from a coma and hadn't quite recalled how to correctly push air through the vocal cords.

*He's awake, then,* was the first thing Gordon thought. Throughout their session together, Ethan had taken a nihilist tack, thinking he was doomed to his fate. So Gordon thought he'd simply awoken again and had jumped back on the defeatist train.

"It's not too late, buddy. Just try to get some sleep," Gordon said, checking the EEG setup.

"I am here now," Ethan said, interrupting Gordon's train of thought as surely as if it had slammed against a brick wall. Gordon turned toward Ethan, and the two of them stared at each other for fifteen seconds. Ethan didn't blink the entire time.

"Who are you?" Gordon stammered.

"The Red," Ethan growled. He bunched his shoulders and looked ready to spring off the bed. "I won't go away."

He ground his teeth, and spittle flecked the corners of his mouth.

Gordon held up his hands, bracing for a bodily tackle, but then Ethan seemed to slacken. He slumped forward, eyes closed, sliding off the bed until Gordon caught him.

"Ethan?" he asked, picking him up and setting him back in bed. "Ethan!" He pressed two fingers against his neck and felt a racing pulse, but even as he stood there trying to count the beats, it started to slow and even out to something deceptively normal.

*Enough of this*. "Ethan," he said, speaking loudly and rubbing the boy's sternum with the knuckle of his forefinger. Ethan stirred, burrowed backward into the pillow, then opened his eyes, blinking. They were bloodshot but otherwise night-and-day different from the eyes that had been staring at Gordon moments before. He looked up and recognized Gordon instantly, then he grabbed his shirt.

"Did I hurt them?" he asked, his voice breaking to a squeak. "Mom? Dad?"

His parents burst through the door, his father with tears in his eyes, his mother sobbing. They came to his bed and knelt down, holding his hands.

"We're right here," Mr. Barret said. "Right here, son."

Gordon knew he had mere moments before the last remnants of whatever spell the boy had been under faded completely, like mist in the sun.

"Ethan," he said, breaking through his parents and standing over him. "What do you remember? Anything? You must think."

Ethan looked up at Gordon through puffy, tearing eyes. "Red mist," he said. "It was nothing but red mist. I breathed it, and it was hot. So hot. That's all I remember, the red and the heat."

Gordon stood back, leaving the boy to the soft words of his parents. "You can all go back home now," Gordon said numbly. "I'll take a look at what we've seen tonight and... and get back with you as soon as I can."

If the three of them heard him, they made no indication. Gordon backed away, out of the room, then returned to the monitoring station and sat heavily on the chair in front of the screens. Red mist. Again. And stronger that time. And he was breathing it. As if he had *become* it.

Before Gordon packed his bags to go, he had to check one more thing, just to make sure. He brought the EEG recording back to the last sleep cycle, the one where Ethan had spoken to him, eyes open. That was awareness. That was self-placement. That was situational comprehension. Lucidity.

But the records didn't lie. The delta waves were big and loopy and irrefutable. He'd never made it to the REM stage, the healing stage, but Ethan had been one-hundred-percent asleep the entire time.

# CHAPTER ELEVEN

G ordon slept from six in the morning until two in the afternoon when he got back from the lab. His last thought before his head hit the pillow was that if he was lucky, all of that activity might spur some movement in his own dream. He wasn't lucky. He slept like a rock. When he awoke, he reached for his dream journal, newly installed on the dusty nightstand next to his bed. He held it for a moment then set it down, having recalled nothing.

He walked past his message machine—a chunky relic from the past he refused to part with—six times as he went about his morning routine before he noticed the message light was blinking. He stopped in his tracks, breakfast pastry in hand. The handful of patients he still had never called him. They'd been lockstep in their appointment times for months. On the rare occasions they needed to contact him, they e-mailed. The message machine was hooked to his business line, which had been gathering cobwebs for almost a year.

He chewed his pastry thoughtfully and pressed the playback button.

"Uh, yes. Hello. This message is for Dr. Gordon Pope. I got your name from the *Baltimore City Tribune* article about that Erica girl. I... don't really know how to say this, so I'll just say it. I have a ten-year-old girl who is sleepwalking like crazy. Quite frankly, she's scaring the shit out of me. Excuse my language. I've called some other psychiatrists, but I don't think they get it. I thought maybe you would. Please, give me a call at..."

"Is this Jefferson and Pope from the article? 'Cause I'm trying to get hold of Gordon Pope? The guy who helped find that girl over in Tivoli? You're not gonna believe this, but my son does the exact same stuff as that little girl. It started probably five months ago, and it's just getting worse. My wife and I haven't slept in weeks. Call me back..."

"I hope this is the right guy because this is going to sound really crazy otherwise, but I'm looking for a psychiatrist named Gordon Pope from the *Tribune* article. It's gotta be you, right? How many Popes can there be? I think my son is gonna hurt somebody. He's sleepwalking just like that girl. I was terrified to call anybody because it sounds... well, it sounds insane. But every night, like, an hour after he goes to bed, he starts acting just... Listen, would you please call me back?"

The pastry dropped from Gordon's mouth. *Baltimore City Tribune* was the free local rag, the kind of thing that was at least seventy-five percent ads. Maybe three or four neighborhood beat pieces that read a bit like high-school book reports. The back page was chock-full of numbers for shady massage parlors.

And apparently somewhere in there was a piece about the Erica Denbrook incident.

Gordon walked around his apartment aimlessly, robe flapping open, orange juice in hand. Warren Duke had made it very clear that Gordon was to have no involvement in that search-and-rescue operation. He was quite sure the lieutenant had scrubbed whatever report was filed and made sure Gordon wasn't listed. He'd nearly been arrested for his trouble that night, so he had a hard time believing anyone down at the police department would willingly speak his name to a reporter, even if they'd been right there next to the dumpster with him when they found Erica.

Gordon gulped down his orange juice. So whoever had written the article likely got shut down by the BPD. Where would they go next? Well, if it had been Gordon, he would have tried to find other, similar cases, like the Ethan Barret case. Then he'd go to the courthouse, hang around, and ask a few questions. The reporters for the *Tribune* might be amateurs, but they were hungry amateurs. They were looking to write that piece that might get them a shot at a job at the *Sun* or maybe something that got the attention of the big boys in New York. They'd be annoyingly persistent.

And if they stuck around the courthouse long enough, they'd most likely run into Dana Frisco.

Gordon could picture the scene now. Dana Frisco would say she couldn't comment about the case at the same time she winked and nodded over at the parking lot. Then she'd say, off the record, exactly what happened. Because Dana was pissed off. No doubt, she'd seen the press conference just as he had. No doubt, she ground her teeth twice as hard as she watched Duke smile sadly in his navy blazer as he applauded his police force without naming any of them specifically, all while his own name scrolled constantly on the ticker at the bottom of the screen.

Gordon fished his cell phone out of the sagging pocket of his robe. He found Dana's number and hit the call button. She picked up after the second ring.

"Gordon?" she asked. She sounded as though she was walking somewhere, probably at the courthouse again. "Everything okay?"

"Dana, what did you do?" Gordon asked, but he spoke through a smile.

"Whatever are you referring to, Dr. Pope?" Dana replied.

"I have three messages on my business line. I haven't had three messages on my business line in a year. To be quite frank, I wasn't one hundred percent sure I still had a business line."

"Well, and this is strictly off the books, of course, but a plucky young kid from the *Tribune* was waiting by my squad car at the courthouse a few days ago. Said he had some questions about the Erica Denbrook case that he wanted to ask me. Off record. Marty damn near had a heart attack, but he got over it after he made the kid swear not to mention him."

"Dana, you beautiful, beautiful woman," Gordon said without thinking. "You didn't have to mention me. I just did what I could do. I got lucky."

"Without you, Erica would be dead," Dana said flatly. She let that hang between them for a moment before saying, "Plus, Warren Duke is a prick and doesn't deserve one ounce of the praise he got."

"Well. Thank you. I mean it. Nobody but my mother goes to bat for me anymore," Gordon said. Speaking of his mother, her one condition for the sleep-lab deal came barreling to mind. Suddenly Gordon's mouth was dry.

"Were the messages for consultations? Maybe you can get some business out of all this?" Dana asked.

Gordon swallowed and felt that it sounded abnormally loud, like a fish gasping. He'd been just fine five seconds before but now felt like a gawky, two-stepping preteen at the school dance.

"Gordon? Did I lose you? Hello?"

"No, no. I'm here. The messages? Yes. The messages. They were asking about consultations. Believe it or not, there are other families out there having similar problems. Sleepwalking kids."

"No shit?"

"Yeah," Gordon said, and the full realization of that truth settled upon him, sobering him and washing the awkwardness from his mouth. "And that was just from the people who picked up that issue of the *Tribune*. Which means that this problem is bigger than Ethan and Erica. Maybe a lot bigger." Gordon stared blankly at his empty glass of OJ.

"Gordon?" Dana asked. "Is everything okay?"

He wouldn't lie to her. He would rather she think him crazy and never speak to him again than lie to her at that moment. The way she spoke, the weight behind the words, sounded as though she already had an idea that things weren't quite right in his head. She was the same woman who had gone along with the Chutes and Ladders idea. He owed her the truth.

"These kids are having the same dream. I'd bet my lunch that if I called back those parents and spoke with their kids, they'd all say the same thing. They'd have different names for it, I'm sure, but Ethan calls it the Red."

Gordon cringed, the phone to his ear, as he waited for Dana to dismiss him, waited for the moment Dana would become Karen, would coddle him out of pity but make it clear that he was delusional. *"Save it for the campfire, Gordon. You did a good thing finding Erica, but this is too much. This has got to stop. These kids are messing with you. Be reasonable."*

But reason had left the building. So far, Gordon was the only person who seemed able to grasp that. Even Ethan's parents thought the boy a one-off sickness, but Gordon was seeing a pattern. The problem was, crazy people also saw patterns. That was a hallmark of schizophrenia. So it was time for Dana to abandon him, too.

"Jesus," she said. "Really?"

"Wait. You believe me?"

"Gordon, I got a little girl of my own. Now, she's not sleepwalking or anything like that, but I can't tell you the number of times I've looked at my baby over the years and wondered if she's actually from the same planet as me. I love Chloe with the heat of the sun, but kids are weird. They do weird stuff. Sometimes they do scary stuff, too. So why not? What do I know?"

Gordon started laughing. He couldn't help himself. Relief swept away his fatigue, washed away his worry that despite what he'd seen the past night, he wouldn't be able to make sense of it. Somebody out there besides his mother believed in him.

And then his mother's one condition wriggled back into his thoughts. His heart rate picked up instantly—he could feel it. The truth was he liked Dana. A lot. More than even he had before, when he took way too many drinks from the rusty courthouse water fountain on the off chance he might run into her again. His mother had only given voice to what Gordon had been pussyfooting around for the past year. It was time.

He felt as though he was breathing obnoxiously into the phone, as though too much silence had passed since Dana had last spoken. Why was he being so weird about this? He was acting as though he'd never asked a girl out before, and a little voice in his head said, *Well, you haven't. You drunkenly made out with Karen in college, and that kicked off that whole disaster. Before that, you mostly read books and collected figurines.*

"All right, well…" Dana began. "I'm glad you got some press. Even if it is Podunk press. You deserve it, Gordon."

That sounded to Gordon a lot like a prelude to a sign-off. His window was closing. He was panicking. So he did what he always did when he panicked. He told the truth.

"Dana, I need your help."

He heard Dana's shoulder com crackle and then clip to silence. He dared to imagine that she'd shut it off for him. "What's up?" she asked.

"Are you busy tonight?" Gordon asked.

"Hmm. That depends. Is this personal or professional?"

"Definitely both."

"Are you asking me on a date, Gordon?" He thought he heard a smile in her voice.

Gordon thanked God they were doing this over the phone. His face was as red as a strawberry, and the OJ was audibly percolating in his gut. "Yes. But it's gonna be a weird date."

"Wow, take it easy, Casanova."

"I'm trying to get in touch with my primal side. But I need you."

Dana snorted. Her com buzzed again. In the background, a low hum of activity echoed down the marble courthouse halls. "Do I at least get dinner first?"

"How about Chinese takeout at the Elliot Sleep Lab at Hopkins? Say eight p.m.?"

"How romantic. I'm guessing this has to do with Ethan Barret."

"I thought so too, but now I think it might have to do with all of us."

In the prolonged silence that followed, Gordon felt irrationally terrified Dana was going to say no. So he didn't give her the chance.

"Please, Dana? If I'm right about this—and that's a huge if, but if I am—these kids don't have much time left before they all start acting like Ethan did that night."

"Who am I kidding? You had me at takeout Chinese."

Gordon almost collapsed. "Thank you. I mean it. Thank you. And be prepared, because I'm gonna keep you up all night."

Dana laughed, full throated and loud. "I'll see you at eight."

When she hung up, Gordon was still smiling. He wasn't any closer, really, to figuring out what the Red was. Ethan was still mere weeks away from forcible rehabilitation at Ditchfield. He now knew of at least four other kids, and probably far more than that, who were going down the same path. It was hot as sin in Baltimore and raining at the same time. He was groggy, exhausted, and still as broke as he'd been when he went to sleep.

But Dana had laughed, really laughed, and she was coming to the lab with him. So in that moment, none of the other noise mattered.

GORDON WAS ALREADY at the lab that evening when Dana arrived. He was waiting in the control room where he'd stood just a day earlier. Two folded boxes of Chinese takeout steamed on the desk by the monitors. Dana took off her raincoat and hung it from a peg behind the door. She was dressed in a linen skirt and purple rain boots. Gordon couldn't help but smile. He'd never seen her wearing anything but her police uniform. Just seeing her dressed like a normal person, he felt as though Dana had let him in on a secret, as if he'd earned the right to see her as something other than the authority figure she was day in and day out on the beat.

"You look great," Gordon said. "We should be out along the harbor. Someplace hip. Not in this old block of concrete."

Dana waved him off but smirked in a way that let Gordon know she pretty much agreed with him. "Is that from Great Wall?" She pointed at the food.

"You know it. Crab Rangoons in the bag there too."

"Nice. I love Great Wall."

"I wanted to bring wine. But you've got to stay awake for a while."

"Don't worry about it. I'm going through a beer phase anyway."

"Well, I've got Cokes. Coke is like beer for kids. It's close."

Dana snickered. "Where is the kid? Ethan?"

Gordon took a deep breath and sat on the desk and was suddenly absorbed in the food. He popped open his box of General Tso's chicken and doled out a generous glob onto a paper plate. "He's not coming today," Gordon said quickly. Then he took a big bite of crab Rangoon.

Dana crossed her arms. "Okaaay," she said. "So you really do think this place is a romantic first date then, huh? Maybe you need your own head examined."

"I think you're right on the money, there, but no, I need your help still. We're using the lab, but the patient is going to be me."

Dana stared at Gordon in silence for ten seconds while

he crunched his crab Rangoon through puffed cheeks. Then she cleared her throat. "All right, Gordon. Enough bullshit. What is going on here?"

"Here," Gordon said, handing her a carton of Chinese food and offering her a seat in the swivel chair before sitting down himself on the same bench where Jane and Andrew Barret had sat last. "It's spicy beef lo mein. Their beef lo mein is a minor miracle. It makes everything easier to take."

Dana took the carton and started eating straight from it with a plastic fork. She paused after the first bite, looked down, and nodded in grudging approval. Then she crossed her legs, chewed, and waited.

"Okay, so you know how I said Ethan Barret and Erica Denbrook were having the same dream?" Gordon asked. "And how I said I'm getting calls now, from other parents, worried because their own kids are sleepwalking? And how I told you I think all of these kids are having the same dream? And then remember how after I told you all that, you didn't run away from me, screaming for a straitjacket?" He hoped she remembered especially that last bit.

"Yes," Dana said. "Although the more you talk about this, the more insane it sounds."

Gordon sucked at his teeth. "Well then, this next bit might really be the straw that breaks the camel's back."

Dana took another bite and watched him through narrowed eyes.

"What if I told you that I had the same dreams as these kids?"

Dana shrugged. "That's not too crazy. If a bunch of kids are having the same type of dream in this city, makes sense the adults would start to have it too. Maybe it's something in the water. Or maybe it's sort of a collective anxiety because

Baltimore is slowly falling apart. Not the craziest thing I've ever heard. You should see some of the shit I dream about."

"Yeah, but I had the dream over thirty years ago," Gordon said. "And I lived in Bethesda at the time."

He let those words hang in the air and went back to attacking his food.

"Huh. Well. Yeah. That's a little bit weirder. A lot weirder. Makes it tough to pin it to something happening here, now. Not if you were dreaming it three decades ago."

Gordon nodded vigorously and started talking through a full mouth before stopping himself. He coughed and swallowed and coughed. Took a big swig of Coke. Wiped his eyes. "That's exactly what I'm saying! I think this stuff might be ingrained. An imprint, something ancient, something Jungian. Have you heard of Carl Jung?"

"No."

"That's okay. Forget it. The point is I had the same type of dream, but then they stopped. I want to know why they stopped. Because if I know why they stopped, I think I can help these kids stop their own dreams, and then maybe we can avert this entire train wreck before we have a hundred— or a thousand—Ethans."

Dana sat back in the chair and appraised Gordon. He knew he'd put a lot on her, but he'd tried to do it in stages, sort of like boiling a frog. The truth was, he wanted her alongside him more than anything. A sort of clarity came to him when he was by her side, a clarity that helped him come up with ideas like playing Chutes and Ladders.

Gordon expected her to scoff or laugh or set down the Chinese and pick up her coat.

What he didn't expect was when she asked, "Why do you care so much?"

She didn't ask it as if she thought it silly that he cared so much. She wasn't mocking him. The question was genuine.

"Do you know how many violent assaults there are in this city every day? Stuff like Ethan pulled, only these guys are wide awake?" she asked. "Hell, do you know how many people die in this city every day? How many kids are essentially doomed, one way or another, before they ever reach thirteen? No sleepwalking required?"

"I can guess," Gordon said softly. "But it'd probably be low."

"And yet here you are, two nights in a row, working your ass off at a sleep lab. You look like you're running on fumes, no offense, but you're still going. Why? Why do you care so much about these kids?"

He almost said, *"Because I can't have kids of my own. I'm a single white male in debt and underemployed. People like me have zero chance of adopting. And zero also happens to be the number of working testicles I have."* But he was prepared to heat the water by degrees, not flash-fry the poor woman.

"I like kids," Gordon said instead, simply and honestly. "And not in the way everyone assumes a forty-five-year-old single balding guy likes kids, either. Not the restraining-order kind of like. Don't worry."

"I know," she said, watching him carefully. She shook her head, but it was a soft, quiet kind of exasperation, and it struck Gordon as more the type of thing you'd do dug into a foxhole with a person than anything borne out of confusion. "And just when I get to thinking that there aren't any of us left." She took another bite. "All right, Gordon. What do you need me to do?"

.  .  .

An hour later, his belly two pounds heavier with Chinese food he was vaguely regretting, Gordon sat on the middle bed of the lab in a threadbare Hopkins Medical T-shirt the school had mailed him fifteen years before, hoping for money they didn't get, as well as a pair of reindeer-patterned boxers that he'd sworn he would throw away three Christmases before. He was already rigged up with the brain-wave hairnet. Dana looked as though she was stifling a laugh the entire time he spoke to her.

"So you understand the waves, right? Because that is imperative. You have to recognize the waves."

"You wear socks to bed?" Dana asked.

Gordon blinked. "My feet get cold."

"It's summertime. It's ninety degrees at midnight."

"I have poor circulation of the feet," Gordon said before stopping himself. "Listen, Dana, you have to be able to recognize the patterns that indicate each of the five stages of sleep."

"I get it. You went over them five times. But I still don't get why you want me to wake you up all the time." Dana sipped her second Diet Coke.

"If you wake me up before I hit REM a couple of times, when I eventually do hit REM, it'll be that much more powerful. Like when you have a stiff drink after a week on the wagon. You wake me up during stage-four delta waves four times. Okay? Then in the fifth sleep cycle, I'll hit REM like a wrecking ball. If I'm lucky, I'll be able to bring back the cave dream as it was back then."

"Back when it was a nightmare that scared the pants off you," Dana said, nodding. "Sounds completely reasonable. You're actually hoping for a nightmare."

"If that's what it takes," Gordon said, swinging up into bed. "Good thing I've got a food coma coming. Maybe I'll actually get to sleep. My mother always threatened me with these sleep labs when I couldn't sleep as a kid. Among other things."

"She sounds charming."

"You'd be surprised."

Dana turned and walked toward the monitoring room, but she stopped at the door and looked around. "Hey, be careful in that crazy mind of yours, okay?"

Gordon held a thumbs-up sign. "I'll see you in fifty minutes. Give or take."

Dana softly closed the door behind her, and Gordon stared at the ceiling while the noise-canceling machine played a steady stream of what sounded like an air-conditioning unit. His last waking thought was that he would never be able to fall asleep to that sound.

GORDON WAS WALKING along the wide perimeter of the back lawn of his childhood home. The grass was rough and thick, overgrown and sprouting seeds at the tips. Everything felt right. Normal. He was dreaming unaware and taking each set piece in its own right. He had a vague sense that he was there to do something, but it wasn't pressing and was quickly forgotten, like that last task left undone on a Friday afternoon. He was walking. Simply walking.

And then he was awake. Dana was shaking his arm gently as she said, "Gordon. Gordon, wake up."

He blinked, groggy, then jerked away from her, his place and purpose lost in a fog. His heart raced, then just as quickly began to calm.

"It's okay. It's just me."

Gordon nodded and yawned hugely then cleared his throat. "How long was I out?"

"Fifty-four minutes. You were just starting to leave the delta waves and settle into REM patterns. I got you as soon as I saw the change."

"Good. That's good. I feel like shit. Which is also good. It means my cycle was interrupted."

"What did you dream about?" Dana asked, rubbing her own eyes but otherwise looking as alert as always. For a split second, he allowed himself to think what it might be like to be awoken by her under other circumstances—say, if she was lying next to him in bed, for instance, in PJs of her own, not standing over him, looking vaguely concerned. He nipped that thought in the bud when the blood flow in his body shifted downward.

"Nothing. I mean, obviously something, but I can't recall, which is also good. Dream recall is at its strongest in REM sleep. If it all goes according to plan, I won't recall anything until you let me. How are you holding up? Bored out of your mind?" Gordon stifled another yawn and gauged if he should pee. He was okay, but he was glad he'd held off on his Coke.

"I'm fine. Reading a trashy romance novel. Trying to stop myself from finishing off the rest of the Great Wall. Sort of succeeding."

Gordon nodded, already groggy again. "Ready for round two?" he asked.

Dana said something that might have been *good luck*, but he already had his head on the pillow, fading, fading, and gone.

Gordon's dreaming from then forward slowly coalesced into something recognizable, like a gradually rising cake cooked for hours in the oven of his brain. He still paced the edges of his parents' estate, but the landscape was unrecognizable. He came upon things that had no place there but that still seemed normal to him as he dreamed unaware: his first car, a beat-up Chevy Nova that was pristine as he approached it then rusted and on blocks as he reached it. Next was the two-story sliding chalkboard Morty Gladwell had used in Psych 101, jammed with medical minutiae, the countless formulas that make up the balance of the human body and brain. He slapped it as if giving it a passing high five, still smiling. The grass of the lawn grew taller, around his knees. He accepted it as a child would and continued to walk. In a blink, he found himself walking through library stacks, the grass still underfoot. He knew Karen was close by—that was where they'd made love once. He felt a pulsing desire and a strange sadness at the same time. Of course he should be in those stacks, of course he should be with Karen. But something wasn't right. That was the first whisper in the corner of his mind that perhaps where he thought he was wasn't where he actually was. He paused and looked toward his feet, but they were swallowed in grass that was nearly up to his waist. Why would there be grass in a library? Why would there be a library in his parents' backyard? Could he be dreami—

His body was slack like a scarecrow as Dana shook him. He awoke slowly that time.

"Gordon," she said, louder, almost stern. "Gordon, you have to wake up."

He didn't jump back this time, no shock, no sense of displacement for Gordon—only an overwhelming exhaustion. His brain was sluggish. He mumbled something, distantly aware of the lab, of the experiment he was concocting on himself.

"This is it, Gordon. Are you ready?" Dana asked.

*This is what?* "What time is it?" he asked, not exactly what he meant to ask, but close enough.

"It's four in the morning. I've broken four cycles. This is it. Number five."

*How could that be?* It seemed he was checking his bladder a moment before. But all of that floated from him. His body was already falling back through the bed, back to the lawn. He heard a shuffling sound and smelled a faint waft of perfume. He felt a tickle of hair on his face.

"Good luck, Gordon," he heard. Or he thought he heard. And then a warm, soft pressing on his forehead. It couldn't possibly be a kiss. It felt too warm. It was like a kitten sleeping on his face. Or was it a kiss? He wanted badly for it to have been a kiss, but by then he was too far gone.

The slice-of-life imagery from earlier in the night disappeared, and Gordon found himself on the lawn outside his house, all alone in a vacuum quiet. Everything was in its place, yet everything had gone to seed. The grass had grown to his chest, and when he turned around, he saw the estate flaking, its whitewash peeling off the wood in sheets. The windows were broken, the doors missing. He placed himself within his mind almost instantly. *This is not my house. This is not my lawn. I am in a dream.* And just like that, he knew what he had to do. He wasted no time in pushing through the grass until he reached the edge of the lawn, where it met the undergrowth of the forest, which wasn't nearly as overgrown. He stepped over the threshold and into the forest, and then he waited. He waited for the pull that would drag him to the cave. He stood still, waiting, but felt no pull that time, either. No drag. No terror.

So Gordon walked.

The journey was tinged in sepia, and the forest seemed to disappear into black nothingness when he didn't stare directly at it. Dream time compressed and relaxed such that he was at the mouth of the cave in a blink while still feeling as though he hiked to it, and there he saw a snaking tendril of red mist float from the opening. He felt fear at first, but more than fear, he felt a sense of a job that needed to be done. He was here for Ethan. He was asleep in a lab right now.

The dream wavered, so he shut down that line of thought. He pictured himself as a child again, brought here countless times. He grabbed on to that fear he'd felt, making it his own again. The cave settled around him. The mist grew thicker. He walked forward, and it parted around his legs as he ducked inside.

Gordon immediately moved to the point in the cave where he'd been when the dream had broken over him thirty years before. He was finally in the REM stage he'd been denying himself, and it focused his sleeping brain like a natural amphetamine. The walls were clearer, the mist a deeper red. The cave closed itself off as it had all those years before, and when Gordon looked behind himself, he saw the stone was smooth again. No scratches.

Gordon sat just as he had then, and he covered his head with his arms. Gordon the boy had done it out of terror, weeping. Gordon the adult did it because it was what he'd done then to make the Red appear, but he didn't weep. He waited. He felt fear, surely, and anxiety as well, but that was because of whatever was happening in the waking world, outside his sleeping brain—because of the things he dared not focus upon, for fear his chance would collapse. His monsters were still there, but they had moved outside of the closet, and some small part of his mind knew that, so he was able to sit still as the mist tugged at him, brushed him, and moved over his closed eyelids and around his face, feeling like a blind man. His younger self would've screamed, *had* screamed, by that point, eyes squeezed shut. But Gordon bit his tongue and kept his eyes open.

He saw a figure in the mist, walking towards him. He did not claw against the cave that time, but he did press his back against it. He tried to grip for purchase on the floor and he had the rough, tearing sensation that the muted psychiatrist portion of his brain told him was night onychophagia: he was biting at his cuticles in his sleep. Then the figure walked out of the mist, and he stopped scrabbling, stopped pressing away, stopped everything.

He was looking at himself as a boy, and the boy was staring down at him.

Gordon's first inclination was to relax. *Where is the beast? Where is the horror?* But a whisper in the back of his mind told him to stay present, to stay alert. Gladwell's voice from another lecture, decades before, manifested like an errant note of the piano on the wind. *"The brain cannot self-actualize, Gordon. This is known. You cannot see yourself in a dream."*

This thing was not what it looked like.

The boy stared at the man still, as if it was as confused as the man was. Gordon marveled at it. He saw the scar he'd gotten over his right temple from when he and the neighbor girl had twisted the swings up until they spun like tops and then collided, only the boy's was still red, still fresh. He saw his chipped molar, a black gap in the boy's mouth. He would get it fixed the next year, just before his thirteenth birthday. He saw his mother's handiwork in the choppy way the boy's hair was cut. All those memories were correct, yet none should have been that clearly remembered. The psychiatrist in him sounded a warning.

"Are you what came for me in the mist?" Gordon asked.

The boy nodded.

"But... how? You're no monster."

"I am changed," the boy said. "You changed me." His voice was a crystal copy of Gordon's as it had been, even down to the tremulous breaking that hovered over each word.

"What were you before I changed you?" Gordon asked.

"You. But a different you."

Gordon shook his head. He'd tortured himself in a sleep lab for more riddles. The dream wavered. He shoved all worry of failure from his mind. Only when he gave up, when he sat with his arms draped over his knees, just as he had when he first spoke with Ethan in his office and simply watched this boy, did the dream settle over him again and solidify.

"This is madness," Gordon said, to the boy in his dreams, to himself. "I'm going mad."

A small smile pinched the boy Gordon's mouth. He stood straight, unblinking.

"Perhaps," the boy said. "Madness is one word for what I am. There are two parts to men. There is the part tied to the beginning and the part tied to the end. I am the part tied to the beginning."

"The beginning? You mean birth?"

The boy shook his head as if annoyed, and Gordon nearly reeled with an intense feeling of sympathy. He shook his head like that when he was trying to make himself understood to his family, his friends, when they just didn't get it.

"Before birth. Before even the knitting together in the womb. I am what you leave behind to go into life. The second you step into life, my grip on you begins to loosen." As he spoke, his face darkened, and the red swirled around him. "I hate it," the boy said.

Gordon saw violence in his eyes, a primitive darkness that he suddenly felt was probably similar to what poor Jimmy Tanner had seen in Ethan's eyes as he came for him —his friend gone, replaced by something else.

Then it was gone, and the boy straightened.

"Why do you come here again and again?" the boy asked as if he'd been watching Gordon for months, as if he wasn't a part of Gordon's subconscious at all but an alien observer. The psychiatrist sliver blared a red alert. Gordon closed it off, focusing on the cave, on the boy—anything to keep the dream together. "You must know that this place is empty for you," the boy said. "I lost you long ago. You are done with me, and I am done with you. Yet you pull me here. Why?"

"There is a boy. A boy who... who wants to be done with you as well. With his version of you."

"Ethan," the boy said, his eyes dark once more.

"Yes," Gordon said, fighting a stammer. His mouth was gummy, falling apart. He didn't have much time. "And a girl—"

"Erica. Yes. I know them both. I will take them both," he said, the cold finality of his words somehow made twice as unnatural by the boyish tone, like a child soldier utterly devoted.

"Why?" Gordon asked. "Why can't you let them go?"

"It's simple. They want the beginning more than the end. They cling to me. They may walk forward in life, but they look backward."

The dream wavered heavily, as if a fault line had snapped. Gordon knew he'd done it to himself. Speaking of Ethan and Erica was bringing his mind back toward the conscious world, and it was tipping the scale. He perhaps had time for one more question, and he wanted it to be *How did I beat you?* but he felt strongly that the boy, the thing, was proud and saw every child that slipped from its grasp as a loss not only for itself but for the child too.

"How did I lose you?" Gordon asked instead.

The boy's eyes glowed with blackness, the red mist swirled up and around him, and he faded, the cave faded, even as Gordon tried to grab hold of the walls of rock they turned to sand in his hands. Only the boy's face remained, Gordon's from thirty years before, floating like the Cheshire cat, inches from Gordon.

"You decided to look forward," said the boy.

GORDON SHOT up from his bed. Dana was there already, sitting next to him on a small padded stool as if she was the doctor and he the patient. She leaned away and let him pant and blink and cough himself into awareness.

"It's okay, Gordon," she said, her voice calm, but when Gordon turned to look at her, her eyes betrayed her. Her mascara was blotted carefully, but she'd been crying. Still, just looking at her and at the way she looked back at him steadied his heartbeat. He could hear his vitals beeping through the walls, but they were slowing, normalizing. He brushed at his forehead and his gnawed fingers came away glistening with sweat.

"What time is it?" Gordon asked.

"Almost five thirty. I'd say you've been in REM for almost thirty minutes."

"You left the control room?" Gordon asked.

Dana looked away for only a moment. "You were a mess. Talking. Crying. Twitching. I didn't know—"

"It's okay, Dana." Gordon touched her hand briefly. "Thank you."

Dana looked at his forehead as if it was a million-piece jigsaw puzzle bunched in a box. "What the hell went on in there? Who were you talking to?"

"Myself. From a long time ago," Gordon said, already going through the conversation word by word, repeating it to himself in the manner he'd taught himself over years of journaling.

"Did you get what you needed? Do you know what to do now? For Ethan? Or any of these kids?"

Gordon took several steadying breaths and reached for his journal. "I don't know what to do to help Ethan," he said. "Not yet."

Dana slumped. Gordon looked up at her, pen in hand. She looked tired, burdened by a load he thought was his own but that she'd taken on with him. Her cute skirt and top were gone, replaced by floppy pajama bottoms and a jersey-cloth T-shirt. Her hair was pulled behind her head, bunched into a clip. She crossed her arms over herself as if embarrassed, but Gordon couldn't think of a single sight he'd rather see upon waking up from that cave other than her, right then.

Gordon grasped her hand again and smiled. "I may not know how to treat him yet, but I know what's wrong with him. And that's a hell of a start."

# CHAPTER TWELVE

A ndrew Barret no longer felt comfortable with his back turned to his son, but his wife was absolutely terrified of him. She spent the entirety of the day after the sleep study at St. Mary's Cathedral on Center Street, starting at six a.m. mass then staying through noon mass and evening vespers, and then she'd gone to her parents again.

Andrew was ashamed of his wife. Her newfound Christian zeal rang hollow. She was a lapsed Catholic. Before Ethan took a turn, she hadn't been to church outside of Christmas Eve in as long as he could remember, but now she insisted that nothing but God could help the boy. As if they lived in some sort of seventeenth-century village where the doctors were shunned as witches. He'd blown up at her in the car on the ride home as she muttered Hail Marys while Ethan stared out of the window through hooded eyes like a drugged dog. Once home, she'd immediately left again to "get her spirit right," and Andrew and Ethan were left together in the living room. The Orioles' game was on low volume, but neither of them was watching. Ethan stared at nothing, and Andrew stared at Ethan.

As much as he hated to admit it, in the silence of the living room as he watched his son pawing blindly at his phone while a low, rhythmic growl came from him with every breath, Andrew had a moment—just a moment—when he allowed that Jane's belief might not be as insane as he'd told her it was before she stormed off to a church she hadn't set foot in for half a decade. Either way, she was missing the point. For some reason, the child who sat across from him was no longer his son. But Andrew firmly believed, as he knew Jane did, that his son was somewhere in there. The question was how to get him back.

*Thank God for Pope.* Talk about possessed—the man worked feverishly. He'd called the house twice already to reassure Andrew that he was close to being able to treat Ethan and getting closer all the time. Without Gordon Pope, Andrew would've been as lost as Ethan seemed. He knew that Pope's insistence that Ethan's condition was a purely medical issue was keeping him scared *for* his son, not *of* his son, like Jane was.

Ethan picked up one of Jane's magazines from the coffee table and slowly started to rip the cover. The sound jarred Andrew even as he saw it coming, overwhelming the murmurs of the baseball game.

"Ethan, put that down."

Ethan looked in the direction of Andrew's voice but seemed to see right through him, as if he'd heard his name called in a crowd of thousands. He started tearing again.

Andrew stood. "Ethan!"

He took a step forward, and Ethan's eyes focused. He dropped the magazine. Andrew sat back down. He watched Ethan for a moment more, sitting, staring, and then took a glance at the baseball game—tied two to two. The heart of the order was coming up to bat for the Os—and then he heard a loud crash.

Andrew's eyes snapped back to Ethan. He'd punched through the glass lamp on the end table to his right. His fist was still inside the bulbous base. He stared at his arm as if it wasn't his own.

Andrew stood again, eyes wide. For a moment, he couldn't say anything.

Ethan slowly withdrew his fist, still clenched. A thin, steady stream of blood fell from his middle knuckle and splattered the wood of the end table. Andrew rushed to his son and grabbed his arm, still outstretched. A sliver of glass was embedded in the skin like an iridescent splinter.

"Here, hold it up," Andrew said. "I'll get the first-aid kit." He pushed Ethan's arm into an upward position, and Ethan held it there dumbly like a mannequin, his mouth open, his eyes unblinking.

Andrew walked toward the kitchen to turn on the sink. "Keep it away from the rug," he said, turning back toward Ethan. "Your mother will kill—"

Ethan was right behind him. A foot away. Standing still and bleeding. How the boy could have been that fast, Andrew had no idea. Ethan stared at him and started sucking at the cut on his fist. Even if Andrew found the words to speak, he doubted anything he might say to his son would register anyway.

When Andrew had been ten, his father got them a rescue dog, an unruly terrier that barked and barked and seemed not even to register a scolding, as if she went deaf whenever anyone raised their voice at her. One day, she took off out the open front door after the neighbor's dog and was tagged by a truck as she bolted across the street, oblivious to his screams. As Andrew faced his son, he was reminded of that dog for the first time in years. He reached out for him and grasped his shoulder, bony even by gangly preteen standards, and he directed Ethan in front of him and to the kitchen sink in a wordless exchange.

One hand still on Ethan's shoulder, Andrew reached up and took the first-aid kit from the high shelf above the refrigerator. He gently pried Ethan's fist from his mouth. His tongue lolled after it for a moment as Andrew put it under the running water in the sink. The glass was gone. Ethan must have swallowed it.

Was that to be their life from then on, his wife and son falling back into the Dark Ages while he walked on eggshells, trying to keep them all from breaking? He saw his son was clutching his phone still, white-knuckled. His son's addiction to the thing felt just as unnatural as his suckling mouth. He could see the screen. It showed that chat program he'd been on for months, the one he and Erica used to use religiously. Her name was on the screen but grayed out, unavailable. He looked back up at his son and found him staring back at him with glazed eyes that were as dilated as an owl's.

Ethan's waking life was looking more and more like his sleeping life. Whatever had plagued him in the darkness was creeping over to the light. And it was getting worse by the hour.

GORDON POPE SPENT a full half of his monthly booze-cash allotment to resubscribe to an online medical journal that he'd let lapse, but even after poring over the published literature on sleep disorders, which he noted was far less extensive than it should be, he still hadn't found anything resembling what he'd experienced the night before at the sleep lab with Dana. The research on shared dream imagery was annoyingly symbolic in nature. What Gordon had experienced, and what he believed Ethan and Erica were experiencing, was disturbingly specific, as if the same thing had appeared to all three of them.

He found countless articles on Freudian symbolism and repressed sexuality, but Gordon's dream wasn't sexual. He'd had plenty of sexual dreams before. He knew them. His life had been something of a repressed sexual existence recently. He would have recognized it. And anyway, professionally speaking, Freud served as more of an academic red flag than a primary source of theory. The new school of thought held that no shared symbols existed in dreams. The hip consensus in modern psychiatry was that people were individually weird, not collectively weird.

For years Gordon had bought that, but not anymore.

The one thing that did stick with him was an article by Crump and Lowe, titled *On the Validity of Freudian Limbic Theory*. The limbic system is the instinctive apparatus of the human brain, the primal part. The whole article read sort of like a backhanded compliment to Freud, but in essence it focused on how he was correct when he asserted that dreams were driven by primitive instincts. It was the word *primitive* that stuck with Gordon. He bookmarked the article.

From there, he went on a wild goose chase of reference hunting and two hours later ended up across the psychological line of demarcation with Freud's colleague and defector Carl Jung. One particular paper was a whopper, over a hundred pages of dripping academia titled *Jungian Analysis and the Evolution of REM Sleep* by Elsworth and Bortles. He read until his eyes blurred and was about to toss it when he stumbled across a sentence that made him stand up from his chair:

"Increasingly, it appears as though Jungian theory may have been correct insofar as the tenets presuppose that certain elements of dreams can reflect the collective experiential history of our ancient ancestors. The commonly occurring survival dream, for instance, in which we experience an intense fear of being pursued, might be said to emanate from a collective ancestral experience that is genetically coded."

It was dripping with *mays*, *mights,* and *insofar*s, but it spoke to Gordon. Could it be that Ethan was being overtaken by his primitive self? That Erica was in danger of being overtaken by her primitive self? Thirty years before, Gordon had made a stand against his primitive self, and he'd won out. They'd called the thing the Red, which made sense. Red was primitive. Red was ancient. Red was basic, like blood. Arguably, the pumping redness of the womb was the first thing a child could see. Medically speaking, these children weren't under attack from a physical red mist or a red monster, but Gordon had good reason to think they might be under assault from their own limbic systems.

As to why, Gordon had some ideas, each as harebrained and farfetched as the last. He couldn't afford to speculate on the why just yet. He didn't have enough time.

As for what could be done about it, Gordon was still in the dark. But he had a medical definition of the problem, and that meant he could call Karen.

Gordon looked longingly at his empty liquor shelf, picked up his phone, and dialed his ex-wife.

.  .  .

ETHAN no longer recognized his bedroom for what it was. He *saw* his bedroom, and the things inside it, far more clearly than he ever had before, but he recognized only that they smelled of him and that they did not threaten him, so he assumed a type of possession by association over them, but they were not his anymore. If anything, he felt most drawn to his bed, but only because it smelled the most strongly of him, of his sweat and grease and urine.

One thing confused him: what he held in his hand. The word for it—

*phone*—was fleeing quickly down the dark corridors of his brain, and in its place another surfaced: *Erica*. It was his *Erica*. But it wasn't acting like his Erica anymore. It was silent when it used to talk. That made him grit his teeth and want to throw the thing, to wound it and make it wake up, but his Erica was delicate, he knew, so he held it as tightly as he dared and refused to let it go. And he sat on his bed, and he watched his father through his eyelashes.

He was lying in wait, like a snake in the grass. Because Ethan needed to leave. The Erica he held in his hand was only one part of Erica. The rest of Erica, the *meat* of Erica, was nearby. This part of her he held in his hand was broken, but the rest of her was not. This part of her wouldn't respond to him. Not to his touch or his taste or even to his squeeze. But the meat part would.

But first, he needed to leave this cave of his. His father was keeping him. Trapping him. Turning his cave into a cage. He sat in a chair across from his bed, but Ethan recognized neither the chair nor the bed nor the book his father was reading. He saw only the threat level that the man posed. Ethan could try to kill him. If he did, he could take the entire cave too. But Ethan knew his limits. The man was old, but he was still strong. Stronger than Ethan, unless

Ethan used something—a weapon of some sort, something heavy or sharp. Even then, Ethan knew the old man was smart. He'd hidden most of his tools from Ethan.

No matter. Ethan could feel his strength growing. And the old man's strength was shrinking. That was the way of things in a pack. A time would come when he could kill his father easily. But not that day. So he was a snake in the grass.

He knew his father was tired. Ethan himself was beyond tired. He no longer needed sleep as his father needed sleep. Ethan slept by never existing fully awake or fully asleep. He slept like a shark. Parts of him were shut down, but others kept him moving forward always. Not so for the old man. The old man needed heavy sleep. Vulnerable sleep. Even his watch over Ethan, which Ethan knew was important to the old man, could not last forever for someone that needed heavy sleep. Trying to overpower him even if he slept still held too much risk. Best just to leave his cave.

Waiting, he watched his father fight against his sleep. He seemed to be asleep several times, and Ethan almost moved, only to find that the old man would snap awake again as if frightened. When Ethan finally rose from his bed, the night had truly come, the moon shining strongly through the window, and the old man hadn't moved in some time. He crept with a silence he didn't know he possessed, one born from a time when noise could get you killed or starve you by startling away your food. The normal distractions that plagued the mind of a young boy were gone. He made virtually no sound as he left his own room and then left the house altogether. He stepped out onto the front lawn, wearing a pair of basketball shorts and a large T-shirt that hung down past his butt. He carried only his phone. Stepping silently, he set off in the direction of the rest of Erica, but he stopped at the sidewalk. First, he needed to make sure that his part of Erica was truly silent and not just a snake in the grass. He took his phone in both hands and squeezed—squeezed as hard as he'd squeezed another member of his pack once before, when he was first waking up to the way of things and felt that he wanted to be head of the pack with only Erica at his side. He bent the phone until it cracked and shattered.

Then he dropped his phone in the grass. No, this part of her would not answer to him any longer, but the meat part would. He was sure of it.

Gordon Pope paced his living room, seven steps each way. Karen Jefferson was on speakerphone.

"Again with Freud? Really?" she asked. "I thought we'd gone over this."

"No, no. Freud wasn't quite right. And Jung wasn't quite right," Gordon said.

"Well that's the first sane thing I've heard you say all this conversation—"

"But in a way, both of them were right," Gordon finished.

On the other end, Karen either made a sighing sound or perhaps just shifted her phone to the other ear. Gordon could hear the nonsensical chatter of Maggie playing in the background.

"So because you talked to your childhood self in a dream, you think you've had some sort of revelation with the ego and the id?" she asked.

"First of all, you know that studies show it is very rare to see yourself in dreams... if not impossible."

"What you saw was most likely an image of a boy. You made it into yourself."

"But the conversation, Karen. You have to admit it was way too prescient. Way too specific and driven. It was a *real* conversation." Gordon flopped down onto his battered recliner, and it popped ominously. He flipped though his journal, reading and rereading what he'd written about his dream in the lab.

"I'm going to be honest with you. You're sounding less and less like a medical doctor and more and more like a witch doctor these days."

Gordon picked up one of several EEG prints of Ethan's brain that were scattered around the base of the television. Much of the printout was dark—the outline of his skull looked like a hedge maze of black—but just beneath the cerebrum were bright white indications of activity, the limbic system.

"The limbic activity in the boy was off the charts," Gordon said. "That's undeniable."

"Now *that* I am more interested in. That is real. That is not normal. But it's hardly indicative of a primal takeover of the boy's brain, as if the limbic system is a virus of some sort." Maggie cooed next to the phone, and Karen continued in a baby voice, "The limbic system isn't a virus. Is it, Maggie?"

Maggie shouted, "No!"

Then Karen said, "That's right!"

Gordon felt a headache coming on. Or perhaps he'd had it for some time but just never noticed it. Say, for the past five years, if such a thing was possible without dying. He set the EEG prints on his head and let them slide down his face and to the floor. Karen was doing the baby talk thing on purpose in order to make him want to hang up, but he wouldn't give in.

"No, not a virus... All I'm saying is, isn't it possible that maybe there comes a point in everyone's life when a switch flicks in the brain—maybe in the limbic system, maybe not—when we, as self-conscious human beings, decide that there's no going back?"

"Back where? The womb?"

"Yes, but more to wherever we came from before the womb. The ether. The goo of oblivion." Gordon was well aware Karen hated philosophical mumbo jumbo, but he couldn't think of any other way for him to describe his theory. *Now we'll see who hangs up first.*

"Gordon, there is nothing before the womb. There is no ether. This type of nonsense should be hashed out with your priest."

Gordon ignored her tone and pressed on. "When I broke that cave dream, back when I was a kid and I ended up actually sleepwalking to the place, that was a watershed moment for me." The words of the boy version of himself rang in his mind: *You decided to look forward.* "It was when my subconscious brain made a decision to grow up, something that very likely came from my limbic system."

Karen was quiet. Gordon took that as a good sign. Karen was only ever at a loss for words when she was struck by something that made her think.

Gordon pressed on. "We know the subconscious is guided by the limbic system. The most primitive part of the brain. The emotion system. It makes no differentiation between the future and the past, age and youth. It lacks the vocabulary. It's guided by something else, something ancient. Encoded in our genetics from the time when it ruled the roost. But it had to give way, at some point, to the waking brain."

"I'm listening," Karen said. "Skeptically. But I'm listening."

"And I think that if it doesn't give way, if it can't be bested like I somehow did in the cave way back when, it starts to exhibit itself more and more. The primal instincts it holds start to claw their way back to rule the roost again."

HOUSES AND TREES blocked out the silver moonlight, and Ethan kept to the shadows they made. He moved in bursts, pausing each time to look and to listen for a change caused by his passing. The night was just as deep, the sounds just as loud. Not even the ripping of the cicadas paused for him. He was as much a part of the night as the birds that slept nearby or the fox that ran silently to his right.

He recognized Erica's own cave by her smell. He hadn't realized he'd been following it until it hit him as he crouched under a wisp of an elm, newly planted and already broken by the heat of the concrete around it. He grasped the thin line of twine that staked it upright and watched the house in front of him. It was dark except for a blue light glowing from Erica's window. The light was low, but it still hurt Ethan. His pupils stretched across his eyes by then, only rimmed by the barest hint of white. He walked onto the sharp cut of her lawn nonetheless and into the pool of light thrown from her window. Then he stopped. He squinted. He recognized that glow. It was the same type of glow as the phone he'd broken. It was her computer, her way of reaching him, as his phone was his way of reaching her. That was the way things used to be. Until she left his pack. Until she broke from him.

Ethan stood in the soft edges of light, faced with his own decision. He felt a strong urge to take Erica back. He knew it only as a need like his need for food or water. Erica was as important as those things. And as he saw her reaching out to others, joining another pack without him, the India-ink black and heavy silver colors of the night faded until all he could see was red.

On the other end of the line, Gordon could hear Karen muttering to Chad.

"Just get her coloring book for her. I'll be in in a second... Yes, it's Gordon. I know what we said. Just watch her, and let me finish this conversation, would you?"

Gordon imagined Chad miming for her to cut the line with a clip of his fingers, and he rolled his eyes. He was running out of time. "Karen, this is serious," he said.

"So what you're saying is that this child is being taken over by his limbic system? Like he's undergoing some sort of human devolution?"

Gordon listened for sarcasm in her voice but couldn't find any. That didn't mean she was on board, but it might mean she no longer thought he was trying some sort of half-baked ploy to work through his own sterility or to get back to the way things had been with her. As for Gordon, he was positive it wasn't the first—not so sure on the second, but she didn't need to know that.

"Ethan is increasingly animalistic. Primal. He is losing all reason and acts on impulse. He has no regard for society any longer. He's increasingly sociopathic. That's the limbic system to a tee. If you could see this kid, Karen, you'd understand. The scans confirmed what I already supposed. The anterior cingulate cortex has gone silent, and the limbic system is lit up like a Christmas tree. He's lost his ability to reason."

Karen drew a big breath and let it out through her teeth. "And you think you were in danger of having the same thing happen to you at that age. Only you beat back this thing. But you don't know how you did it."

"That's right. And it's not just me and Ethan, either. I have about twenty messages from frantic parents on my machine, so many I can't even call them all back." Gordon looked over at his answering machine. The message indicator had been blinking red twenty-four hours a day. He knew what each one said, more or less. He also knew that if he could help Ethan, he could help all of them. And if time ran out for Ethan, it most likely meant it had run out for all of them.

"Why?" Karen asked simply.

"Why what?"

"Why is this happening? Why now? Kids have been sleepwalking for thousands of years. As far as I know, there's been no evidence of this extreme limbic activity. What the hell happened?" It was a question and a challenge. Gordon knew she wasn't on his side yet. She was a scientist even more than she was a therapist lately. In Gordon's experience, the more entrenched you got in the science of the brain, the less likely you were to make the leaps of faith you needed in therapy. But still, she sounded intrigued. Almost angry. Because scientifically speaking, this wasn't the way things were supposed to be, and it pissed her off. Gordon could see her, sitting at the kitchen table, leaning on her elbows, her hand massaging her temple, stray wisps of brown hair escaping her tight ponytail.

"I think it's this place," Gordon said.

"Baltimore?"

"Well, yeah, but also this place in time. You said kids have been sleepwalking for thousands of years. But think how vastly differently a child sleeps now from when they did then. Did you know that Ethan can't fall asleep unless he's on his phone? Unless he's listening to something? He chats with his buddies until his phone drops from his hand. And he's not the only one, I guarantee it. Light pollution. Noise pollution. Sensory inputs of all types. These are things that even kids a hundred years ago didn't have as prevalently as we do now, to say nothing of a thousand years ago. I bet if a kid from a couple hundred years ago saw what our night looks like, he'd think it was more like day. There's never a true night anymore. I think it's hindering the development of the anterior cingulate cortex, and the limbic system is compensating."

Gordon found himself shaking.

"And then there's Baltimore itself. I kept thinking, *Why would it be here?* If what I thought was true about Ethan, why would this mess start here? Then I picked up the *Wall Street Journal* the other day. You know what was on the front page?"

He waited for Karen to answer. She was quiet. He could hear her breathing, though, so at least she hadn't hung up on him.

"Okay, I'll tell you," he said. "It said 'Baltimore Grapples with Blight Problem.' Did you know that nearly ten percent of the houses here in this city are classified as unlivable? Ten percent! And then you got the houses that are livable but empty. Have been for years. They can't even get accurate figures on all of them, there are so many. The foreclosure crisis wiped out entire neighborhoods here, and nobody wants to come pick up the pieces and start again. Ethan lives in one of these neighborhoods."

That reminded him that he was supposed to be hearing from Andrew Barret soon. He'd told the man to call twice a day, once at noon and once at ten p.m., to update Gordon on the boy's status while he worked. His watch said ten forty-five.

"That doesn't mean the city is breeding monsters, Gordon," Karen said evenly.

"No, no it doesn't. But it does mean that parents these days aren't exactly keen on letting their kids run around and play. When you can't play outside, you play inside. The Internet is these kids' playground now. But it's a different sort of playground. It doesn't tire you out like the ones you and I had. It stretches different parts of the brain. Creates a different kind of exhaustion. Maybe even a different kind of sleep altogether."

Gordon stared at his watch as he spoke, and he got a sinking feeling in his gut with each second it ticked. He fumbled with his phone, with Karen still on the line, to check his call log. No missed calls.

"What are you doing?" Karen asked, her voice muffled and small as Gordon held his phone out in front of him.

"I gotta go, Karen," he said.

"Whoa, wait. Hold on just a second. You drop all this on me and ask for my help, and then you just *gotta go?*"

"I think something's wrong. I'll call you back."

"Wrong? What's wro—"

Gordon hung up and dialed Andrew Barret. He picked up on the first ring. His voice wavered as if he was barely holding back a lake of panic.

"He's gone, Gordon. I've been looking everywhere. I can't find him."

.   .   .

ETHAN WAITED, pressing himself down into the earth, until a cloud passed over the moon. Then he moved, crawling to Erica's window. He pushed through the bushes at its base, ignoring the thorns and pricks, until he pulled himself up inch by inch from the overhang of her window sill. His muscles ached, but he dared not move faster. Slowly, he rose until his bleeding forehead and then his eyes were at the base of the window.

Outside the soft glow of the computer, the room was completely black. But that hardly mattered to him. He was able to see more clearly in the dark than ever before. Erica wasn't here. His nose confirmed it as much as his eyes. The sense of smell that had brought him here also told him she had left. And he knew immediately where she'd gone.

A part of his brain wondered why he was here, at this window, sinking back down into the bushes, pushing through and flattening himself against the grass, waiting for the moon to disappear again. That part said that Erica was his neighbor. His classmate. His friend. But not *his to have.* That strangled cry in the back of his brain was enough to make him think for a moment about his pain and his weariness, and there in the grass, he almost closed his eyes to sleep. But that voice faded, faded, and was soon like a whisper. And as it faded, his eyes opened slowly, more and more, until they were pits of black again, and all of the times he'd spent sitting next to Erica in school, walking with her, laughing, watching movies, holding her hand when she cried, texting and messaging late into the night, then sometimes scrolling through everything she'd typed long after her parents made her sign off... all of that faded away.

He knew where she was. He would make her part of his pack again, under him.

He set off under cloud cover. The only eyes he felt

watching him were those of the birds in the trees, who settled quickly again after he passed.

DANA FRISCO SAT in her idling squad car under the bug-swarmed halogen lights of a 7-Eleven parking lot that had seen better days. She tried to ignore the pattering of the moths and thumps of larger things on her windshield as she ate a microwaved hamburger she already regretted buying from the mousey teenage clerk inside. Marty sat in the passenger's seat, picking through a bag of home-mixed nuts and dried fruit and watching her unwrap the plastic.

"How can you eat that garbage?" Marty asked, crunching loudly.

"I didn't have time to pack a dinner before getting Chloe to her grandma's for the night." Dana lifted up the burger and inspected it. "Believe me, I'm not super happy about it. But after a night shift, you feel like shit no matter what you eat." She took a bite and shrugged. *Not bad. Better than squirrel food, anyway.*

As if Marty could hear her thoughts, he popped another generous pinch of trail mix into his mouth. "What you eat always matters. If you wanna stay sharp, stay cut, stay at the top of your game, it starts with what you put inside your body."

"Thanks, Dr. Oz."

"I'm serious. I know you've been trying to bust out of the beat, make detective and all, and—"

"Yeah, *that's* why I haven't made detective." Dana rolled her eyes. "It's what I eat. Thanks, rookie. I've been trying to figure it out for years now."

Marty was quiet. Dana closed her eyes. She'd overstepped. She never called Marty *rookie*. That was a shitty thing to do, a total cop-show thing, the exact type of marginalizing that she'd been fighting her whole career at BPD. They were supposed to be partners, for Christ's sake, equal. Plus, Marty Cicero might be a gym rat, but he was a sensitive gym rat. He put on the East Coast cop-swagger routine as good as any of them, but it wasn't him, not exactly.

"It's shit like that, you know, just like that. Acting like you know better than anyone else. Just going off on your own right in front of Duke's face." Marty jabbed angrily for a peanut.

Dana started to speak through a full mouth, but Marty stopped her.

"I know how it ended up. We found her, and then you got another red flag on your file. All I'm saying is, if you'd talked about it first, told me about Pope, maybe, then we coulda gone through Duke, found her, and you'd be closer to detective instead of sitting in front of a friggin' 7-Eleven at midnight, waiting for dispatch to send us to some domestic dispute or whatever."

The heat behind his words gave her pause. *"We coulda gone through Duke."* No partner of hers had ever said *we* like that before. But he didn't have the history with the department that she did. When God pushed the "cop" button on the great vending machine in the sky, he was the type of guy that popped out. She wasn't, but she felt called to the job, and the more it pushed back at her, the more she was determined to make it work. She didn't blame Marty. She'd been like him in her first year too. But he hadn't been squeezed by Duke for seven years—first, in their class at the academy together, her and Duke; then, on the beat at the same time; then, as he had been promoted on a whim to detective. Dana had taken years even to hit corporal, and that's where she'd stayed. Duke was a sergeant in four—lieutenant two years later. The rumor was that a phone call from his venerable father was all it had taken. Duke Textiles was a big supporter of the police union. And at every promotion, with every handshake, he looked at her. He found her in the crowd, just for a second. Not out of malice, either. Not quite. Malice she could deal with. The "Aw shucks" look that was somehow pitying and knowing at the same time was what got to her, as though he felt sorry for her that she would even question why he was where he was, with the big badge at his age, while she would still be in a squad car on a night beat, parking lot bound, with huge Maryland-summer bugs pinging off the windshield.

She wanted to snap all that off at Marty. He was caged there next to her, with nowhere to run. But she clenched her jaw and bit it back.

"Don't worry, Marty. You'll be right up there with all of them soon enough," she said instead.

Marty looked out the window. "That's not why I asked to be partnered with you," he said quietly.

Dana paused midbite. She'd thought Marty Cicero had been paired with her just as the rest were: regretfully but with promises from up top that Dana Frisco's partners turned into some of the best cops in the precinct. She could hear Duke: *Put up with her. We'll make it worth your while.* But Marty had *asked* to be put with her? She swallowed a mouthful of spongy burger and was about to ask him what he was talking about when her cell phone rattled in the cup holder. She picked it up, expecting it to be Chloe telling her good night, way past when Grandma knew she was supposed to be in bed... but it wasn't Chloe. It was Gordon Pope.

"Hey..." she answered tentatively. One day, she hoped, Gordon Pope would call her, and the sight of his name wouldn't drop her stomach an inch. But today wasn't that day.

"They can't find Ethan," Gordon said in a strained tone, forced into evenness.

Dana's stomach dropped another inch.

"Andrew Barret said he's looked everywhere in and around the house. He's gone."

"How long?" Dana asked.

Marty stopped munching and cocked an eyebrow.

"He's not sure," Gordon said. "But no more than an hour. Barret guesses thirty minutes. He was up with him in his room, watching him, but he fell asleep. When he came around again, Ethan was gone."

"Thirty minutes? Maybe he's just... I dunno... taking some air?" Dana asked, cringing.

"You haven't seen this kid recently, Dana. He's not the night-strolling type anymore. He's more the night-crawling type. We have to find him."

"We? Gordon, I'm on patrol right now." She looked at Marty pointedly. "If you want help from the BPD, you can call 9-1-1. Dispatch is all over the missing-kid calls these days. Duke says it's great publicity."

Gordon sounded as though he was working moisture into his mouth. "Ethan's on parole pending an appeal. If I call 9-1-1, he's going to jail. It's game over for him."

"Gordon, don't you think..." She paused and reworded her thoughts. "I mean, isn't it possible that Ethan might need to be somewhere under twenty-four-hour care?"

"Twenty-four-hour care? That's the nicest way I've ever heard an insane asylum described in my life," Gordon said. "And the answer is no. I'm positive that Ethan does not need to be at Ditchfield. His limbic system is attacking him. You helped me figure that out at the sleep lab."

He wasn't accusing. He was pleading. Hearing it pained Dana because she did believe him. She didn't know what a limbic system was, but she'd have believed him even if she hadn't seen the way he struggled in his sleep that night, the way he seemed to be in a chess match with his own brain. She believed him because she trusted him. He wanted to help those kids more than anything. She could see that in his eyes when he'd woken up from that last sleep cycle and reached for his journal. But that was the problem. She didn't want to see him fail. He was unflagging and very bright, but he'd pinned his heart to the Ethan Barret case, and she knew his heart was brittle. He was one bad crack away from becoming a cynical asshole like the rest of the men she surrounded herself with, cops who'd seen too much, gotten hurt, and had no recourse but to think the only reason people messed up in life was because the world is garbage.

She wanted to say that the real reason she hesitated was that if Gordon tried and failed and fell and then gave up—if a man like him could give up—then she had no chance whatsoever to keep fighting her own battles.

"Nobody is giving this kid a chance," Gordon said, his voice husky. "His mother thinks he's possessed. His father is starting to accept that he'll never see his son again. And worst of all, the kid has given up on himself. Don't you give up on him too. Don't let me be the only one here, screaming at the clouds."

"God dammit, Gordon," Dana said, the curse coming out like a sigh.

"Is that a good 'God dammit' or a bad 'God dammit'?"

"What do you need from me?" Dana asked.

Marty narrowed his eyes.

"I need you to help me look for him, for one," Gordon

said. "But more than that, I think this could get ugly. If Ethan is out there in the state I think he is, there's a good chance the cops are going to be called anyway. If they are, I need you to run interference until I can figure out what's going on."

Dana pinched the bridge of her nose but nodded.

"Can you do that?" Gordon asked.

"I'll do what I can," she said and hung up. She looked straight out the window as the silence in the cab fell heavily over them both. Then she cleared her throat and gripped the gearshift to go into reverse when Marty stilled her hand.

"What the hell are you doing?" he asked.

"Checking something out."

"With Gordon Pope?" he asked.

Dana stared at him. She knew she was going off the track again. She had no recourse.

"And I suppose you're not going to call this one in, either?" he asked.

"There's nothing to call in," she said. "The kid's been gone thirty minutes. Just checking up. That's all."

Dana could tell Marty didn't buy it. He was a lot brighter than he let on, not that she was exactly good at hiding things. He just shook his head, looking as though he wanted to say more, and she vaguely recalled wanting to ask him something, on a partner-to-partner level, before Gordon had called—something that felt important. But it had fled her mind when the phone rang.

"Are you with me?" she asked.

"Or what? I get left at the 7-Eleven for the night? I'm your partner, Dana." He plucked his hand from hers. "Like I could have kept you anyway," he said.

Dana backed up with force, the tires squealing faintly.

The cashier inside looked up from his phone, his reaction time a full five seconds off.

"I'd just like to point out, though," Marty said, "for the next time you wonder why you're still bug-watching at the 7-Eleven parking lot, that while you may have a point of sorts vis-à-vis management at the department..." He was stumbling over his words, holding on to the *oh Jesus* handle above the window as Dana shifted into drive. "That at least *some* aspect of all this," he continued, "might be on *your* shoulders."

Dana smirked. That was about as antiauthoritarian as she'd heard Marty Cicero get in the eight months she'd been riding with him. She cut him off with a conciliatory raise of the hand. "Yeah, yeah. Buckle up."

She threw on the siren and peeled out onto the street.

# CHAPTER THIRTEEN

Gordon Pope almost forgot to throw his car into park before jumping out into the Barrets' driveway. He had to skip back inside and jam the brake to keep the car from plowing through their garage. *Wonderful start. Why not just bring the whole house down?*

The neighbors were already skittish in the area. He could see dim lights and dark outlines behind ruffling curtains in the scattering of occupied houses around him. He'd told Dana to run interference with the cops, but he doubted even she could play gatekeeper for long if the neighbors got spooked.

Gordon trotted up to the front door. It was open a crack. He knocked once. It opened farther with his pressing.

"Hello?" he asked. "Mr. Barret?"

No answer. He walked inside. He stood in the small foyer of their ranch house. It looked quite similar to the Denbrooks' nearby, which he'd been tossed out of. Ethan's shoes were pushed haphazardly up against a shoe rack to his right. A small table stood to his left, strewn with mail. A leafed-through newspaper sat on a chair. A window AC unit sweated onto the windowsill, working overtime, still failing to beat the heat. The domestic trappings of the family home seemed so normal that, for a brief moment, Gordon thought maybe they'd found Ethan. Maybe the kid was just taking a long leak. Maybe he'd gone out to look at the stars and the fat orange moon. But Gordon knew better.

A strange murmuring sound came from around the corner, someone whispering in an unbroken string.

"Mr. Barret? Andrew? It's Gordon. Hello?"

No answer. Gordon walked inside. He'd watched the clock religiously on his drive over. Twenty-one minutes had passed between when Barret told him his son was gone and Gordon had shown up at his door—no time at all and an eternity all the same. Every situation had run through his head, from finding the boy asleep on the floor, to a blood-bath spreading over the tiles he walked on, to finding nobody at all. But he wasn't expecting murmuring.

Gordon turned the corner into the family room. It was a well-kept space, the type of place nobody ever went. It was just offset from the kitchen, where Gordon supposed most of the actual dining occurred. But it was here that he found Jane Barret.

He froze as soon as he saw her, and his mind stumbled over forming an apology at the intrusion, but she didn't even seem to notice him. She was on her knees on a small decorative pillow in front of what looked like an altar set flush against one corner of the room. A decorative sculpture of the Virgin Mary had been placed on a small desk there, surrounded by votive candles that put off a cloying vanilla scent. Different objects were scattered in front of the sculpture: a cup of wine, a gold medal on a blue ribbon that glinted in the firelight, a tattered leather bracelet, and a broken cell phone.

Gordon's first instinct was to back slowly out of the room, but then she spoke to him without breaking stride.

"I know you think me a fool, Dr. Pope," she said. "My husband does too."

Gordon nearly jumped. "I... I don't think anything, Mrs. Barret. I'm just trying to find Ethan."

"Ethan is gone. Andrew went after him."

"Where did they go?"

She stood from the pillow in a fluid motion. She took a votive candle in one hand and walked to Gordon. "Andrew thinks he's at the old theater. At the top of the hill. Ethan has always been drawn to it."

Gordon nodded and turned to go, but Jane grabbed his arm and turned him back around. Her eyes were wide and glassy, her makeup layered over dark bags beneath them. "Take this," she said. She poured a dollop of hot wax onto her fingers. It sluiced through and spattered red on the floor. Before Gordon could object, she swiped a cross on his forehead in wax.

Gordon tensed and blinked away the burn that she didn't seem to feel. He sensed her watching him for his reaction. "Okaaay" was the first thing out of his mouth.

"Save my son," she said, releasing him.

Gordon backed out of the house, nodding continually. Jane Barret watched him go to the door then turned back to the altar. Gordon flipped around and walked outside. He stood on the porch for a moment, wax on forehead, hands on hips, wondering what the hell had just happened. His first instinct was to wipe it all off, but he knew she was watching through the window. The medical professional in him scoffed at her. The frightened kid in him thought maybe it was best not to get cocky. He knew his mother would be appalled if she saw him. He could hear her now:

*"Act like a professional, for God's sake. You didn't go to fifteen years of medical school to have your face painted."* Which was another reason he kept the wax on as he took off at a run toward the upper neighborhood and the bleak skeleton of the half-restored theater that sat atop the hill there.

He followed the Chutes-and-Ladders path from before, starting with the sidewalk that led him past Erica Denbrook's house, but then he stopped. The milky moon was high in the sky, and most of the lights in the neighborhood were going off, but the lights were coming on in each of the rooms at the Denbrook house. He recognized Marcus Denbrook through a window. He was tearing through Erica's room. His voice was muffled as he threw open her small closet. He was speaking to his wife across the house. She was doing much the same thing, moving frantically from room to room, flicking on the lights. She moved to a window and looked out into the night, and for a moment, Gordon thought he'd been spotted, but whatever she was looking for she didn't find, and she turned away. Gordon knew then, recognized it in the frenzied, disbelieving look in her face, as if she'd just rebroken a bone in her body that she'd spent months nursing back to health, that Erica was missing again.

And Gordon had a very good idea of where Erica was.

If those dreams and those kids had taught him anything, it was never to discount coincidences. He turned to go down the first chute when a snippet of panicked conversation drifted through the window.

Marcus Denbrook said, "She's not here. I'm calling the police."

Gordon thought about barging in to hold them off. Maybe he could convince them to let him take care of things. He'd found their daughter once, and he could do it again. But then again, they most likely knew nothing about his involvement. For all they knew, Warren Duke had returned their daughter with the help of Officer Dana Frisco. Why wouldn't they call the police? What could he say to them? *"Your daughter is in danger of being swallowed up by her own brain. And she's most likely with Ethan, you know, the boy that tried to kill his friend Jimmy? The one you've been telling your daughter not to speak to? How do I know this? Glad you asked. I've been having a series of vivid dreams that I believe are connected to Ethan and your daughter and in which I spoke to the thing that is consuming them."*

What a wonderful conversation that would be. Very productive, shortly followed by Gordon asking, *"Who are those men in white, and why do they have a straitjacket?"*

No, he would have to leave the Denbrooks to Dana and pray that she could step in between the call and the dispatch. He felt a strange calm. He realized, to his amazement, that he had faith in Dana because Dana had faith in him.

He set off again, running as softly as he could in loafers and khakis toward the path that would take him up, up, up. Time was short, and he couldn't bear to let them down. Not Ethan, not Erica, and not Dana, either. Especially not Dana.

DANA CAUGHT the call just after Doreen—their dour dispatcher on duty—rolled off the address. The moment Doreen paused after the code, Dana chimed in.

"This is zero seven seven eight. We're out east already. We're on it."

"That was quick," Marty said acidly, but he left it at that.

Dana neither blared the sirens nor flashed her lights, ignoring Marty's brief but smoldering stare. She wanted to keep as low of a profile as possible. She knew the lights alone would bring out half the neighborhood... or half of whatever remained.

The place looked even more decrepit and shuttered than it had when they'd first visited only weeks earlier. The BPD was pushing a department-wide initiative called Broken Window Policing. The basic idea was that if a place looked like shit, it would attract crime. Fix up the windows, get rid of the dark alleys, whitewash the graffiti, and the theory was that less shady activity would occur. Dana didn't know about all that. In her experience, crime found a way, but as she drove up to Ethan Barret's house, her first thought was that maybe the policy had its merits. Tivoli Estates just felt bad. But fixing broken windows and power-cleaning a few fences was one thing. Fixing what was essentially an entire abandoned neighborhood was something else entirely, something the city of Baltimore had yet to figure out. An abandoned house couldn't be whitewashed.

"I knew something about that address was familiar," Marty said as Dana pulled onto Ethan's street. "It's the girl. Erica Denbrook. It's her house, not Ethan's."

Dana slowed the car to a stop and picked up her com. "Dispatch, this is zero seven seven eight. Say again on that Tivoli address?"

Doreen repeated the address, twice as droll. Marty was right. That was the girl's house. Again. Instantly, she knew the two were connected. The two kids used to play together. That they would go missing together made a macabre sort of sense. Marty picked up on her line of thought almost instantly.

"You're telling me both kids are gone?" he asked. He turned to look at Dana, and for the first time, his face showed open confusion. Not the rock-solid I'll-take-whatever-shit-this-city-can-throw-at-me look that rookie officers liked to affect. And she saw some fear there, too.

*The man surprises at every turn.* Dana opened her door and stood, settling her belt and gun. "C'mon. And let them do the talking. Say nothing about Ethan."

She knocked quickly on the door three times. McKayla and Marcus Denbrook opened the door as one. McKayla looked up at her, recognized her, and broke into tears at once.

"It's you! You can find her!" She grabbed Dana by the shoulder and started weeping.

Dana held her awkwardly, at a loss for words.

Marty stepped in. "Erica's missing again?"

Marcus nodded. His eyes were tired, his face sallow.

"No sign of break-in?"

Marcus shook his head. "It's just like last time," he said. "I thought it was maybe a one-time thing. The sleepwalking, I mean. I should have stayed up. I did, for two straight weeks. But I thought she was good. I thought she was all good." He seemed to be talking more to himself than to Marty.

"How long has she been gone?"

"An hour at most," Marcus said.

McKayla was still holding on to Dana for dear life.

"I went in to make sure she wasn't on her computer, like I always do," Marcus added. "She was gone."

Dana felt her phone buzzing in her pocket. She set

McKayla standing again and took a step back while Marty jotted down information on his notepad.

"We'll start at the construction site where she was last," he said.

Dana pulled out her cell phone. The text was from Gordon Pope.

*Theater. Top of hill. Meet you there.*

The theater was just past the construction site, along the same path. Dana considered that Erica might have been trying to get to the theater all along the first time and had just fallen into the construction site along the way. She touched Marty on the shoulder and nodded toward the door. "Mr. and Mrs. Denbrook, we have reason to believe that your daughter might be at the theater up top. Am I right in thinking that she occasionally went there?"

McKayla and Marcus gave her blank looks. Marcus shook his head. "That broken-down place? I don't think she's ever been there in her life. You think she might be there? Why?"

*Never underestimate what your kid won't tell you.*

"I need you both to stay here in case she comes back. It's important. We'll be in touch, okay? We're gonna find her." McKayla nodded while Marcus was apparently trying to reconcile that newest piece of information with what he knew of his daughter.

She pulled Marty out after her before either parent could think too much about her source of information.

"Top of the hill," she said. "C'mon."

She took off at a run. Marty was right behind.

By the time the hill leveled at the top, both Dana and Marty were huffing in the still air, their uniforms damp at the neck and drenched at the back. Behind them, the south end of Baltimore County glittered in spotty bits and pieces like bunches of glowing algae in a sea of black. In front of them stood the remnants of the Tivoli. It was a tattered patchwork quilt of a structure, a collection of several buildings that stretched back and out of sight down the far end of the slope. The original bones of the classic theater were still recognizable; extravagant concrete moldings turreted the top of the building, and old red brick ringed the bottom. The redeveloped accents and additions here and there—a big bay window on the second story, a large dome addition to the back—might have looked lovely, had they not been shattered and rotting. The whole place had been left for scrap, and when the scrap was stripped by tweekers, what remained was given to the birds. Dana would have liked a better look at the perimeter of the place, but as they stepped toward it, the one remaining streetlight in the area popped off as if to say, *"Forget it, cops."*

She thought Marty was reaching for his gun, but he clicked on his Maglite instead. Its beam was absurdly bright under the scattered cloud cover. "I don't know what the hell is going on here," he said, "but after this, if I never see this neighborhood again—or anyone in it—it'll be too soon. Understand?"

Dana heard the unspoken ultimatum in his words. Marty was saying, *"If this is how you're gonna operate, I'm out."* And she knew, also, that Gordon Pope was who Marty never wanted to see again. And she could have blown her top—railed at her rookie partner and told him to sack up and do his damn job, but she didn't have it in her. She felt sad and was surprised at the sadness, surprised at how it hit her. Forty-five minutes before, he'd been lightheartedly ribbing her about her choice of late-night dinner. Dana sensed a thunderhead on the horizon, one felt but not seen, and its looming silence was pulling the strings of her life until they were fraught with tension. One wrong step, one wrong word, and the strings would snap.

"All right, Marty. Just hang with me here, okay?"

Marty might have been expecting a lot of different responses from his partner, but not that. Dana knew it from his silence. Then he nodded. They walked toward the Tivoli, two sweeps of bright white in a sea of shadows and strangled moonlight.

"Gordon?" she called, tentatively at first, then full bore. "Gordon, where are you?"

No answer. A dog barked in staccato bursts somewhere below. She plucked out her cell phone. No service. *Naturally.* She wasn't surprised. The Tivoli felt like the kind of place that plucked every sort of call for help right out of the air. Nothing about this investigation came easy. The whole phenomenon, the sleepwalking, the dreams, it was all part of a thing buried deep. Digging was always hard work.

Getting inside the theater, at least, was not hard work. The front façade was entirely open air. Apparently, the plan had been to have big double doors flanked by bay windows, but none of it had materialized. Dana and Marty stepped over plywood and onto the trash-strewn concrete floor inside. *Better than rotted wood. Small miracles.*

Marty swept his flashlight from side to side, catching snippets of graffiti and the glitter of glass bottles and aluminum cans as he went. He lingered on a pile of rags in the corner for a moment. "Anyone here?" he asked, his voice booming.

Dana heard scurrying, then silence, then she heard Gordon's voice.

"Over here! Hurry!"

Both officers snapped their beams forward. The voice

had come from the other side of the building, out of what was supposed to be the back doors. A courtyard was wedged there.

"Hello?" Dana asked, walking carefully but quickly through the bones of the theater out into the skeleton of a decrepit atrium. The plan might have been to cover it with a paned dome, but it, too, was unfinished and forgotten, stretched above them like a brittle honeycomb.

"Here!" Gordon cried, his voice coming from the courtyard's far side.

A dirt-strewn path led from where Dana and Marty stood down a shallow flight of stairs to a flat space that, in a better time, might have held a playground. Instead, it looked more like a massive, empty altar. Beyond that, the path reconvened near an exit tunnel. There she saw Gordon kneeling over what looked like a pile of clothes. Gordon waved them over. The clothes groaned. Dana took off at a run and spanned the atrium in moments. Gordon had his sleeves rolled up, his hands darkened with blood. He stepped back as they came. Dana bent down as Marty watched her back. The pile was Andrew Barret.

Dana dropped to one knee and checked his pulse, her light scanning him from head to toe. She didn't notice anything immediately wrong with him, and his heartbeat was steady, if a bit weak, but then she saw the dark red corona in the dirt under his head.

"Sir? Can you hear me? Hey, Mr. Barret. Andrew."

"He's been struck in the head," Gordon said.

His lips fluttered, but no sound came. Dana gently lifted his head and peered behind. A flap of scalp as wide as a baseball started to pull away from his skull at the back of his head. Marty saw it as soon as Dana did. He unbuttoned his uniform shirt and whipped it off then gently placed it under Barret's head, settling the flap just as Barret's eyes fluttered open... then closed.

"I found him like this. Maybe five minutes ago. I tried to call out," Gordon said, showing his mobile phone streaked with blood, as if he needed proof. "I got no service. And it's a shitty phone. So I've just been trying to talk to him."

"Mr. Barret, stay with me. You've got a concussion, buddy," Marty said. "You need to stay with me here." He rubbed Barret's sternum vigorously with the callous knuckles of his right hand.

Barret's eyes opened. He cried out and tried to move, but Marty's hand kept his head still.

"We're with the Baltimore Police," Marty said. "Can you tell me who did this to you?"

Barret's eyes were alert, but he kept his mouth closed.

"We're not here to arrest Ethan," Dana said, dropping all pretense. "We're here to help him. Did he do this to you?"

He looked into Dana's eyes for a moment then over at Gordon.

"It's okay, Mr. Barret. They're with me. Tell them what you told me."

"He hit me from behind with a rock," he whispered.

Dana could barely hear the man. "Ethan did? Sir, I need you to speak up. Stay alert, okay?"

Barret shook his head and winced sharply from the pain before Marty could brace him again. "Shhh," Barret said. "Be quiet, or he'll hear you."

Dana heard a heavy smack in the near distance and the scattered-sand sound of concrete chips falling from above. Both officers snapped their beams upward. Gordon crouched a little closer to Barret, as if to protect him. Dana found the brick, shattered and still dusting through the cold white of their flashlights. It had hit smack dab in the center of the open altar space. She traced her beam up to the top of the atrium, but it went through and out and caught only the scudding black clouds of the night sky. Had it been thrown?

"Ethan? Ethan it's me, Gordon. Why don't you come out, buddy?"

Silence. Gordon looked over at Dana and shook his head. Dana knew already, could tell by the flat tone of his voice that Gordon was under no illusions that the boy would walk back to them in his present state. If they wanted Ethan, they were going to have to go get him.

"Dana, I'm calling in an ambulance," Marty said. He glanced at Gordon, who was still scanning the broken ceiling. "I don't give a shit if it does mean the kid goes downriver. This man could die if he's not treated."

Dana almost argued, but she caught herself. When the medics arrived, they'd have to file a report, which might open up a case, which meant the jig was up. Marty was watching her carefully, and she knew he was testing her. He'd already said he was as much as gone after this case. Maybe how she answered would determine if he would be taking her down on his way up the ladder. How far was she really willing to go for the boy's sake? For Gordon's sake?

In the end, Gordon spoke up. "I'm not some sort of fanatic, Officer Cicero. I tried to call an ambulance myself before you arrived."

"What the hell is on your forehead?" Marty asked.

Gordon looked at him, puzzled, then seemed embarrassed and wiped at his brow. Dana looked closer. Dirt? A smudge? It looked like a cross.

"I'm not a fanatic," Gordon said again, less convincingly that time, still scrubbing.

Marty looked unconvinced. He pressed his com and

calmly ordered an ambulance to the top of the Tivoli district.

Barret tugged at the crease of Dana's slacks. "He's in there still," he whispered while Marty gave details. "Through the tunnel. I heard him when I called. He cried at me."

*Cried at me?* The image gave her shivers. He wasn't just telling her. He was asking her. His eyes were pleading with her. His son had just brained him with a brick, but still he was pleading with her to help him. It brought tears to her eyes. If Chloe had been the one in there, Dana would do the same thing. Her daughter could literally shoot out both her knees and run off, and she'd still crawl after her.

Dana stood. She looked down the open tunnel in front of them, which appeared to lead to a second structure on the downward-facing side of the hill. It was as wide as a bus and sloped gently into darkness, wide enough to accommodate a crowd it would never see.

"Marty, stay with Mr. Barret," Dana said. "You too, Gordon. I'm going in after them." She hadn't forgotten about Erica, the little Houdini. She was in there too. Dana couldn't see the little girl's footprints this time, but she felt strongly that they crossed paths with Ethan's somewhere back there nonetheless.

"I'm coming with you," Gordon said at the same time as Marty. The men looked at each other.

"No way," Marty said. "No way am I letting you go in there alone. You're my partner."

She held up a hand and turned to Gordon first, only to find that he was already running toward the tunnel. "Gordon!" she called after him. She let her hand drop. "Shit." She turned to Marty.

"Are you serious with this guy?" Marty asked. "I mean,

really? He's nuts, Dana. Nuts."

"He has a lot invested in this," Dana said. "But he cares about these kids. He really does."

"I know what you're gonna say. You're gonna say, 'Marty, I gotta go in after him. Marty, I gotta find them. Marty, I need you to stay here with Barret until the ambulance gets here.' Well, that's bullshit. Gordon Pope put himself where he is on his own. We should both stay right here. The kid can wait ten minutes."

Dana heard the slimmest crack in his voice and knew he was fighting to keep his composure. What he'd said to her back while they'd waited at the parking lot surfaced again in her mind. *"That's not why I asked to be your partner."*

He'd asked because he cared for her. Maybe he was even falling for her.

She found tears in her own eyes and unabashedly blinked them away and down her face.

"Marty—" she started, not knowing how to follow up, not knowing if she could.

"No," he said, cutting her off. "No. Dana, I'm waiting until I know this man has the medical attention he needs. If you go in there without me, I'm walking up to Duke tomorrow and requesting a transfer." He looked away as he spoke. His voice was as quiet as she'd ever heard it.

Dana hung her head. "He's a brilliant man, Gordon Pope. He thinks he can save them. And I believe him because I think he has a bit of whatever insanity is going around already inside him, like a vaccine. It makes him do shit like that." She waved over at the tunnel through which Gordon had disappeared moments before. "But this isn't his pretty little sleep lab. This isn't his office stuffed full of books. This is real life, and the bricks are already flying—"

Marty shook his head like a dog pulling rope. "If you go

through that tunnel without me, I'm going to Duke to—"

"He's gonna get himself killed," Dana said. She was horrified at how much she believed it.

"If you go through that tunnel—" Marty repeated, more loudly.

"This isn't about you, Marty!" she screamed.

Marty was silent. He held her gaze for a moment in which she was determined not to look away, then he dropped it, and she was ashamed. But she'd been crossing lines all day—for most of her life, really—and she wasn't going to pull back now.

"Call me on the com as soon as he's packed away," she said flatly. She couldn't even look at him. She knew how he was watching her. She was reminded of Chloe. Chloe hated vaccines, hated them more than anything on earth. It got so bad that Dana had to trick her to get to the doctor or else she'd work herself into a hyperventilating fit. One time, days before she would have had to delay starting first grade because she hadn't gotten a physician's approval, Dana resorted to saying they were going to McDonald's just to get her in the car. When she parked at the doctor's office, Chloe gave her a look. It was that look. That look was coming from a thirty-one-year-old man.

Dana couldn't deal with it. She took off into the downward-sloping darkness, and as she was engulfed, she understood a little bit of why Gordon had done the same.

Some things are better left unsaid.

## CHAPTER FOURTEEN

As Gordon ran down the tunnel, he thought how ironic it was that he was less afraid of whatever monster lay at the end of it than he was of whatever was going on behind him, between Cicero and Dana. He knew his presence had something to do with whatever beef was between the two officers, and he wasn't up for it—not right then. Better to turn tail and run. Not his finest moment, relationally speaking, he knew. But was running away from feeling things really cowardice if by running he actually was careening *toward* uncertain danger? Didn't the one cancel the other out? Wasn't there a case to be made for hightailing it? He'd have to run it by his mother. She had a good grasp of those things.

What awaited Gordon at the other end of the tunnel he could only describe as Chernobyl meets Barnum & Bailey. It was the lobby of the theater proper. The design committee for the Tivoli was clearly going for a vaudeville revival look: big marquee signs stuffed with lightbulbs the size of grapefruits, glittering mirrors, dramatic murals of exotic places, loud wallpapering in stripes of gold and black and red polka dots. The problem was that when vaudeville broke down, which it undoubtedly had, it left a funhouse-of-horror look. Almost everything made of glass was shattered. The sharp moldings were either crumbling or never there to begin with. The wallpaper was molded and sagging. The murals were bloated with damp and chewed through in places. Gordon held up the weak light from his phone and panned the room, cursing himself for not thinking to bring a flashlight. The corners were still in darkness, but he couldn't see anyone. *This would make a prime crack den in a more lively area of the city.* But not at Tivoli Estates. Apparently, even the bums and the dealers didn't think the place worth their time.

Gordon heard the voices of Dana and Cicero behind him, yelling at each other, but he easily tuned that out. He'd had a lot of experience doing that as a kid. He thought he could hear something else... something softer but noticeable. He tilted his left ear forward. There it was again. A crying sound. It came from the back corner, an area that looked as though it was supposed to have been the ticket office. It'd been designed to look like a circus tent, set flush against the corner of the room. Two shattered windows gaped where pimply-faced teens might have sat, bored, punching tickets and giving change. An unfinished door led back behind. Creeper vines, the tough New England bastards that never went away, had come in through the unfinished ceiling and draped the ragged tenting like a frozen rain of green leaves.

The crying was coming from back there. He looked behind himself. Dana and Cicero were still going at it. He turned back to the ticket booth. Ethan's time was about up. He couldn't wait any longer. His shoes scraped on the debris as he walked forward, and the sound echoed like slips of sand down a canyon.

"Ethan?" he called, trying his best to sound conversational but failing. He coughed and tried not to think about the mountain of mold and asbestos he was most likely walking through. He peeked his head through the gaping ticket counter. Nobody. But the whimper was clearer there. It sounded distinctly like a girl's, too soft and high for Ethan, almost like a constant sigh. Between the rats' nests, he could see the outlines of two sets of footprints leading through the employee doorway at the back and into the darkness beyond. It looked an awful lot like a cave.

"Erica?" Gordon called.

The crying cut off abruptly, as surely as if someone had pressed pause on the girl. Gordon held up his cell phone and waved it around as if he was trying to catch a signal.

"Erica, honey, I'm over here. I'm here to help you, where are you?"

Silence.

*Shit. Am I really gonna have to go back there?* But even as he thought it, he was swinging around the outside of the ticket booth and walking through the doorway, generously overstepping the rats' nests until he was engulfed in darkness. No moonlight. No open sky. *Typical. The one part of this place they do finish is where we end up.*

When the light on Gordon's mobile doubled up and shone back on him in the form of another looming shadow, he nearly screamed. He clipped his shout to a yip as his brain registered his own reflection in front of him in a mirror, a big one. And not just one. As he panned the hallway, he saw it was lined with mirrors, many of them unbroken, resting at an angle against the walls, forgotten materials for construction. His dim light was reflected back at odd angles through the thick dust that coated each as he walked past.

His heart hammered so hard he was seeing the pulse of the veins at the back of his eyes. He nearly screamed a second time when he thought he felt a spider the size of his fist tickle the back of his head—or perhaps it was the first kiss of a brick from Ethan's hand. He swatted it away only to find his hand grasping a creeper vine. He yanked it out of frustration and heard an ominous tumbling sound. He scampered forward.

Gordon found himself in what he guessed was a storage room or, judging by the continuing echo, something more along the lines of a storage warehouse. An unholy storage warehouse. He pledged to himself that if he got out of there and somehow managed to get Ethan and Erica out too, he would stop bitching about the tax increases it would take to level all the shitholes in the city like the theater. Rip everything down and plant a whole mess of columbines or something. Gordon liked columbines.

He fully recognized that his brain was running at a breakneck pace to keep up with his racing heart. That was an old mental fail-safe Morty Gladwell had called "scattershot thinking." When the heart races, the mind often skips all over the place. That was sometimes the precursor to a panic attack but also often the mechanism that kept the panic attack at bay. Gordon hoped for the latter. Dana was somewhere close behind, and the last thing he wanted was for her to find him crying right next to Erica.

He stopped. He could see the girl now... or at least what he hoped was her, a small bundle curled up on the floor near the center of the storage room. His low light picked up on the sparkles of her pink pajama top. He waved at her and saw his own reflection waving back again from the rear of the room. More mirrors. They were stacked side by side in front of a big, rotted canvas replica of a vaudeville playbill.

It read OPENING IN PARIS! MILAN! MONACO! BALTIMORE!

Erica's face was streaked with tears and she held her arms around herself, but she no longer cried. She was staring right at Gordon.

"Erica, sweetheart, do you remember me? Are you hurt?"

Gordon started walking toward her but stopped when she held up one finger in front of her mouth. Her eyes grew wide with terror, and Gordon heard a strange pattering, fast, like many moths batting against a screen door at the same time, and before he could turn around, he was blind-sided by pain. He staggered to the ground, too surprised even to cry out. His vision jarred, and after he felt the back of his head, his fingers came away wet and red. He heard another flurry of pattering, Gordon looked up again, still on his knees.

Ethan was standing with his legs spread over Erica, an old, rusted pipe in his hand. He was staring at Gordon, his lips pulled back from his teeth in a grimace. A low, constant growl came from somewhere within him. His face was streaked with dust, his hair white with it. His hands were dark red with mud and blood, and his knees and feet were black with filth.

Gordon held out one hand to stop him, but the boy made no move to advance. He only watched Gordon, but not in any way Gordon had been watched before. The stare was purely analytical, weighing the cost of attacking again with the risk of getting captured or struck himself. He saw no recognition in Ethan's eyes—and not only of Gordon as his therapist but of Gordon as a human. Gordon hadn't realized just how much that spark of the eye meant, how much it softened a face, until he looked upon Ethan and found it missing.

"Ethan, it's me. You remember me? Gordon? Think, buddy. There's some part of you in there that knows this isn't right."

Gordon staggered to his feet again, which seemed to unnerve Ethan. He looked Gordon up and down as if sizing up his bulk, determining his threat level. He gripped the pipe again and tensed. Gordon realized the boy must be thinking he wanted to take Erica. More than that, to *claim* Erica. He was standing over her as though she was a possession he didn't want to lose. And in the next moment, he was running at Gordon again, pipe held above his head. He didn't growl or yell, and his odd silence made his charge all the more surreal and terrifying. It was business to him. He was eliminating a threat. Still shaky, Gordon shifted to try and take the blow and maybe catch the boy, but he was dizzy, and his neck was wet with blood. He held his hands up and winced, waiting for the pain, but Ethan stopped on a dime and jumped back, his eyes on the hallway behind Gordon.

"Don't move, Ethan," Dana said. She had her Taser out. The red button indicating a full charge glowed angrily in the darkness. Ethan didn't move, but Gordon didn't think that had anything to do with the Taser. He was simply reassessing. He looked back and forth between the two of them. On the ground, Erica saw Dana and did recognize her, and she started to cry, either from pain or relief or both, but when Ethan turned at the sound, she stifled it with her own fist.

Ethan backed up to stand over Erica again, watching them the whole time, but when he stopped over her, he also looked down at her and cocked his head. An awful thought struck Gordon. The way Ethan looked at Erica had a cold, zero-sum air to it. It was the look of someone who has been pushed to the ropes of a bridge, cornered with the loot—the jig is up, but there's still one option left: the nuclear option, taking the loot down with him.

"I don't want to tase him, Gordon," Dana said, her voice shaky. "But I will."

"It's okay," Gordon said, speaking as calmly as he was able. "I know. But not yet." Gordon understood her hesitation. He knew as well as she did that if the boy was hit by a Taser, it wouldn't go well for him. He was skinny to begin with, and his ordeal had hollowed him further. He was a reedy, feral husk of a boy, and Gordon had the distinct dread that fifty thousand volts at that particular moment stood a good chance of killing him. But he also knew Dana had a job to do, to protect the innocent, and if she had to make a choice between the two kids in front of them, one looked more innocent than the other.

Gordon's theory was that Ethan was living in a constant dream. He had a hunch that if the boy was hooked up to an EEG monitor, the readout would be deep delta. His mind had been denied REM for so long that it had settled into stage four functionally. The boy was sick, not a monster. He kept telling himself this in his mind, again and again, but doing so was getting harder, especially when the boy looked at Erica as he did, especially when he tightened his grip on the pipe. Ethan shifted his flat gaze to Dana, who Gordon realized was crying, yet somehow the red target dot stayed true on Ethan's chest.

And then the barest hint of hesitation crossed Ethan's brow. A tiny pinching of the eyes. Confusion. A distinctly human look.

"Wait, Dana," Gordon whispered. "Here, move slowly toward me."

Dana sidestepped toward Gordon, but Ethan didn't follow her. He still stared forward, past where she'd been, where his reflection was illuminated in the light from Dana's shoulder rig.

"He sees himself in the mirror," Gordon whispered. As soon as he spoke, his mind raced back to Gladwell's proseminar on "The Mind at Night."

*Mirrors and dreams. They just don't mix.*

They'd read a case study of a Vietnam veteran suffering from horrendous PTSD nightmares back when nobody knew what PTSD was. Gladwell himself wrote it. The man was terrified he'd fall into his nightmares at any second, so he kept cutting himself. He figured that pain was the only way he'd know for sure he wasn't dreaming. Gladwell had a better idea.

*"Look in a mirror. If you see yourself clearly, you're awake. If it's hazy, murky, or swimming, you're dreaming."*

The clarity of Ethan's reflection, of the boy that stared back at him, was throwing Ethan for a loop, making him realize he was in a real place, in real danger. Dana turned to follow his gaze. Her shoulder lamp lit up his reflection crystal clear, and Ethan staggered backward, along with his reflection.

"Ethan," Gordon said clearly. "Read the words on the canvas. Read them."

The faded marquee was just above the mirrors. And enough of Ethan had surfaced so that his eyes shifted to the words. His voice was weak, croaking—but he read. "Paris. Milan. Monaco... Baltimore."

He barely got the last word out before he dropped the pipe and then dropped to the ground like a stone.

Gordon stood in shock. Written words had the same effect as mirrors on the dreamer. He'd never been so happy in his life that he stayed awake for those first seminars.

Dana wasted no time getting to the kids. She knelt down, and Erica grabbed her around the neck, at the same time pushing feebly away from Ethan's body draped over her. Dana picked her up. The girl seemed all too ready to be carried, and she buried her head in Dana's shoulder, her nose pushing the com aside, tears cutting rivulets in the dirt on her face.

"Are you hurt, Erica?" Dana asked. "Did Ethan do anything to you?"

Erica coughed and responded, "He pushed me down. That's all."

"Did he bring you here?" Dana asked.

Erica shook her head, a small keening cry building itself in her chest.

"He didn't bring you here, Erica?" Dana asked again.

"I wake up here sometimes. But I always go back before Mom and Dad know."

Dana sagged a little at that, nodding. Gordon was relieved as well. Ethan hadn't physically stolen her away. That was something, at least. Gordon moved to Ethan and knelt down. He felt for a pulse and found it easily, hammering against the side of his neck, but his eyes were closed.

"Ethan," Gordon said clearly. No response. He pulled back the boy's eyelids and saw they were rolled back to the whites. "He did this before," Gordon said, turning to Dana. "It's whatever passes for sleep for him now, sort of an emergency shutdown. Last time he came out of it with some lucidity. I don't really want to wake him right now, not if I don't have to."

"We've got to get him out of here," Dana said. "Maybe we can still salvage this shitshow without writing him up for kidnapping and assault. Because this looks like kidnapping and assault, Gordon—even if she says she woke up here and all he did was push her down. There's no way around it. Not for a kid on ice this thin."

"I'll carry him. I had to practically slap him awake last time. He'll be fine. I mean, all things considered."

Dana shook her head, amazed. "That kid looked like he wanted to eat your neck five seconds ago. Now you want to carry him like a baby?"

"Well, yeah. How else should I carry him? Like a sack of potatoes? That's not good for his back."

"You are a piece of work, Pope. Get to it then."

Gordon gripped Ethan under the armpits and lifted him up then held him to his chest with one hand around his waist. The boy was terribly light. He didn't even stir. His head lolled onto Gordon's shoulders. Dana was already on her way out, her light bobbing steadily in front of him as he followed. He ducked under the dripping ivy and pivoted out of the ticket box, sweating a lot more than he was accustomed to. Ethan was breathing a mile a minute on his neck, which felt like getting blasted by a hairdryer.

They passed from the outer yard back under the bridge to the ill-fated atrium, and Gordon knew something was wrong. He could see the lights. When every streetlight is out for a block in every direction, swirling red and blue are hard to miss. Still, Gordon held out hope that the commotion was just the medical response to Andrew Barret.

Dana passed through the tunnel first, and when he followed, his heart sank. The only person not arrayed in a swirling arc of red and blue in front of him was Barret. His ride had come and gone, back to the hospital and, hopefully, to nothing more than a boatload of head staples. In his place were two more ambulances and the slowly mobilizing efforts of what he guessed, at first glance, were fifteen policemen. And one lieutenant, of course. One ever-present asshole of a lieutenant.

In front of him, Dana tromped to a halt and dropped her chin, her body sagging again, but not, Gordon guessed, from anything resembling relief. Not that time. Not as they were surrounded.

"Put the girl down, Dana," said one bull-necked officer.

Another tall cop didn't even give Gordon the courtesy, charging toward him with hands out. If a team of medics hadn't brushed their way past the police and taken custody of Ethan first, Gordon had no doubt the officer would have pulled the boy from him by force and then probably taken Gordon to the ground for good measure.

One of the medics that tended to Ethan, a young woman, looked Gordon in the eye and said, "We'll take care of him, Dr. Pope. I promise." Still, his hands had to be removed, and still, he gave Ethan up reluctantly, like a farmer carrying the best of his crop to town, only to be robbed on the road.

Dana didn't go so easily. She knew the officers personally. She spoke each of their names as they squared up to her, reaching for Erica.

"Don't touch me, Halloran. If you touch me, I'll break your goddamn arm. You too, Vick. Hey. Victor, yeah, Victor Garcia, I'm talking to you. You know me. Put your hands down. What are you gonna do with that Maglite? Huh? You gonna swipe at me, you chickenshit?"

Each of the men refused to meet her eye and then faltered. For a moment.

Then one young man, a big fellow with his hair buzzed

within a centimeter of his head and his uniform still creased at the seams, grabbed her by the lapel and screamed, "Put her *down*, Frisco!"

Then others bucked up. Gordon could see it in their eyes. They wouldn't be outdone by the rookie. They moved in again, and the rookie gripped Dana harder, balling her uniform in his fist until Marty Cicero popped a clean hook right across his jaw. Then he was on the dirt and not moving.

"What the fuck is this?" Cicero asked, staring down at the man as if he was a drunk on the sidewalk, then addressing the rest of the policemen. "See, this is funny because for a second there, I thought you boys were treating my partner like a criminal. But I must have been mistaken, right?"

Cicero stared at each of them in turn. They backed up. Victor Garcia looked cagily back toward where Warren Duke was standing, holding back Erica's family. The fear in Garcia's eyes was clear.

"Right, Vick?" Cicero asked. "Am I right? Because if I'm right, then my hand sorta slipped there with Packman, and we can leave it at that. But if I'm not mistaken, then maybe my hand keeps slipping."

An older cop with thinning gray hair and a slight stoop stepped forward. "It's all right, Cicero. No harm, no foul." He looked down at Packman—who had rolled to his stomach and looked to be shaking some wits back into himself—as if the young officer was his neighbor's dog shitting in his yard. "We'll let Lieutenant Duke take care of Officer Frisco and her friend. Meantime, let's run a preliminary sweep and button this up before even more press arrive. Chop chop."

The officers dispersed slowly. One shouldered into

Gordon on purpose then held up his hands. "Sorry, guy."
The older one stared Dana down as he passed her by.

For a moment, only Gordon, Cicero, and Dana
remained with Erica. But the second team of medics was
already moving in, flanked by Erica's parents. McKayla
Denbrook was grasping for her child as if an imaginary rope
could pull her more quickly to her side. Behind them all
walked Warren Duke.

In the brief interim, Cicero turned to Dana. He looked
furious. Gordon thought he looked even angrier at Dana
than he did at Packman, who had to sit down about forty
feet away and seemed to be rethinking his career. Cicero
spoke quickly and quietly.

"I know you think this circus was me, that I called it in. I
didn't. Maybe I should have, but I didn't. The Denbrooks
lost it. Ran up here themselves. Woke the whole damn
neighborhood. Someone called the cops—a couple of some-
ones. There's only so much mess I can eat for you, Dana.
Then it's *my* career on the line, *my* life you're fucking with,
and I can't abide by that."

Dana's face slackened as surely as if she'd been punched
in the gut.

"Keep it together in front of Duke," Cicero whispered.
"You can sink your own ship if you want. Fine. Just do it
away from me. If for no other reason than I put Packman on
the ground for you, keep it together right now. We're in
enough shit as it is."

Before Dana could muster a reply, the medics were
there with a stretcher. The Denbrooks reached for Erica,
her mother saying, "Baby, baby, baby" over and over again,
and Dana let go. Only Erica didn't seem to want to let Dana
go. The medics tried to take her, but she burrowed deeper
into Dana's arms. It took her mother whispering and softly,

shakily brushing her fingers through the girl's hair to get her even to look up. Warren Duke stood behind them, his hands clasped behind his back, the badge on his hip reflecting the flashes of red and blue. He looked annoyed with Erica's reluctance. Gordon had the feeling Duke was hoping the girl would spring from Dana's arms, screaming and pointing back at the three of them with confused horror. He got no such thing.

In fact, separating the girl from the woman who had twice come to her rescue proved so difficult that Duke stepped away, toward the medics who were still treating Ethan. He spoke with them briefly, and the young woman who addressed him responded as if confused. Duke spoke more forcefully, and the woman stepped back, her hands up. She shrugged and took out a four-point restraint rigging. The second medic prepped a shot that Gordon recognized as a quick-punch benzodiazepine.

"Whoa, whoa," Gordon said, stepping forward. "The boy is completely unconscious, deeply unconscious, and he will be for some time. Is that really necessary?"

He quickly regretted his words. Warren Duke turned toward him with barely veiled disgust. All he'd needed was an opening.

"Ah, yes. Mr. Pope. Here again."

"It's Dr. Pope, Lieutenant."

Duke nodded as if he could not care less while his tie, with its golden clip, stayed motionless. "I can't expect you to understand these things, no more than I could understand your..." He twirled his index finger while looking for the words. "Kiddie therapy or whatever it is you do. But this boy has proven to be a danger, and he is under arrest. Thus, the restraints."

Duke took the four-point rig from the medic himself

and clipped them around Ethan's feet and wrists, looping the connector below the rolling gurney. He did it like an old pro. Ethan never moved, never gave any indication he felt a thing.

"The sedative there is in case he wakes up en route to the hospital and tries to kill any of these hardworking medics like he nearly did that poor Tanner boy. Or like he very nearly did to his poor girlfriend."

"He didn't try to kill Erica," Gordon stammered. "And he wasn't in his right mind when he attacked Jimmy Tanner."

Duke held up a hand and gave that same dismissive nod again, as if it was all the explanation he needed to offer. "They'll keep the restraints on and the sedative ready until the boy is safely in a holding cell at the city circuit courthouse. There he will stay until his appeal is... sorted out."

He might as well have said denied.

"You can't just take him like this. He's very sick."

"Mr. Pope, if I were you, I would be far less concerned with little Ethan here and far more concerned with yourself."

Duke turned toward Dana and Cicero. Erica had finally allowed her mother to take her and set her gently on her own gurney. The medics were smiling at her and trying to get her attention while they logged her vitals. Erica reached for Dana, and Dana almost reached back, but Cicero pressed gently on her shoulder and nodded toward Duke.

"Frisco, Cicero, get over here," Duke said.

Cicero led Dana over with a barely evident series of presses. Dana stared at Ethan, cuffed to the bed like a young Hannibal Lecter. She breathed carefully through her nose.

"Frisco, you're the superior officer here, so I'll ask you.

You wanna tell me how you and Cicero showed up to this call well before your backup?"

Cicero started to speak, but Duke held up one finger and silenced him with a sharp stare. Then he settled back and looked at Dana.

"It was a non-violent disturbance call... sir," she added, as if she had to pull it from her own mouth. "I thought Cicero and I could handle it."

"It was a missing persons call—"

"Not even thirty minutes old, Lieutenant," Cicero said. "Book says check it out before calling in for—"

"*Fuck* what the book says." Duke leaned over at the waist directly into Cicero's face. "I *am* the book. And you both knew goddamn well what was happening here."

Dana started to speak up, but Duke held up a hand. For one terrible moment, Gordon thought he was going to slap her. But he wiped his lips instead.

"I don't want to hear it, Frisco. I've already called for a full internal review of this dispatch. Of this case. And of the two of you."

Duke dropped his hand and shook his head like a disappointed father. "I don't know what has gotten into you two. Frisco, I'm used to this bullshit from you, but Marty, I expected better. I don't know who pulled the strings here..." At that, he looked right at Gordon. "But I've got a guess. As to why? I cannot fathom."

He turned his back on them and walked past Ethan, trailing his hand on the metal rail of the gurney. His signet ring popped up and over each chain restraint.

"Sir, please. Marty had nothing to do with this," Dana said, calling after him.

"Both of you will cooperate fully with the investigation.

They will take control of your desks tomorrow morning. As of now, you're on administrative leave."

He looked back at them out of the corner of his eye. "Paid, though. For the time being. So the three of you can enjoy a nice night out together. Maybe talk over your relationship. Because if internal affairs finds that either of you or your friend..." He pointed right at Gordon. "If *any* of you are found to have obstructed justice in any way, you two officers will be fired, and this clown is going to jail."

None of them had any response. Dana stared after Duke as if he'd taken her heart with him and still held it in his grip, trailing intermittent spatters of blood on the way to his black Suburban. Cicero dropped his head and propped his hands on his hips.

Gordon watched his patient, the patient that had brought him back to life even as his own hung in the balance, as he was carted away toward the ambulance. The medics pressed the rig slowly against the back of the vehicle, and the legs folded as the gurney slid inside. The medic that had spoken to him turned and saw him and must have understood something of the slow self-hatred he felt creeping across his face, his anger at his own failure. She gave him a sad smile. Then she slammed the doors shut, and Ethan was taken away from them in chains.

# CHAPTER FIFTEEN

K aren Jefferson woke early. She always had, even
when she was married to Gordon and lived in Baltimore, which she thought somehow seemed dreary even
when the sky was crystal clear and the sun was shining. In
San Diego, getting up with the sunrise was easy. She never
wanted to miss a single one of them.

When Maggie had been born, her New Mom Circle
told her to get ready for the frustration of sleepless nights
and early mornings. She'd loved all of it, the sleepless nights
and mornings both, because it gave her more time with
Maggie.

Maggie was nearly four, and both she and Karen had
fallen into a wonderful routine, one that got Karen up an
hour before even Chad awoke. She used that time as her
own with her little girl. She crept into her daughter's room
while she still slept and carried her out to their living room,
where she set her in her "happy corner" of their big
sectional couch. She had her toys there and a second, identical version of her favorite blankie. She was soon fast asleep
again, facing their big bay window with its view of the

purpling Pacific Ocean. Then Karen poured herself a cup of steaming black coffee—just one—and either wrote, wrote, wrote, or revised, revised, revised while sitting on the couch next to her daughter. When she got stuck, she looked at Maggie, and her mind freed itself up again.

Lately, she had so much material already written that she was mostly doing revisions. She'd finished her largest research study four weeks before—two hundred days of intensive analysis of over one thousand children, aged five to twelve, who suffered from acute Obsessive Compulsive Disorder. Her theory was that OCD could be linked directly to what she called "achievement pressure," a term that was colloquially accepted but still hard to define medically. Karen believed she could define it as abnormal activity in the central amygdala of the developing brain and then link it directly to newly exhibited OCD symptoms.

The experiment was massive, one that required a detailed medical history and full workup for each child, along with an extensive OCD-barometer tool she'd developed herself along with three members of her UCSD team over the course of a year. That was the crown jewel of her Davis Grant, and it was going to make one hell of a journal article, but even if it didn't—though she knew it would—the Davis Foundation had already short-listed her for a continuation grant and a teaching position, should she want it.

She had her career, she had Chad, and best of all, she had Maggie. In short, Karen Jefferson hardly ever spared a thought for Gordon Pope any longer. Unless he called her. Which he did a little too frequently for her comfort and certainly too frequently for Chad's. But even when he did call, she was surprised by how *surprised* she was to be thinking about him. They'd been married for two years and engaged for two before that, and they had dated on and off for five years as they both went through school together. Shouldn't she be pining, even a little? Shouldn't she get annoyed at the things Chad did every now and then that Gordon had never done? Things like looking down his nose at her on the odd Tuesday when she decided to have another glass of wine. Or when he decided to eat nothing but blended kale and vitamin B for a week and then blended a week's supply of said kale at ten at night on Sunday when she was trying to put Maggie to bed. Shouldn't she have a wistful moment, at least?

Probably. Most women in her situation would. But not Karen. And she knew why. She'd thought she loved Gordon, once. She was wrong. She loved her child, a child that had been waiting to spring from within her and that Gordon could never do his part to bring forth. Her choice was black and white and couldn't have been easier. In her experience, when a choice was easy to make, she rarely revisited it.

No amount of subtle accusations or cold looks from their circle of Baltimore friends—truthfully, *her* circle of Baltimore friends that he also happened to inhabit alongside her—could persuade her otherwise. Not even Deborah, Gordon's mother, who was more of the overt-accusation type of woman, and for whom Karen still felt begrudging respect, could persuade her to stay. And she had tried. Then promptly sworn Deborah to secrecy about her trying.

The proof that Karen had made the right decision was there in front of her, sleeping soundly with her arms spread out above her head, her pony pajamas slightly askew.

Gordon and Deborah could say whatever they wanted about her. Gordon couldn't give her this. This moment. This feeling.

Gordon was a good man. They had been young and in

what she liked to call "stupid love," but still, something might have come of it if Gordon wasn't sterile. Bottom line.

Maggie was waking up just then. That was a slow, droopy process that Karen loved watching. Maggie scratched at her mouth, changed her breathing, and rolled over on her side. Her eyes opened to slits then to half-moons. She stretched like a cat and smacked her mouth and then just lay there.

"Mommy," she said, smiling.

"Hi, honey. How'd you sleep?"

"I flew," Maggie said.

"Flew? Yeah?"

"Yeah. Jenny said she could fly in her dreams, and everyone called her a liar."

"Jenny Burgess? From school?" Karen asked, but her mind had already started to flit back to the spreadsheet she had open on the laptop in her lap.

"Yeah, they called Jenny a liar, but I didn't." Maggie rubbed at her eyes and looked out the window at the sunrise.

"That's good, honey," Karen said, somewhat absently. "You can't call people liars unless you know they're really liars." She highlighted a row and marked it red for *check source data*.

"So I tried and I tried to fly, and I couldn't for a long time. It was hard. I just couldn't do it. Like my head was..." She looked for the right word but couldn't find it. "My head said no."

Karen paused and looked at Maggie. "You had a lucid dream?"

Maggie was still looking out the window. She shrugged.

"Did you have a dream where you were flying? Or did

you have a dream where you wanted to fly and then you flew?" Karen asked. She set her laptop on the coffee table.

"I dunno," Maggie said. "Both. But it took a long time. I had to practice. Like at my books. Because at first my head said no, you know?"

And that was when a thought occurred to Karen that brought her troubled ex-husband rocketing to the forefront of her brain so quickly that it startled her.

Maggie saw the change come over her mother's face, and she furrowed her small brow. "Mommy?" she asked.

"It's okay, honey," Karen said, her mind racing, her eyes unfocused. "You just gave Mommy an idea."

"What idea?"

Karen brushed Maggie's hair back gently with one hand while the girl dangled her legs over the couch. "An idea that you should have some breakfast. How 'bout it? Any cereal you want. Even the good kind because Daddy's still asleep and he'll never know. Sound good?"

Maggie smiled and hopped down to the carpet. She tiptoed to the pantry as quietly as she could. Karen stood and followed, but she paused at the edge of the coffee table, where her phone sat. She eyed it, thinking of her last clipped conversation with Gordon. God knew the poor man had his problems, but he had some good points too, especially that bit about the effect of rapidly changing sleeping conditions on a slowly evolving brain. That had been intriguing.

*What the hell.*

Then Karen Jefferson did a rare thing. She actually picked up her phone and called her ex-husband for once, instead of the other way around.

·  ·  ·

Gordon Pope turned his tumbler of scotch round and round on the table and stared absently at his Cobb salad. He'd very nearly slept through lunch. He'd considered bailing on it, but sitting around his apartment and staring at the wall was doing him no good either. He needed a distraction. From his job. From failing as Ethan's psychiatrist. From his life in general. Plus, his mother's drinking habits made him feel less guilty about having a scotch at eleven in the morning, and he'd never needed an eleven a.m. scotch so badly in his life.

"I don't think you've blinked since you sat down, Gordon," his mother said, eyeing him over a frosty martini glass.

"If I blink, I may fall asleep," Gordon said.

"Eat something."

"I'm not hungry, Mom. I just came for the scotch."

"And the company, of course," she said.

"Of course," Gordon replied, nodding wearily.

His mother stared down her nose at him, and he recognized the look. It was the one she used before giving Gordon a piece of her mind, the one she wore with one foot on the soapbox. Gordon stifled a sigh and tried to buck up. No need to ruin her day with his failures.

"I never said thank you for the lab time," he said. "It helped me to diagnose Ethan."

"You don't sound thrilled."

"I couldn't treat him in time. I was too late. He had another episode last night."

His mother set one manicured hand flat on the table, and her silver bracelets clinked gently. "Did he...?"

"He bonked his dad pretty good, but we were able to calm him before anything really terrible happened." Gordon tipped his drink back until the ice tapped his teeth.

"I mean, nothing more terrible than him getting arrested after all and him being held at the courthouse without bail until his appeal, which is in a week, which is essentially a formality now because it will be denied and he'll go to Ditchfield, where his life will become a living hell of four-point restraints, sedatives, and antipsychotics that he doesn't need and that will do him no good. So. Nothing more terrible than that. Oh, also, I may or may not be going to jail myself, depending on the results of an investigation into my involvement in this whole thing."

His mother drummed her nails on the wood. Gordon set his drink down with a smack that turned Caesar's head from where he was standing near the bar. He popped a questioning eyebrow, and Gordon nodded for another.

"Did you ever follow up with this Dana girl like you promised me?" she asked.

"Seriously? That's what you want to know? That's what's got you most concerned? Not the fact that Ethan is screwed? Or that I might be going to jail? Or that I have fifty messages on my machine, and I can't answer any of them?"

"So you *didn't* follow up with her. Like you promised."

Gordon held his head in his hands. Caesar gently slid a fresh scotch into his view and patted his shoulder lightly before sliding off. Gordon didn't even look up.

"I did," he said. "Even convinced her to help me with Ethan. Although it didn't take much convincing. She's a good person. So she was there. Front-row tickets to watch a psychiatrist fail his patient."

"Sounds to me like you saved the day. You de-escalated the child. You quite probably saved his life," she said.

Gordon couldn't help but notice she sounded an octave more chipper upon hearing the Dana news. His mother was a difficult woman in many ways, but in many others she was remarkably easy to please. He could be going to jail, but as long as he was dating someone, that was okay in her book. Gordon took his glass and pressed it to the golf-ball-sized knot at the back of his head. He felt his long-simmering headache resurging.

"He's done for, Mom. Maybe it's good I can't have kids if this is what my help gets them."

Her right eyebrow arched so severely Gordon thought she might be able to chop his salad with a look. "First of all," she said, "I'm not going to dignify that with a response. Second of all, unless I'm much mistaken, you told me you still have a week."

"Mother—"

"You're my son, and you have a week."

"What's that supposed to mean?" Gordon asked but was distracted by a buzz in his pocket. He fished out his mobile phone, on its last gasp of juice. He'd forgotten to charge it when he'd passed out as soon as he got back from the Tivoli fiasco. He saw a missed call from Karen Jefferson, and she'd left a voicemail.

Gordon almost dropped the phone in shock.

"Is everything okay?" his mother asked, but Gordon was already listening to the message. "What did I tell you about those phones at the table?" she asked, but Gordon ignored her. She sat back with her martini, looking more intrigued now than angry.

"Gordon, it's Karen." She sounded perplexed, as if she was as surprised to be calling him as Gordon was to be listening to her voicemail. "Listen, I was thinking about what you said last time you called, when you had to go. What you said about taking ownership of your subconscious. I don't want you to think that I was lying awake at night or anything, but... Maggie said something to me this morning. She said that she had a dream where she was flying, a lucid dream, although she can't know what that is. But what struck me was that she said she had to work for it. Now, I don't know if it means anything or if it'll do you any good, but I felt that I had to call you. Maybe there's something there. Maybe you ought to ask this Ethan kid if he's ever had a lucid dream. I dunno. Just thinking out loud. Wish I could be of more help."

Gordon stared at nothing. *Lucid dreams.* Most people lucked into one or two of them every now and then. They were very liberating. Gordon had had to deprive himself of REM and quite literally medically induce his last one, wherein he spoke to his child self in the cave. But before that? It had been years earlier, and it had involved sex. Most lucid dreams he had did those days. He'd been in a bit of a dry spell in real life, but on the rare occasion he was in control of his dreams... well. And that lucid dream had been with Karen, too. Some habits were hard to break.

So his last had been lab induced. But when had his first been? When he was very young, like Maggie? Or maybe Ethan's age? He couldn't remember. But what he did remember was a final paper he'd written years before for Gladwell. He'd sought to define the sensation that occasionally happens in dreams when one floats above one's own body. He'd submitted it and gotten a C minus. That he'd passed the class at all was more due to Gladwell's friendship with Gordon than anything, but that paper came back to him in a rush. In it, he'd done a study on disembodied dreaming that took into account dozens of documented doppelganger experiences where he'd found one common theme: When the subject was able to take ownership of the dream, the doppelganger experience ended, often with a violent, sucking sensation and a panicked awakening.

*Taking ownership...* What if that was the cure? And the only way Gordon knew of to take ownership of the Wild, Wild West that was the human subconscious, was through lucid dreaming. When he told his subconscious brain to do something, and it did it. If lucid dreaming could bring a floating brain back to a body, might it also piece Ethan's fragmented brain back together?

Gordon realized he'd been holding his silent phone to his ear for minutes. His mother had her arms crossed, waiting patiently with a droll look on her face.

"I have to go, Mom. I'm sorry. It's about Ethan."

She smirked, but it was a kind smirk. "What happened to 'He's done for'?"

"I... I dunno. Maybe there's one last bullet. But I gotta go now."

"Then go," she said. "Go, my son."

As Gordon passed from the pleasant music and temperate air of Waterstones out into the driving heat of late summer, he marveled not at Karen or at his own recall but at his mother. She never seemed to know when to quit.

And more often than not, she was right.

# CHAPTER SIXTEEN

E than's dream of running free, of taking claim of what was his by strength, of rising to the top of his pack, was cut abruptly short. When he awoke, he was splayed out on a thin mattress, chained at his wrists and ankles to the short walls of his bed. He was not himself by any means, nor was he the thing he'd been the night before. That waking dream had fled, but another was already building in strength, and to Ethan, they were seamless. The night before, his vision had been entirely consumed by the Red. That morning, the Red was floating around the edges of his sight and his thoughts like a flitting shadow, but it was growing.

His first inclination was to lash out, to test the strength of his bonds, but as he tensed to snap, he heard voices. They were vaguely familiar. He stilled and feigned sleep.

"Of course I can," said one voice, coming nearer, already booming. "Check the ledger again. It's Thomas Brighton. B-R-I-G-H-T-O-N. Think illumination. Think awareness. I'm his attorney, Officer... Belmont is it? Where is Dana Frisco? She usually oversees this lockup. You know what? Never mind. Why would you know that? You apparently are unclear about even the *basic tenets* of attorney-client privilege, which states that I should have been notified upon the boy's arrival as the appointed attorney in an ongoing case where my client is unable to act on his own behalf, which—"

Ethan could hear them right outside the bars.

"Good Christ. Is he in four-point restraints? Tell me he is not in four-point restraints."

"Lieutenant Duke made it very clear that the boy be kept under strict supervision."

"Oh, did he? Is that what Lieutenant Duke said? And I suppose that means 'chained like a dog' these days? My client must have resisted arrest then, to a violent degree. And you must have that on record. Or did Lieutenant Duke neglect to give that to you, to give to me?"

The officer cleared his throat.

"Give me the keys to the shackles. Despite what Lieutenant Duke thinks, in the eyes of the law, for at least the next week, Ethan Barret is still a twelve-year-old boy, not some sort of pig trussed up for slaughter."

Ethan heard a heavy sigh. "Fine. Here." A chime as the keys were thrown and caught. "But just you, not this guy. He's not any sort of lawyer."

"I should hope not. There are far too many of us in the world as it is. No, this is the boy's court-appointed psychiatrist. He will also be staying. If you have a problem with this, I suggest you find Lieutenant Duke, if you can pry him away from whatever press conference he's no doubt gargling salt water in preparation for."

The officer paused for a long moment. "Make it quick."

"We'll take as long as it takes," Brighton yelled after the

man. Ethan could hear the slow, heavy steps of the officer receding down the hallway. Then silence.

"Is he out cold, or what?" Brighton asked.

Then a voice Ethan recognized. A friendly voice, one that awoke a calm part of his brain by nudging it ever so slightly. "I doubt it. I think he can hear us right now. He'd better be able to. If not, we're screwed."

Ethan snapped open his eyes. Both men were standing next to his bed, and both men jumped back a good foot, as if a mouse had scampered across their shoes.

"Gordon," Ethan said groggily, as if the name was mud in his mouth. And he winced because as he spoke, the Red perching at the edges of his vision screamed at him. He would have sworn the two men could hear it. They must have. But they were steady, peering down at him.

And Gordon was smiling. "Hi, Ethan," he said simply. "You remember me."

The Red receded, but it deepened, like a dug-in tick suffused with blood. Ethan knew it was furious, but it was also confident that it was going nowhere and that Ethan would exhaust himself again, and it would be waiting. Soon, he would live entirely within the Red. That's what it wanted. That's what Ethan wanted, too, when it had control of him.

"The keys," Gordon said.

Brighton looked at the keys in his hand and then handed them over, but with none of the bravado of before. "Are you sure this kid isn't going to... I dunno... go all silver-back gorilla on us?"

"No, we've got a small window of time. He lives in a waking dream now, but it has stages just like any other. He's still in the dissociative part, stage one. But he won't be for long."

Brighton looked as though the medical description shot right over his head, but he couldn't care less. "You got that right. I filed a motion for dismissal and a few other tricks that'll keep them busy for a while but won't do any good, so I think you'll be able to work with him for a little bit, but they could yank us both at any time. Especially since you pissed off Duke. Everyone knows he's the prodigal son of the precinct." He looked at his watch, a big, glinting thing. "I gotta go. I got a hearing in twenty."

"Thomas, thank you."

"Don't go thanking me just yet. You owe me. And you might not be thanking me when I call your ass to the stand on the next whale of a case I get."

Brighton walked out of the cell then paused behind the bars. "Doc. Good luck, hey? This could be major for my career."

With that, he passed by and out of Ethan's view. Ethan snapped back to Gordon, watching him carefully.

Gordon moved to the restraints on Ethan's feet and clicked open the clasp there, threading the chain back through the cuffs until Ethan could freely move his feet. Then he moved to work on his hands, one at a time. The quietly screaming part of Ethan's brain told him the time had come to act, to overpower this man, to establish himself as above this man. But that part was still pushed aside for the time being. Instead, Ethan felt an odd fondness. The fact that Gordon seemed blindly to trust him when everyone else was afraid of him only strengthened the feeling.

"Why don't you try just sitting up, feet on the ground," Gordon said. "Gently."

Ethan pushed his feet over with a groan. He was sore everywhere. How had he gotten so sore? He put his feet on the ground and winced, seeing for the first time that they were covered in gauze. *This isn't real. This is a dream.* The Red in him grew.

"How do you feel, Ethan?" Gordon asked carefully.

"Like I'm sleeping," Ethan said.

"You're not. See that? What is that?" Gordon asked. He pointed through the bars at a wall clock the size of a dinner plate. It had two big black hands for the hours and minutes and a slowly ticking red second hand.

"It's a clock," Ethan said. His voice seemed far away, and his vision swam, but whether that was from this dream he thought he was having or from having sat up too quickly or from the mere fact that he could no longer place himself anywhere for sure, he couldn't tell.

"What time is it?" Gordon asked.

Ethan blinked, his head lolling about. It seemed heavy. He heard voices, strangely amplified.

"What time is it, Ethan?" Gordon asked, louder that time.

Ethan squinted. "Four fifteen." And just like that, the world snapped back into place. The Red faded to the edges again, where it pulsed angrily. He could see the veins of his eyes like tiny streaks of white lightning where it crept, but the rest of his vision cleared.

"That's right. Wanna know something funny about dreams? You can never tell time in dreams. Even if you're standing right in front of a clock, it never tells time. Look again."

Ethan did. "Four sixteen."

"That's how you know you're not dreaming. We're gonna use that test a lot, okay? In the work we have to do here."

"Where are my dad and mom?" Ethan asked. He felt as

if he hadn't seen them in forever. The last time he'd seen his dad was... watching baseball, maybe? He had a vague memory of the drone of the play-by-play. As for his mom, he honestly couldn't remember.

"They're on their way here," Gordon said, but he looked away. Ethan knew he wasn't telling him everything. But then again, even if he did, Ethan had the feeling he wouldn't get it, the way a person waking up from a coma after a long time wouldn't get it if he was handed a cell phone.

"Where's my phone?" Ethan asked.

"You broke it," Gordon said. "You haven't been yourself lately."

That much Ethan knew for sure. He hadn't been right for quite some time. He remembered. He reached for the chain that had been around his ankles.

"You have to put these back on me," he said, feeling hot tears well in his eyes. "Forever. Understand?"

Gordon crouched down in front of Ethan so he could look up at him, and even though Ethan wanted to look away, he couldn't. Gordon's eyes kept following his.

"I'll put them back on you if you need it. But let me decide that, okay? And it won't be forever, buddy. Not if I have anything to say about it. And not if you work with me. If you work with me, there's a chance you might never feel like you need these again."

Ethan wiped away his tears with the shoulder of his shirt. "What do I need to do?"

Gordon sat next to Ethan on the cot and turned to him. "Have you ever been able to change a dream?"

"Change a dream?"

"Yeah, like, have you ever been dreaming and then realized you were dreaming and decided to change that dream up? Say, decide to fly or drive a racecar or talk to a pretty girl and be really good at it."

Ethan thought back. He recalled some times when he thought he might have realized he was dreaming, well before his long, waking nightmare fell over him, but as for changing it? Flying? He was pretty sure he'd remember something like that.

He shook his head. "I don't think so."

"I don't think so either. In fact, I'm about as sure as I can be that you've never had a lucid dream in your life. And we need to change that."

The Red twitched. It went the dark shade of heart's blood for a moment and tunneled his vision before receding. Ethan had to steady himself on the bed.

"You okay?" Gordon asked quietly.

Ethan found he was breathing heavily—panting, really. He had to force deep breaths to slow down his heart. He found his jaw clenched as well, grinding. He pried it open with effort.

"We don't have a lot of time," Ethan whispered.

"Story of my life," Gordon replied.

FOR THE NEXT FOUR HOURS, Ethan and Gordon played with a pencil.

Gordon started by dropping the lid to the open-air toilet in the corner of the cell with his shoe, and setting the pencil on the closed lid. He turned on his heel, walked back to the bed, and sat down next to Ethan. He wormed back on the bed until his back was against the wall and his legs kicked up. He motioned for Ethan to do the same. If anyone had come by, they'd have found a grown man and a young boy sitting on a prison bed, staring at a toilet.

"I don't get it," Ethan said.

"If we were in the lab, I'd have other tools, other things I could use to try and get you into a pattern of lucid dreaming. But we're not, so we gotta make do."

"With a pencil?"

"For the next thirty minutes, we're going to play a little game," Gordon said, setting his watch. "It's called 'Who can stare at the pencil the longest without blinking?' If I blink, you win the round. If you blink, I win the round. We'll keep score. For every round you win, I give you a buck."

"And every time I lose?" Ethan asked, a small smile on his chapped lips.

"You give me ten bucks."

"No way!" Ethan said and laughed once. The sound was so foreign to him that he was nearly startled.

"C'mon, I'm broke."

"A buck for a buck," Ethan said.

"Deal. Ready?"

Ethan set his hands on his thighs and got to staring as Gordon did the same to his left. "No cheating," Ethan said.

"I wouldn't dream of it," said Gordon, still as a statue. "Remember, stare at the pencil, okay? Not the toilet or the gross stains under the toilet or the wall or the gross stains on the wall—"

"I get it."

Ethan stared until his eyes watered, then he stared some more. He stared until he had to squinch up his mouth to keep from blinking, then he stared some more.

"Damn it, I blinked," said Gordon.

Ethan smiled and blinked and blinked and blinked. He still saw the pulsing Red at the edges of his vision, but he also saw an imprint of a bright white pencil on the inside of his eyelids.

"That's Ethan one, Gordon zilch."

"Nice," said Ethan.

"Again, ready?"

Ethan wiped the tears from his eyes and set his hands on his thighs. "You bet."

"Okay... go."

ETHAN COULDN'T REMEMBER the final score because at the end, a strange thing started happening to him. The pencil stopped being yellow and started becoming red. It stopped being a game, and Ethan started to focus on the bars of the cell. Then the bed. What was he doing here, again? And this man beside him... He knew the man, right? If not, if this man wasn't of his pack, wasn't under him, then he was against him, and Ethan needed to—

"Ethan, what time is it?" asked Gordon.

Ethan looked up at the clock, his face heavy, as if small weights hung from his cheeks. But he still saw the clock. He still saw the hands.

"It's four fifty-two," Ethan said.

The room popped back together. Gordon was looking carefully at him. After a moment, Gordon patted him on the back. "That's right, buddy. It's four fifty-two. And I owe you twenty-two bucks."

Ethan laughed weakly. They'd been playing a game. That was all.

Gordon stood up, walked over to the toilet, and picked up the pencil. He pulled a white piece of paper from his pocket and drew a big circle on it, then he propped it up against the low metal headboard of the cot, between the slack chains.

"I think we'd better stand up from here on out, okay, champ? You're getting a little tired."

Ethan nodded. He tried to shake the fuzz from his brain, and got it most of the way clear, but he noticed the Red had advanced. It no longer lingered in the periphery. It was pulsing in the side of his vision proper, pacing like a lion in a cage.

"Pencil," Gordon said. He tossed it to Ethan.

Ethan barely caught it.

"This is big money time. We're playing a fun little pastime I like to call Pencil Chuck. Every time you throw that pencil through the bull's-eye, you get five bucks. Every time I do, I get five bucks."

Ethan nodded.

"Thing is, you gotta stare at the pencil in your hands for thirty seconds before each throw. Got it? Them's the rules. You're up first. Start staring. I'll tell you when to throw."

Ethan liked that game. He pretended he was in a quick-draw competition—staring, staring, staring, then *snap*. He'd throw it like a ninja star. The first ten or so times each, neither of them got anywhere near the paper. Once, it nearly rolled outside the bars, but Gordon stopped it with his foot. Then, Ethan nailed the paper. It was a flat-sided strike, and it didn't go through, but he whooped anyway, and Gordon laughed. The next shot Gordon careened way high, hit the wall, and bounced under the cot. Ethan scrambled to grab it, barely noticing the pain from his bandaged feet, but once he was underneath, in the darkness, the Red surged within him. The smells and sounds of the holding cell assailed him. He could smell Gordon's sweat and his anxiety. He was putting on a good face, Ethan knew, but he was frightened. And frightened was weak.

"You okay down there, Ethan?" he asked. Gordon

tapped his leg, and Ethan almost snapped at him. And Gordon knew it, too, because he withdrew. Ethan knew the man was wily. Ethan inched his way back out from under the bed, lying flat with his knees splayed, like a lizard. When he was backed out, he climbed up the bed until he was standing. Gordon was watching him carefully.

"What time is it, buddy?" Gordon asked.

Ethan looked at the clock. "Five fifty," he said, but his voice was flat and his eyes slits. The Red was expanding, as if it was taking in great big breaths and puffing itself out to cover everything in his brain. Very little of his vision was as it had been that morning. His memory of that time was distorted, as if he'd seen everything through rippled glass. The Red was so much clearer.

"A few more tosses then?" Gordon asked, his voice even. "I bet you could get up to fifty bucks."

Ethan nodded and held out his hand for the pencil.

"Stare at it for thirty seconds, now."

Ethan stared at it without moving, without blinking. Then he threw it right through the middle of the paper in one snapping motion.

Gordon looked at it for a second then turned to Ethan. "Nice work, my man," he said. But his voice was flat.

Ethan walked over to where the pencil lay and he picked it up. He walked back to the throw line.

"It's my turn," Gordon said, holding out his hand.

In a flash, Ethan struck at him with the sharpened point. He felt the pencil catch in Gordon's forearm, and he ripped down, nearly shuddering with the pleasure of the feeling. But then he stopped. He looked over at Gordon, who had jumped back and was holding his arm but, incredibly, had neither cried out nor fought back. He just watched.

"I'm sorry," a part of Ethan's brain said, some small part, getting smaller.

"One more time, Ethan," Gordon said, wincing, blood running down his arm.

"Okay," Ethan said slowly. He set his feet, rubbing the pencil until he felt it nearly splinter. Then he saw the target. It was red. He flicked out his hand, and the pencil ripped through the paper. Then he felt a ring of cold metal click shut around his ankle. He heard a clacking sound as it tightened, and Ethan turned to see Gordon stepping away, his face drawn.

Ethan growled at him. He tried to jump but fell face-first. Gordon rushed in and then leaped back just as quickly because Ethan was already up again, kicking against the restraints. Heedless of his bandages. He could hear other noises from outside the cage. Yelling. Running.

"Remember the pencil, Ethan!" Gordon said.

Then the Red took Ethan under.

ETHAN WAS IN A STRUGGLE. He was caught like a coyote in a trap. He tried to gnaw his arm off, gnaw his leg off. He kicked and screamed until he couldn't any longer. Then he played possum, hoping to lure one of the men around him close, so that he could strike out with his teeth. Those men meant him harm. They were trying to dominate him, take his pack from him, take him under them, make him subservient. He would not allow it. He was stuck in their cage, in their cave, but that didn't mean he was theirs. Not yet.

But the men didn't get close. They were all wily, just like the bald one. Nobody came near his mouth, not until he felt a hot pricking sensation on his leg. Then his consciousness and his subconsciousness melted away. Then he remembered nothing.

Ethan awoke to a man speaking, a man he recognized again. Gordon Pope.

"None of this is gonna be worth a damn if they sedate him when he starts to go under. He needs to do things in his dream. He can't do things in his dream if he's in a medical blackout."

"I'm working on it, Pope." This from the other man, the slick man in the suit. "You never told me what a pain in the ass you were when I started billing you out for expert-witness jobs. You should have done that. It would have saved me one hell of a headache."

"We gotta stop the sedatives, Thomas. And I need a longer visitation."

"It wasn't the end of visiting hours that caused that circus last night. If I recall correctly, it was the boy trying to kill everyone."

"The cops were breathing down my neck the whole time. I saw them in the wings," said Gordon.

"I called in some favors. You'll have your time," Thomas said. He sounded weary.

Ethan wanted to see, but he also wanted them to keep talking. So he'd struck out at people? Tried to kill them? He remembered nothing properly after the staring game. Vague memories of throwing a pencil. Then the Red. He saw it now, and with his eyes closed, it was doubly apparent. It was halfway across his vision already and gaining ground. He hated it, but he loved it. He was torn. His brain felt creased in half, ready to rip. The Red was warm. Safe. Without a care for these people, he was free. More and more, it felt natural.

"He's very ill, Thomas. And we have very little time. Four days."

"That fact, and that fact alone, is why they keep letting you in here. If word got out that they refused a mentally ill boy his medical counsel on the eve of his parole, they'd all be strung up. So you got your time. What's left of it. Good luck, Pope."

The lawyer walked away. Ethan heard the tapping of his shiny shoes. The cell door closed, and someone grunted then clomped away. He heard Gordon shuffle in. Was that a sigh? He snapped open his eyes. He felt a strong urge to reach out to him, but when he did, he was cut short by the restraints. Gordon looked down at him, but Gordon was smiling, and Ethan could tell from Gordon's eyes that almost all of that smile was genuine while the rest was putting up a good front for his benefit. Then he saw the bandage on Gordon's forearm. He didn't remember doing it, but he knew he must have done it. That was his life now.

"I'm sorry," Ethan said.

"Forget about it," Gordon said. Then he pulled a pencil from his back pocket, the same in every respect to the one from the day before save one: it was unsharpened.

"What time is it, Ethan?" Gordon asked.

Ethan looked up at the clock. Saw the sweeping hand. Saw it true. "It's four fifteen."

"Good. Let's get after it."


GORDON'S VISIT on this second day seemed to Ethan like a living memory. He viewed it from afar even as it was happening. He was cold, distant, uninterested in the pencil or the games, but Gordon didn't care. Or at least, he acted as if he didn't care. He kept thrusting it into Ethan's hands. He kept a tally of numbers and dollars that was difficult for Ethan to understand now. They were trappings of a life he no longer cared to be a part of. Why had he ever cared? What mattered was freedom, and he was chained. If he ever hoped to get out and take charge of himself again, he would have to break everything: the bars, the doors, the people. Even Gordon. He would be easiest, Ethan knew, because Gordon felt a fondness for him. The Red said that fondness was weakness. The Red was right. It was as easy as that. The boy Ethan sank, and the Red rose.

The day ended the same as the one before, with Ethan in chains although this time, it came sooner. Ethan snapped the pencil, snapped it right in his fingers, like the delicate bone of a bird's wing. And just as soon, he felt the cold snap of the manacle around his leg. He lunged at Gordon, swiping at him with his fists and his free leg until he fell back on the bed. He cut his head and could smell the copper tang of blood stronger than anything else in the room. Stronger even than the rancid toilet.

Gordon rushed in to help him, and Ethan let him closer, closer, until he was within his grasp. Then he ripped at his face, his eyes. Gordon yelled and fell backward, away, but Ethan knew he'd hurt the man, and he laughed. Gordon was the agent of his capture, the reason he was caged. He was the one keeping him from his place with Erica. From his own cave. Gordon pushed himself against the far wall, but he reached out to Ethan as though he still wanted to be by his side. Why the persistence? Why did he care? Didn't he know how vulnerable this made him? How predictable?

Ethan heard commotion then. Noises. Others came permeated with strong smells of alcohol and strange, unnaturally clean smells of bandages. Men that grabbed his free leg and both hands at once and chained him again. Then came one man with the strongest smell of all. Most of it was locked in a syringe, but some of it leaked from the razor point, dripping onto his hands. He gripped at Ethan's thigh, pinching a hunk of it between his thumb and forefinger.

"I certainly hope that is not what I think it is, good sir!" came a breathless voice, yelling but trying not to yell. A drowning part of Ethan's brain recognized the slick man. The lawyer.

The man who pinched him paused.

The lawyer waved a piece of paper around. "Because if it is, and you stick my client with that poison, you're gonna need a good lawyer yourself. May I give you my card?"

Ethan understood little. There was yelling, then whispering, and then, somehow, Gordon speaking to him.

"What time is it, buddy?" he asked. Ethan felt a drop of blood splatter from Gordon's face onto his own. It was warm and then quickly cold. Ethan turned toward the clock.

"It's..."

He looked at the sweeping hand, trying to see the numbers, but they were melting.

"It's..."


HE WAS BACK in his cave now. His own cave. The cave they'd ripped him from when he stood over Erica. The one he'd fought for. That he'd marked as his own. He remembered now. His Red memories opened like snap shades as his other memories closed. His body was chained, but here, he was free. He ran the perimeter of the mirrored room like a loping colt, stretching his legs and jumping. He stopped in front of one mirror and saw right through it. Not himself, of course, but what he was before he was forced to awaken into the world that had chained him. The mirror reflected a world where nothing that men built stood. Where there was no care in his mind but of survival and continuation. How freeing that was. How light he felt, staring into it. It was as it should be. He knew. Not least because it was dripping in red.

He would make his home here. With the mist. He would let it take him where it would. If chains were what awaited him moving forward, he wanted to fall backward. The mist seemed to understand this. It growled with pleasure and expanded around him, filling his mouth and his eyes and his nose. Ethan lay down in his cave and let it wash over him.

But something was wrong. Something was in his cave that shouldn't be. He sat up, breaking free of the red as he twitched left and right, looking for what did not belong. There, in the corner, propped up against a mirror.

Ethan stood. The mist protested, gripped him like tendrils of seaweed at the bottom of a lake, but it couldn't quite hold on to him, not yet. So Ethan walked. He stopped in front of the mirror. It still showed the red infinity, but Ethan didn't gaze into it again. He stooped down, crouched, to find his intruder. He grasped it in his hand.

It was a yellow number-two pencil.

Ethan looked back at the mirror, and he saw in its reflection a clock.

"Five fifteen," said Ethan. "It's five fifteen." He felt outrageously weary, as if he'd been placed on a tilting table in the middle of an ocean. Stay awake and you can balance. You live. Fall asleep and you drown. Or perhaps he'd fallen off long ago and had been drowning this entire time.

Beyond the cell, underneath the clock, he saw his mother and father. His mother muttered prayers. His father had a bandage around his head, a bandage that Ethan knew hid his own handiwork.

"I'm sorry," he mumbled. That was all he seemed to say these days.

His father leaned in, gripping the bars.

"I'm sorry, Dad." He wasn't asking for forgiveness. Ethan knew now that he was beyond that. It was a goodbye. He had to stay away from them forever. He knew now that this was where he belonged. Alone and in a cage.

Except that he wasn't alone.

"You saw it," Gordon said, his face swimming into view, and he was smiling. "You saw the pencil. I heard you."

"It doesn't matter," Ethan said. "The Red is there. It's too strong. A pencil can't save me."

Gordon stood and walked over to his bed. He began undoing his shackles. "You're wrong, buddy. That's what you need to understand. Your Red, your mist, it's as strong as that pencil is. No stronger. The same brain that created that mist created the pencil. Get it?"

Ethan stretched his neck and turned back, only to find his parents had disappeared. He wondered if they had ever really been there. He shook his head. Gordon handed him a glass of water, and he drank it down in one go. "I don't get any of this," he said. His head throbbed. His vision was already clouded with red. His hands tensed. Part of him already itched to rip at Gordon where he was wounded. At his arm and at his face, which was striated with four raking scabs that he knew he'd given him.

Gordon knew it, too. Ethan could see in his eyes. But Gordon stood with him. That made no sense to Ethan. Any other creature would have put Ethan down long before or, at the very least, left him to die there in the cage. But not Gordon. It confused Ethan. It confused the Red.

Gordon chained him again, reluctantly. It must have been Ethan's eyes. He felt that they were red on the outside now as well as the inside, and maybe Gordon didn't want to take any chances. Ethan reached out to Gordon and pawed at him, gripping him. Gordon allowed it but pulled Ethan's hands away after he started squeezing, his fingers dimpling into the skin of Gordon's arm. Ethan felt an urge to keep him safe and to destroy him at the same time.

Gordon pushed him down on the bed. Slammed the pencil into his hand. Moved Ethan's head to stare at it. Held it there. Forced his eyes open until they swam with tears.

"Remember. The. Pencil."


ETHAN WAS BACK in his cave of mirrors. He was unsurprised. He transitioned seamlessly. It seemed to Ethan that he'd always been in this cave. The mirrors swam in red smoke. They reflected a host of seething images when he gazed into them as he walked his perimeter, but none of them were of Ethan himself. This didn't bother Ethan. All was as it should be. The cave shed everything from him that no longer mattered. The trappings of life sloughed off like dead skin. No need for any of them. All that mattered was ownership of this place. Of his cave. Of everything in it.

Except that damn pencil.

What *was* that pencil doing here? It felt out of place. Worse, it wouldn't go away, and every time he saw it, he felt he should do something with it.

*It means nothing,* said the Red. *It is of as little consequence as your things in the waking life.* And Ethan wanted to believe it. But he couldn't quite forget it. Something pricked at him.

The Red tried to cover it, to wipe it from the cave, to shroud it, but even underneath the mist, a glint of yellow could still be seen. It troubled Ethan.

*It is a thing of the world you leave behind*, said the Red. *Stop thinking of it as a pencil. Strip its name the way you have stripped the name of your mother and father. The way you stripped the girl's name when you took her. If you strip it, you can kill it.*

Yes. True. All good points. Ethan nodded. He even tried to forget it. He walked to the other end of the cave. He knelt in the mist, breathed it in and out, let it suffuse him.

But why was it here in the first place? The pencil?

Ethan stood, the mist falling from him.

*What are you doing?* asked the Red.

"This thing is out of place."

*Don't touch it. Forget it, and it will go away.*

Ethan tried to believe, but he couldn't. "It has to go," Ethan said, and he started to walk toward it.

And he awoke.

He sat up in his cot, and he saw Gordon. Gordon smiled at him. He crossed his arms the way he had the first time he met Ethan, when he was the only one who decided to help him.

"You did it," Gordon said. "You're free."

Gordon gestured around the cell, and Ethan found the cell door open. His father was behind it, on his knees, waiting for Ethan to come to him. His mother was there too, weeping with joy.

"Where is the pencil?" Ethan asked.

Gordon's face faltered. He blinked. And with his blink, a wisp of red leaked from his eyes. "There is no pencil anymore. Walk out and into your new life, Ethan. Take your place above your father. Take the girl as well. Everything you can take is yours now."

Ethan stood. There were no chains. His mother and father, smiling, prostrate with hands wide open, were also misting with red smoke. Ethan reached the cell bars and grasped them and they smoked in his hands. They felt more like sand than steel. He paused.

"I want the pencil," Ethan said.

Gordon screamed at him. It was an inhuman sound, and it took the shape of a plume of red mist as it came from his throat. Ethan saw why. The pencil was behind Gordon. Gordon wanted the pencil for himself.

"It's mine!" Ethan said, and he ran for it. Gordon exploded in a puff of red as Ethan reached through him to grab the pencil. But once it was in his hands, he had no idea why he wanted it so badly. It was just a pencil, after all. As for the rest of this place, it was mist. His life was mist now. He knew he could give the pencil back to the mist. It would take it, gladly. It snapped at it now. In the form of his parents, inching toward him on their knees with their hands out. In the form of Gordon, back together again, reaching for him. Smiling. Leaking red. It was all mist. Nothing more.

Except for this pencil. This pencil was something more. It meant something. Ethan looked from the pencil to his parents to Gordon and then, behind them, to the clock. It was four fifteen.

"See?" said Gordon. "The clock doesn't lie. Give me the pencil."

Ethan looked at the pencil. Then back at the clock.

It was midnight, on the dot. Ethan blinked. That was weird. He felt it important that he take a minute to think about the clock, but again Gordon was there, stepping in front of the clock. Ushering Ethan through the cage doors. Grasping for the pencil. Nodding eagerly, his eyes bright with mist. Gordon placed a hand on Ethan, and it felt as though it was fusing with him. A jolt of adrenaline pulsed through him. His vision darkened to a deep red, an ancient red.

*Yes*, said Gordon. *Yes*.

Ethan's heart raced. He felt himself grow stronger, more aware, as the connections of his frontal lobe, the noise that made everyday life every day, the noise that made life *life*, fell away from him. The connections between his parents, his friends, his house, his school, all started to break. He felt Gordon place a second smoking hand upon his shoulders, and it sank into him with the surety of a deep heat.

*Yes*, said Gordon. Although it wasn't Gordon anymore. Ethan cared less and less about Gordon. Less and less about the names and titles of anything. It was the Red that was sinking into Ethan now. And Ethan let it.

But now Ethan could clearly see the clock. And it no longer told time of any sort. That was not normal, was it? For a clock to tell two different times, and now to be a swirling fog of dripping numbers? Was that normal? And if not, what was happening?

The clock face dripped down the cell wall, and the numbers plopped in smoking red dollops right onto a bright-yellow number-two pencil. He'd thought it was in his hand, but the mist must have taken it. Everything around it was red, but nothing was red about the pencil. He remembered that pencil. How it felt, how it looked. He remembered it because...

Because he was supposed to.

Because he was dreaming right now.

The Red froze as if it physically felt when Ethan came to that conclusion. Its arms, wrapped partway around Ethan's brain, tensed. Waiting. Like an intruder in the corner of a dark room freezes when glanced at, in the hopes that the gaze will pass on, the door will close, and he can get back to work. But Ethan turned on the light.

"I'm dreaming," Ethan said.

*I will not lose you,* said the Red. *I have all the time in the world to claim you. Your waking mind will break soon enough.*

The cell began to melt after the fashion of the clock. Then his parents began to melt, like wax figures in the heat, smiling and prostrate all the while. Only the Red remained solid. Even the pencil began to melt. Even Ethan began to melt.

*It's waking me up,* thought Ethan. *It's kicking me out of my own dream.* And Ethan despaired. Because the Red was right. He was losing more and more of his waking mind with each moment his exhaustion deepened. If he left this dream, he might never understand when he inhabited another. His whole life would become one long, endless, red dream.

Unless he got that pencil. But it was behind the Red, and it was melting. It was almost gone, a puddle of yellow paint in his dreamscape of red, when one word struck him.

*Spin.*

Gordon's word. Not the red Gordon but the man who was trying to help him. The man who believed he could get better. So Ethan spun. He held out his arms and spun like a top, and at first, he tilted with the dreamscape, but then he righted himself. Faster and faster he spun, and the world around him pulled itself together like a centrifuge, filtering out the noise and returning the substance. His mother and father picked the pieces of themselves from the air and were patched together again. The clock ran back up the wall. The clock face still swam, but it swam with substance.

*You can never tell time in a dream*, thought Ethan. Gordon had told him that too. Ethan smiled now as he spun.

He smiled wider when he saw the pencil clump itself together, connecting to pieces of itself like yellow quicksilver until it stood practically shining yellow, right behind the Red.

But the Red glowered now. It seethed.

*Come with me, child. I won't ask again,* it said. *You want the world I offer. Of oblivion. Your connections to this life only bring you pain. When you don't know death, you cannot fear death. I am the beginning. I can spare you the end. You will never lose anyone if you never come to love anyone. Never know pain. Never know despair. You will be free. If you come with me.*

No fear would be nice. He'd been so afraid recently. And no loss? That would be nice, too. He knew these things came with growing up. He knew adults all dealt with fear in their own ways. His mom held on to faith. His dad held on to family.

But it would mean no Mom or Dad. No Erica. No Gordon.

"Give me the pencil," said Ethan.

The Red seethed in laughter.

"Give it to me!" Ethan commanded.

*I will not. It is not mine to give.*

No, of course it wasn't. That's because it was Ethan's to take. It was his dream. That was his Red. That was his pencil.

And just like that, the yellow number-two pencil was there in his hand. Ethan made it happen.

*No!* screamed the Red, and as it reached out to Ethan, a sucking sensation followed, pulling the Red back, vacuuming the mist from it in tendrils.

"My pencil. My dream," said Ethan, and with one sharp push of his thumb, he snapped the pencil in two. His dream world compressed, and his stomach dropped. The red mist was sucked entirely away, and Ethan found himself standing in front of himself. Not himself shrouded in the red, just his own reflection. But he knew it was the boyhood version of himself, the part he'd just chosen to leave behind. The part attached to the beginning.

It held out its hand and smiled sheepishly. Ethan hesitated to take it.

The boy nodded understandingly. "You have made your choice. The Red has no power over you any longer."

"And you?"

"I am always a part of you, a reflection of your past, of the moment you chose to stop looking backward," it said. "But I am no longer you anymore."

Ethan tentatively reached out his hand, grasped its hand in his own, and with one final, ear-popping jolt, he shot up in his cot, in the Baltimore City Courthouse jail cell. He awoke so fiercely he jolted against his restraints, and he started to cry.

Only after his father placed his hand on Ethan's head and his mother grasped his sweating hands in her own was Ethan able to slow his hammering heart. He met both of their eyes, and what they saw there must have been good because they started to tear up as well. Then he searched the room for Gordon. He found the man standing away and behind them, peering around his dad, his hands balled into tense fists.

"I found the pencil," Ethan said. "And I took it."

Gordon wiped at his own face. He seemed to know already, and he nodded. "Yes, you did."

"And you told me to spin."

"You heard that?"

Ethan nodded. "It fought back. It wanted to break the dream. So I spun it back together."

Gordon nodded vigorously, tears streaming down his face.

"Why is everyone crying?" Ethan asked.

"Your eyes, buddy. They're as blue as the sky."

Gordon moved from legs to wrists and clicked open all the restraints. "I don't think you'll be needing these ever again," he said. Then he rubbed at his face, checked his pockets for his things, grabbed his pad and pencil, and turned to go.

"W-wait!" Ethan cried. "Where are you going?"

"To get some coffee. And then some more coffee. You're better, Ethan, but you're still in jail." He checked his watch. "I got about eight hours to write down the plan of care I have for you that's gonna get you out."

## CHAPTER SEVENTEEN

### ONE MONTH LATER

Gordon arrived at lunch to find his mother smiling and waving. She motioned him back to the patio, martini in one hand, and Gordon watched as she nearly dumped it when she saw he was not alone. Gordon cringed a little, his palms sweaty. He let go of Dana's hand and wiped his own off on his slacks.

"Gordon, it's okay. She's your mother. This isn't a job interview," said Dana.

"There is a way we could do this, you know, without you ever having to meet my mother. It would take some scheduling, but—"

"Gordon. Stop it. It's gonna be okay."

His mother still stood, her slender, jeweled hand pressed lightly to her chest. She looked from Gordon to Dana and back at Gordon, as if he had grown horns.

Gordon cleared his throat. "Mom, this is Dana Frisco, the woman I've been telling you about."

His mother stared but smiled so widely that it jangled her earrings.

"Well, how about that. He wasn't lying," she said, extending her hand. "Praise the Lord. Dana, I'm Deborah Pope."

"Nice to meet you. Your son talks a lot about you," Dana said, smiling warmly. "It's obvious you mean a lot to him."

"Oh, phooey," his mother said, waving her words off and basking in them at the same time. Then she turned squarely to face her. "You know he's sterile, right? Medically. His testicles don't work right."

"Jesus, Mom. Can we at least sit down first?"

Dana reddened but didn't flinch. Gordon thought he saw the subtle upturn of a smile at the side of her lips.

"Yes, I do," she said.

"Good, because the last woman he was with couldn't deal with it. She was a bit of a bitch. Brilliant woman, but a bit of a bitch."

"Mom, enough. Caesar!" Gordon looked around, calling out desperately. "Drinks! More drinks. Please and thank you."

The three of them sat. Dana gave Gordon a look of complete understanding that settled him, a look he was increasingly falling in love with. The look said she got it.

"Gordon has told me," Dana said, "about his condition and his ex-wife. So we're all square there," she leaned in to his mother conspiratorially. "I already have one beautiful little girl. And one is plenty for me."

His mother leaned in to meet her. "Tell me about it," she said, nodding her head toward Gordon. "He's my one. He was plenty. Still is."

That settled, both women leaned back out. Gordon looked between them as if he'd seen dogs and cats curl up next to each other.

"I like her," his mother said. "Let's eat."

HIS MOTHER and Dana talked comfortably for the rest of the meal. His mother was engrossed in Dana's recollection of how they met, a story Gordon had told her himself several times, but she was riveted nonetheless. She even forgot about her martini for a bit. Gordon piped in every now and then, adding details from when Dana couldn't be there, like in the cell with Ethan.

The truth, however, was that the battle, such as it was, had taken part in Ethan's brain. He'd spoken to the boy about what he'd seen and done and so had a picture of it, but from Gordon's perspective, he'd sat watch over a tossing and turning and gnashing and growling young boy for three days and nights. He'd played games with him when he could and kept him safe when he couldn't. He'd told him to spin when Ethan started to mumble that the dream was collapsing. Spinning was another old Gladwell trick. He'd had no idea if the boy could hear him, or if he could help, but all he knew was that Ethan was thrashing one moment then sitting up the next, the red having fled from his eyes. Gordon knew in an instant Ethan had beaten it.

Gordon explained that after the ordeal in the cell, he went home and sat down in front of his computer. He spent the next six hours writing nonstop. He needed an official definition for the affliction. "Scary Mist Monster" wouldn't fly. Not even "The Red" was up to standards. What Gordon ultimately settled on sounded like it read right off a prescription bottle. Ethan had suffered from "cerebral self-aversion," an autoscopic phenomenon that manifested itself in a child's prepubescent years. Preliminary signs included violent parasomnia, particularly of a kind that involved sleepwalking.

Its root cause was as yet undefined, but Gordon laid out what he thought was a very compelling case that pointed toward radically disturbed sleep patterns in the modern era. Light pollution and noise pollution levels were drastically different from those under which the human brain had initially developed, and continuous neural bombardment by said pollution was the likely perpetrator. Not only were children not developing under "normal" sleeping conditions, but our society had changed to such a degree, and so quickly, that "normal" sleeping conditions were unattainable, perhaps gone forever.

In short, modern children were not developing their subconscious properly because what they thought was sleep wasn't sleep, not in the sense that humanity's ancestors knew it.

Gordon found the hypothesis compelling enough to include it. That wasn't necessary for a plan of care, but it did give his case more presence. Karen agreed. She said so after he shared his outline with her and gave her a brief rundown of what had happened in the cell.

As for the cure? Lucid dreaming, which was simple enough in theory but a good deal more difficult in practice, as he'd found out. He could only speak to his experience with Ethan, but he outlined his yellow-pencil technique in detail. He called it a "carry-through symbol."

"A yellow pencil, huh?" Karen had said. "Very clever. Another Gladwell trick, perhaps? You always loved that old coot."

Gordon smiled then because that hadn't been Gladwell's at all, actually. When he was struggling to come up with a symbol Ethan might be able to carry through into his dreams, he remembered one late night in college when he and his roommate had played Tetris for almost six hours straight. That night, he'd dreamed of dodging a nonstop array of falling Tetris blocks.

The good news was that once the carry-through symbol appeared and the subject was able to actualize a lucid dream, the disorder had apparently disappeared completely. Poof. The Red was blown away. After that night, Ethan slept for twelve straight hours like a dead man, and his parents said that his eyes were flitting all over the place under their lids. Although he didn't have the machinery to guarantee it, Gordon was certain Ethan had finally fallen into REM sleep, working to balance a dreadfully empty bank and succeeding.

Since then, Ethan hadn't had any further parasomnia occurrences. His symptoms stopped just as Gordon's own had, years before. The difference was like night and day. He had normal dreams with normal themes thereafter. The Red was gone.

The plan of care he'd dumped on Thomas Brighton's desk fifteen minutes before the appeal was hasty, full of spelling and punctuation errors, badly formatted, and poorly footnoted. However, it had been peer reviewed, more or less, by Karen Jefferson herself, and she found it held water. Gordon believed in it wholeheartedly. Brighton seemed to have expected it. He looked down at it, shuffled through some of the papers, returned them to Gordon, and dusted his hands.

"Can you take the stand?" he'd asked.

"You better believe it."

. . .

ETHAN'S SENTENCE was reduced to six months of probation, and he was court ordered to submit to psychological evaluation once a month for the next year, after which the entire affair would be expunged from his record. The opposing council was stunned, not at the overturning but at the revelation of the nature of the disease. Jimmy Tanner's father even came over to Ethan and wished him luck in his treatment. He said that Jimmy had woken up a week before and was recovering at home. He suggested that the best thing for everyone would be to close this dark chapter and go their separate ways. Andrew Barret hugged Gordon right there in the courtroom. Jane Barret flashed him a knowing smile, as if she'd always known the Big Guy Upstairs would come through in the end, and all He'd needed was a man like Gordon working on His behalf.

Ethan wept with joy when he heard the verdict. Gordon would have also, if he weren't focused as intently as he was on simply staying upright.


HIS MOTHER MARVELED at the story. With Dana to help tell it, it sounded remarkable even to Gordon, more the type of thing a spy or a mad scientist would go through, not a scruffy psychiatrist. Without her, he knew he'd be knocking on Thomas Brighton's door right now, begging for work, not filling his planner with consultations and appointments. Dana, who kept one hand resting lightly on his leg while she spoke to his mother. Dana, who didn't think he was nuts. Who never had, even from the very beginning. Dana, who had brought the entire Ethan Barret story to her plucky contact at the *Tribune* and then taken the ensuing article to Warren Duke's desk. The way she told it, Duke's eyes practically crackled with fire and brimstone, and a purple vein pulsed at his tanned temple, but he smiled and politely congratulated her because the captain of police had caught wind of what had happened in Duke's department and had called him a day earlier. He'd suggested Marty Cicero be put up for a commendation and said that since Officer Dana Frisco seemed so good with kids, maybe they ought to put her in for one of the detective slots that would be coming up in the new unit, the one the mayor had suggested after all the sleepwalking hubbub. They were planning on calling it the CPI unit, for Child Protective Investigations.

Dana said Duke had told her all that through gritted teeth, then shook her hand limply. Outside, Marty Cicero was waiting by her car. She told him he was going to get a commendation, but he shook his head and said he didn't deserve it. What he really wanted to know was if she was getting a new partner since she was going to be a big-shot detective.

"They let me choose," she said. At that, Cicero nodded his head. He turned to leave, but she stopped him. "And I asked for you, Marty."

Dana said the big man had teared up then. He had shaken her hand and held it and looked as though he wanted to say something more, but all that came out was "I'm sorry."

Dana told him to shut that crap down right that instant. He was right to call her out when she was out of line. She hoped he would again in the future because she didn't doubt the day would come around again.

"One of us has to keep the both of us alive," Dana said.

Gordon had the feeling that she was leaving something out, something about the moment the three of them had outside of the tunnel. Gordon suspected Cicero had other reasons for wanting to be Dana's partner, not all of them professional. He liked Cicero, even if Cicero didn't like him. He thought Cicero was good for Dana. Still, Gordon envisioned a storm in the distance on that front, but a storm for another day.

Over the last of their Cobb salads, Gordon told his mother and Dana how Ethan had visited him earlier that week for the first time since the appeal. The boy that he saw was nothing like the one he'd treated four weeks before. Compared to the new Ethan, the pallid, frightened Ethan that Gordon remembered from the cell was nothing but a shade. A shadow of a memory. More like the mist he'd chased away than anything. The new Ethan's smile, along with the way he hugged Gordon, was weighty. It had heart.

Ethan had said he'd told Erica about the pencil, and she'd found it herself not long after. They were hanging out again. Both of their parents were there the whole time, but they were together again. Bit by bit, things were getting back to normal. And then he gave Gordon a pencil of his own, a bright-yellow number two with the words *World's Best Doc* engraved on it. Gordon kept it balanced carefully on the top of his computer monitor, where he could see it every day.

Since that visit, he hadn't heard from Ethan. He doubted he would until Gordon evaluated him for his next monthly review. Then Gordon guessed there would be more radio silence until the next. After a year, it was Gordon's strong hope that he'd never see Ethan again. That would mean he was healthy, and Gordon believed the boy was indeed healthy.

"So that's that," Gordon said, as Caesar cleared their plates.

His mother sat back and took a sip of her martini, cooled in a frosty new glass. She appraised both Dana and Gordon. "My son once told me that if he couldn't save that young boy, if he let him down, then maybe it was good that he couldn't have a child." She looked pointedly at Gordon, who looked down and spun his cocktail tumbler slowly. "He seemed to think that he didn't deserve a child."

Dana squeezed his leg.

"What I believe," she continued, "and what I should have told him then but didn't, was that I think the reason he is not able to have a child, unable to care for his own child, is because he was meant to care for hundreds. For thousands."

Gordon looked up when he heard her voice break slightly. His mother was a loving woman, but she wasn't exactly *caring*. Gordon believed that was perhaps the most heartfelt thing he'd heard her say.

Then she waved her words away and finished her drink. "That's what I think, anyway." she said, as if she'd been speaking of nothing more than when the leaves would change color.

"Me too, Deborah," Dana said, squeezing his knee again. "Me too."


THAT NIGHT, Gordon Pope put the finishing touches on his journal article. It was titled "Violent Parasomnia and the Preteen Cognitive State," and it was based largely around Ethan's plan of care. He'd already submitted the abstract to several journals. The Johns Hopkins University Press had picked it up in short order and slated it for publication in the journal *Philosophy, Psychiatry, and Psychology*. He hadn't told anyone other than his mother, who promptly asked him why he hadn't waited to hear back from the *New*

*England Journal of Medicine* first but then congratulated him nonetheless with a big kiss on the cheek and another round of drinks. He wanted to see it in print first, to really know it was there, with his name on it, before he told Dana. Part of him still believed it didn't exist. He'd stared too long at a blank screen, deleted too many words, and crumpled up too many outlines in disgust over the years. But that was before he'd stumbled into a court case involving a troubled young boy, looked in his eyes, and seen a bit of himself where everyone else had seen a monster.

He printed out the final draft then e-mailed the digital copy to the *PPP* editorial board and sat back in his chair, threading his hands behind his head. He hoped others would be able to see the warning signs in their own young patients and craft similar plans of care. Maybe those kids could start to sleep soundly again.

Because he had messages.

Oh boy, did he ever have messages. He was booked solid for the next two months. He actually had to go out and get a new kids' chair and a couple of new pairs of pants. He realized how unemployed he looked when he'd gone through his closet the week before and thrown out everything over five years old and found he had nothing left.

He'd also finally been able to replenish his scotch collection. Or lack of a collection. He had a nice array. Nothing crazy. He wasn't a huge fan of the expensive stuff. A simple, good old-fashioned sipping blend had always set him right. He poured himself one then, a celebratory dram, as he pressed the play button on his simple, good old-fashioned message machine. He sat back down and took out his pad to write down numbers.

Three messages awaited him that time, two from Baltimore residents. They'd heard about the Ethan Barret case.

They were desperate. He'd call them back. Gordon lifted his tumbler for a big tipple when his business line actually rang. He decided against answering. They could leave a message too. That day was for relaxing. For celebrating. The machine picked it up, and Gordon took a sip as it recorded then started to play on delay. When he heard it, he paused with the glass to his lips.

The caller was a woman, and her voice had that strange, high-pitched timbre that only came out when someone was fighting to keep their voice in control, to hide how frightened they actually were. He knew that tone well. He'd been speaking with it for some time, up until recently.

"Dr. Pope? Are you there?"

Gordon paused. She was waiting for him to answer still.

"No? Please. I know you're extraordinarily busy, but if you're there, please pick up."

Still Gordon paused. He had the distinct feeling that if he picked up that phone, it might flip the switch that shifted the train track of his life. He'd only recently hit a straightaway, one that promised easy work, decent money, and modest rewards. The Ethan Barret case was a once-in-a-lifetime thing for a psychiatrist. Something you could coast a career out of. Gordon had to understand that. Didn't he?

He was at the phone in the blink of an eye. "This is Gordon Pope."

The woman let out a gasp of either shock or relief. "Thank you so much for picking up."

"What can I do for you?"

"It's not me, it's my daughter."

"Is she sleepwalking?" Gordon brought his pen to his pad again. He was almost relieved. He wasn't quite sure what had first spooked him about the call—maybe the way she had sounded initially on his machine, that was all.

"No, no. She sleeps just fine."

Gordon stopped writing on his pad.

"Well, then what... what's wrong?" It sounded harsh, but he was caught off guard. He knew he shouldn't be. Sleepwalking wasn't the only thing afflicting kids, after all. Maybe she had an anger issue. Maybe she was OCD. Maybe she was getting things pierced and wearing too much black for her mother's taste. It could be any number of those completely ordinary, completely explainable things. The straightaway tracks.

"It's hard to explain." She laughed, high and nervous. "To be honest, I don't think you'd believe me if I told you."

No straightaway then, it would seem.

"You'd be surprised at the things I would believe," Gordon said.

"I know. I've heard. That's why I called you. It's just that... Listen, I'm staying at the Marriott on Center Street in town. Both of us are. I was really hoping you might just be able to come over and see for yourself."

Gordon found himself caught in a moment in time that seemed heavy, thick with portents. Another turning point. He'd picked up the phone and started the fuse, but all he had to do was set it down again to tamp it out. Straight and narrow. Decent income. Modest recognition. Pleasant life. He finally had a girlfriend, for God's sake.

*And what would Dana say about this?*

"When can I see her?" Gordon asked.

She thanked him again and again. She gave him her number and told him she'd meet him in the lobby. Gordon wrote it down and hung up, and all of a sudden, the fuse was burning bright. Snaking into the unknown. He looked at his scotch, still on his desk. He took it to the sink and dumped it out.

Straightaways were well and good, and Gordon knew they had their time and place. Just not then and there. As Gordon picked up his keys, he could almost feel the ground shift under him, but he stood tall. He smiled. It was time to get back to work.

## ABOUT THE AUTHOR

B. B. Griffith writes best-selling fantasy and thriller books. He lives in Denver, CO, where he is often seen sitting on his porch staring off into the distance or wandering to and from local watering holes with his family.

See more at his digital HQ: https://bbgriffith.com

If you like his books, you can sign up for his mailing list here: http://eepurl.com/SObZj. It is an entirely spam-free experience.

## ALSO BY B. B. GRIFFITH

**Gordon Pope Thrillers**

The Sleepwalkers (Gordon Pope, #1 )

Mind Games (Gordon Pope, #2 )

Shadow Land (Gordon Pope, #3)

**The Vanished Series**

Follow the Crow (Vanished, #1 )

Beyond the Veil (Vanished, #2 )

The Coyote Way (Vanished, #3 )

**The Tournament Series**

Blue Fall (The Tournament, #1 )

Grey Winter (The Tournament, #2 )

Black Spring (The Tournament, #3 )

Summer Crush (The Tournament, #4 )

**Luck Magic Series**

Las Vegas Luck Magic (Luck Magic, #1)

**Standalone**

Witch of the Water: A Novella

Made in the USA
Coppell, TX
13 October 2021

64029369R00152